Enter

A novel

Ahsan Zahid

No part of this book may be published anywhere without written permission.
Legal action may be taken in the event of such instance occurring.

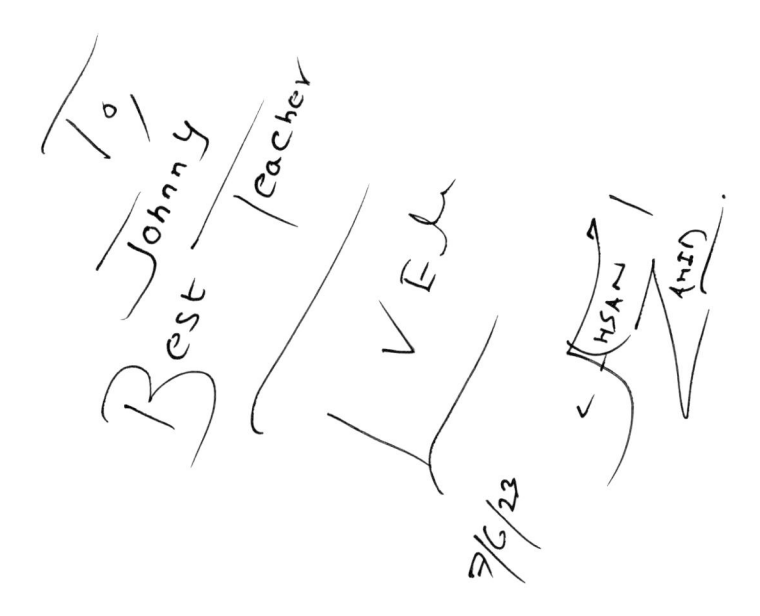

To *'the hand of the unknown'*

Love Destroys Everything

When was the last time that you were in bed... with someone? Someone you don't love, someone who isn't attached to you, someone who loves you... not for who you are but for the kind of *pleasure* you give? And yes, as a dirty gigolo, a fancy man in service, I must serve several sorts of joys... as required, demanded, or pleaded...
But before I go into detail, could you please recall... when the last time was that the person you love... loved...was in front of your eyes but wasn't there in that room where you were, naked with someone else? Shuffling intimacy to forget your significant other? Trying to lose yourself, lose your mind into this new body. Working *hard* to kindle your thoughts in the friction of the lustful desires, striving... to put up the smoke, and wishing the ignition would burn the memories, turn them into ashes, so no longer would be the pain, no longer the soul of the love would be alive. But...did you realize that the harder you try, the quicker you fall?
And I was falling...
"Can you lick me stronger?"

A weak voice came from somewhere above. Yet, in my closed eyes, Rita was smiling... the illusion was so real that I could hear her laugh, laughing naked, laughing breasts moving with her chubby belly. The feeling of being loved was all over, the warmth of just ended lovemaking (what she always called *freshly fucked feeling*) was running through our blood. Her eyes were smiling from all the happiness of this world, from our nasty jokes. When she said "My mad pervy..."
"Can you lick me harder?" A less intoxicating voice reached me. It wasn't an order but wasn't less than that either.
Rita was laughing, with tears, and her tears were so real that they flowed into my eyes... running after her naked in the bedroom with the pillows, jumping over the white sheets in the semi-dark room was good fun, jokes in the air, the world was shut out and it seemed that the bombed world, the world on the edge of a third world war was losing all its poison just outside our doorstep... Prague 9.
The sun rays evading our curtains weren't enough to brighten the room, but they were enough to brighten up our weekend. She was laughing at my evergreen dirty jokes... she was...
"For God's sake. Harder! Play with my clit!" The angry order opened my eyes; as drop or two of salty water ran from my cheeks to her lower lips. A volcanic wave raised and calmed within.
I wanted to slap this bitch; this horny slut spread in front of me. I wanted to push her face into the wall, pull her hair and then slam her against it.... again, and again!

And before she fell with her bloody face, I wanted to shout while throwing my anger into her eyes "Bitch I am not yours. I am not your slave. I belong to Rita. Ritaaaaaaaaa!!!!"

The madness of love roared within to behead thyself.

A noose flashed to choke undone sins and fear to lose all chained life to a grin.

"I'm sorry honey, I'm sorry," I swallowed, to bring energy to my voice.

"Actually... I was trying something different with you today," I threw her a gaze with my red eyes. "I was thinking another way around; I will follow your pleasure... strictly now." And before she replied, I went back down using all my concentration, skill, experience, pain, hate, professional responsibility to get pounds, dollars, Euros, Czech Koruna...whatever would be given to me by the middle-aged mama for my *hard work*.

What is more Halal than the money of a sex worker, for which you don't just have to break a sweat but must kill yourself every second to earn your living?

Fearing...where life can take you with its next spin? Famished, broken in a corner of the police station, or at the bottom of a pit in a sinking graveyard?

Fear shackled every inch of me, ruined me, my dreams... my love, lost!

I... Meer...a Pakistani gigolo. My days are over when I used to enjoy the adventurous work, thrilled to get women to those skies of pleasure where they never tripped before or after. I was... *the man with the skills*, equipped with sweet charms, soft words, and so much romance. But... love destroys everything.

Destiny Lure

"So, what do you do?"
She asked me the same question for the third time that evening and mind you, that was not a date, wasn't a pre-arranged meeting, not any escorting job. That was... just a chance that destiny brought us... here, in the heart of central Europe, in Prague.

The old town square was over-rushed by tourists hoping to see the world-famous astrological clock, and a picture with the clock was a must. Restaurants and coffee houses were full and noisy. People were running over people. It was July, the peak season of tourism, or, in other words, springtime for Euro travelling. Every colour, race, and size of tourist swamped Prague. Backpackers searched cheap dorm hostels and creatures of comfort luxury five-stars. Not only that, but one finds all types of artists and performers here too, entertainers who stand on the street and play their act to the ones who are surrounded by hundreds in a moment.

One of them…one who wasn't surrounded by hundreds, nor performing on squares to a few people…was Rita. Rita, the Harp player. Rita, a chunky middle-aged girly woman, dancing somewhere around her 4Os with her stout body, her blue eyes over which loose skin cried for an eye lift, her blonde hair which needed much more care and attention, and her exhausted mind juggling a million thoughts together, slowly draining the life out of her. She was a Kiwi, raised in England… playing in Prague 8 that eve with her band, when I saw her for the first time, spreading her arms around harp... like beloved in union with the other half. Her eyes were closed. And she stroked every string gently as silk phalanges kissed and played a soulful, spiritual rhythm.

And how did a person like me end up in this off-centre, dull local theatre near Křižíkova? Guess. I was escorting an inked woman whose friend was playing keyboard for the same band. The whole evening, I kept my eyes fixed on Rita while my hands were locked onto the palms of my customer, who had already booked me as a birthday present for the tattooed keyboardist. (I never knew girls shared birthdays and men too!). Anyway, God knows which songs they were playing but I knew exactly what this girl with the thick legs sliding out from her long red polka dots skirt was doing. And before I left, I made sure of it; I was here again… tomorrow.

In my business, sleeping every day with tired, old, rich, frustrated, overly youthful women is normal. Women who didn't have enough sex in their lives, who were overly excited about having some illegal fun. Women who are booking us as revenge for their husbands' affairs with ones younger, prettier, thinner. Women who want some *extra effort* (which their partners refused to make). Women who want to try something *new*! Women who want a bit more confidence in their sexuality, women who want to learn some new tricks from us. Women who seek advice about their partner, about their capability of giving pleasure. Women who are frustrated by their husband's early sexual retirement. In brief, there are many reasons and many women… who want *someone* to handle them… *differently*.

So, sleeping with new women at this point of my service life cycle wasn't enthralling. Good days do come, and I escape from the bedrooms of the weird ones to find someone sexy, beautiful. But even that fails to excite me ('though it does put a nice, unprofessional smile on my face). In the passing years, I had learned how to finish my work quickly… if I don't *like* my work!

"So…. what you do? You haven't told me yet," Rita asked as she was stirring a teaspoon in her half-empty cup. Her eyes threw me a look, that "why the hell did you bring me here to this quiet coffeehouse when you don't want to talk and only want to mingle around your thoughts, huh?".

What could I tell her? Who am I?

"I… am…" I spoke slowly and looked deep into my cup, where dark espresso sat, as jet black as my life.

"I'm… a pimp."

"What?" I couldn't see her face, but her tone made an impression on the surface of my coffee.
"Yes, I am…a pimp… Dark deeds, full of pleasure, passion, and adventure." I spoke hypnotically and returned my gaze to her lost face with a cheeky smile.
"What should I say to him?" was written all over her face.
"Was that a joke?" Rita stared into my eyes.
"No. I am serious." I kept the smooth calmness in my voice, enjoying the discomfort and confusion on her face. There was a pause between us. A pause… which she took to compose herself. A pause I took to discover new lies, new sentences to cover up my stupid answer. I had broken my law, my "no truth" law!
I tried to bring the conversation back to life… so I re-started, with a new voice, a straight face, and my eyes directly on hers.
"I am a salesman in my father's company…. The official representative here in Central Europe. I just freaked you out by using the word *'pimp'*, but if you think about it… I do nothing different…offering, arranging, and taking a percentage of the business conducted."
"Yes! People in sales are salesmen, not pimps though!" I heard an iron wall in her voice. "But… what dark deeds you are here to offer me? *Sir? Pimp?*" A smile conquered her lips as she drummed her fingers on the table in quest of revenge.
"So, tell me why you asked me out for coffee? You are a handsome young guy, at least ten years younger than I am and without children and wife I assume?" Rita looked closely at my face.

"Why do you want to hang out with an old fat woman with a kid? And before you lie, let me say... that you have been coming to the theatre for the last four days and sitting in the same seat in the second row. I also believe you were staring at me." She smirked as my poker face continued to stare blankly back at her.
"Yes! Yes! I know that my eyes were closed. But be sure my brain works supersonically after a joint. And I can feel things better than men. God created artsy women superior – interior & exterior. So, tell me... what are your intentions *young man*?" She raised her left eyebrow and smiled mischievously.
Rita thought she had confused me, but she didn't understand what I had tossed at her. My eyes, my mind, and now my words were all into this game.
I took a deep breath, finding the traces of cannabis that she hadn't inhaled.
"Yes! I agree women are superior to men," I smiled, and won the argument by just surrendering myself. As all the Adams did... opposite of their Eves, bowing to their wishes...to lay them.
"And I asked you for a coffee because I'm interested in you, your harp, your music. As a new fan...*thank you!* For giving me a little time from your busy schedule." I smiled as she accepted the utter truth coated with sweet lies.
And before we reached the steps of her temporary studio flat, I had her phone number.

I wish never to walk on that same path again, the path over which man destroys his self, to be loved and cared for. Destroying himself to be with her again and again… for that intimacy which is an illusion. Ending up with the burden of tiring responsibilities, with a bag full of broken crystal glass dreams. We wish to have families, to build homes. But reality sucks. And we never know if we love the other person because of her or we love someone because we want to be praised too… we want to feed this monk who praised that God, whom he never saw. We breed this lover who gets his peace by worshipping *'the love'* he never knew exactly. We create the illusion, we feed the illusion; we protect and reinforce the illusion… just to satisfy us, that we are in *love* and loved back (praised, sexed, and pampered)

'Love' is one of the cruellest words in human history, bringing more hatred and destruction with itself than any other word.

Love... world's most misused word with dual meanings and fluctuating standards.

A cunning, double-faced four-letter word who sold its soul to the devil and body to all.

Love was following me on the empty street where its echo disturbed the darkness.

Love was following her on the busy road, where the sweet sound of wind chimes overruled the noisy horns.

Circus of Choices

A red alert siren buzzed in my head.
Something was wrong…maybe me?
Since I had met Rita, an unknown fear warned me against her, against me... cautioned about the unsettling new self, fighting… in opposition of fearful happiness, fiercely confronting the unusual behaviour of a reluctant self.
I knew I wasn't completely being *me* in the last few weeks. I had turned down three trips to my regulars within a fortnight and I was sour.
In my business, what else do we have except good relationships and clientele? The money from these clients paid the ever-increasing bills. In this city where no one knew me... who could tell that I was an illegal immigrant, an overstayed tourist, and it was money that spoke on my behalf everywhere. But now, I was saying *no*! To that paper God which protects me from smaller two-legged gods.
I was angry with myself. Why on earth was I losing my sanity over someone so opposite my standard of beauty - Rita? What the hell was so special about her? I couldn't figure it out. I sat two nights alone without distractions, trying to understand, to seek the rationality of the madness that consumed me. I was sure Rita knew about the craziness she cast like a spell, as now when she looks into my eyes, her eyes are so different.

We hadn't had sex. But without even touching her body, I could see through to the furry coat worn by her Goddess Venus in its natural dress. My trained eyes took the liberty to frame her body and soul, to know her more, but every time we walked to her door, silent seconds wiped us out, our memories, our breaths, our words.
The whole world was a silent drop hanging breathlessly over a leaf's edge…quiet as the night in mountains under the moonlight, saying nothing but breathing in mystery. Speechless, as relaxed as the air of heavens. Emotions, puffing like a volcano reaching its climax.
Last Saturday, over a pint at a local pub, she told me… she isn't going to Warsaw with her band. She loved Prague and would stay. She had found a job as a teacher in a local music school. And while she was telling me all, she kept reading my eyes in the candlelight, which was the only thing between… keeping us apart by *burning*.
I smiled. I guess I smiled a lot these days.
Yes, I know. The alert siren is still buzzing in my head... Something is wrong…destiny, maybe…
Playing a hand with me, letting me win…or? But what was the reality, who could tell? The reality that we see against the reality of what we feel, against what we would feel, who could say? Even the changing calendar can't simplify but rather complicate the answer, with the passing years bringing only more dust over dust to the facts wrapped in the dirt of time.
I know something is wrong. The direction, maybe?
Saying no to money wasn't easy before I met Rita. Turning down someone was so difficult… with apologies and sweet words I juggled situations, but losing the business was always hard.

My life is by chance. To the world, I'm an American-born Pakistani whose father is an industrialist in the States, here temporarily to help my dad's business. My illusion's magic was playing its charm. My accent, my clothes, my confidence and above all this 'paper god' made it easy for the world to believe.

Nowadays on the nights when I'm alone till my *busy hours,* where I exhaust myself in some hotel room to satisfy some *whorney,* my mind often slips to Rita. I check my phone and write her, complaining about my slave master father.

And what was the truth of my family?

My dad, shot dead by political opponents in Pakistan. My mother, likely killed by my dad immediately after my birth. My brother, a drug addict, murderer, a puppet politician.

And all this lunacy was eliminated by showing an old picture of me and my friend's family from his wedding. I introduced them as my parents and brother. So, who in this city could tell her differently? Rita didn't know anyone in Prague, nor did she speak the language. That made me anxious when she went alone to places, but more I was worried about the pile of lies, lies, and more lies. But I was desperate to be with her, to be close, to be near... So, I kept making up stories, kept hiding behind lies, seeking refuge in delusion and fantasy.

Did I have a choice, any choice?

Was I in love? I wasn't sure, but something I did know was that we hadn't had sex since we met. I wasn't starving, but that doesn't mean I didn't want it either. That also doesn't imply that I'm sexually exhausted by my trips. I have my secrets... secrets apart from my high sex drive. But lately, stress was killing that too. Rita, Rita, Rita was on a loop in my head. When I first took her out, it was some kind of fatal attraction that made me pull her into that coffee shop. I didn't take her seriously, a musician playing with a band on tour. I saw myself waving goodbye to a bus carrying Rita away. Sex? Why not? If life and time bring an opportunity, then why not? Apart from being a sex worker, I'm a human too... I too like one-night stands, night outs with pretty girls. I am not a 'gigolo gigolo' all the time.

But this Kiwi-British Rita was becoming an enigma. She was shaking my grounds very quietly. I had always thought that I was directing us, but later I understood that Rita was captaining the ship of our destiny. What else I could call it, if not fate, to find a person with whom one's entirely able to talk about everything and anything of this world. I could listen to her lecture about European kings and the history of the Austrian-Hungarian Empire without yawning, and Rita would forgive me for dragging her to watch a documentary about Indian history. Somehow, we could talk about bullshit in a most meaningful way for hours and hours without getting tired. We shared the dirtiest jokes, talked about our travels, told stories about the funny incidents and unusual people we met on the journeys of our lives, our dirty secrets from childhood, our crushes and love affairs, sexual fantasies, drunk one-night stands. Unknowingly we could brew philosophy from ordinary and absolute non-practical nonsense that made us so proud of our findings, and while discussing this like badly drunk scholars, we reach Rita's flat and suddenly as we approach the door… my feet froze, our laughs went silent, and we shared a moment of complete consciousness revealing the unknown known. And the tranquillity of those seconds made us calmer.
A moment.
A bit longer, sometimes… a bit shorter, a pause, in which we silently talked to each other, with bowed heads… thinking, that is it, another day's over.

She quietly kissed me on my cheek, and I never looked up, waiting for the sound of the bunch of keys, the noise of hinges, opening and shutting of the door. But that night I didn't hear her heels. She stood there, waiting for me to give her some cue to walk away.
Was she more helpless than I, more deprived of happiness with a darker lifestyle? Was there something I didn't know about her? After all those long conversations about life and time, still… she decided to hide herself behind the door of silence and pauses? Did she lie to me too? What did she want from me? Did she want a toy-boy or she was looking for a companion? A better father for her daughter? What else might she want? Did she wish to enslave me? Yes! Love means controlling another, capturing other psychologically, physically, sexually… demanding an emotional bond, voluntarily or involuntarily.
Love romances us, sways us…and the fantasy guides us to be faithful slaves. Art and long-gone rotten love stories condition us, prepares us for forthcoming chains.
 Clank... Clank... Clank...
Am I ready for monogamous chastity, for heart-shaped handcuffs? And no, it's not true that you enjoy them every time. Blindfolds, either.
Whip! Crack!
Did you hear it? Did you hear it too?
That is love… cracking its whip around me, around my sins. Making me a submissive bitch. Bonding me with darker truths. Choking life...

Silent Scream

"My dad was gay."
Her sentence melted the silence within my ears.
The glass walls were sweating from the warmth of the crowd gathered inside the pub, chattering away around clinking glasses of beer and joyful cheer. Was it the warmth of happiness galloping with the number of pints, or was it the heat of hatred and politics between the people? Was it the lust and greed collecting on the glass? Or.... was it just me, struggling to see through Rita's burnt heart?
Mist over the glass wall or the frozen fog jamming the illusion of life, when things get blurry, you can't surely tell what's outside in the actual world. Until you decide to rub your palm against the vapours, unless you decide that your hand will give away its warmth for the wet, cold, ice glass feeling. But who thinks all that, who wants all that? Discomfort, effort to come out from delusional cosiness, hiding us behind the untrue, unreal perception creating a new lie on the outside.
All of us are blinded in part by our failed, inherited human ego, ignorance.

I was blinded by evaporating dreams, dreams to live a normal life, have a respectable job, a wife, a child, a house to live in... just a regular, unimpressionable common man's life. I wished for a romantic intimacy with someone who loved me. I was looking forward to becoming a proud dad of an intelligent child, I was looking forward to... But all was a dream. Dreams come true, they say, but in which world? Not in my world, at least not nowadays.

We were sitting at the corner table with our ales, and I was struggling to see outside. The glass, covered by melting little, tiny drops, was blurring my vision.

Today is 11th November, and the first snow of the season turned Prague into a wonderland. Leafless trees, streets, streetlight poles, traffic signals, rooftops, doorsteps...everywhere is snow-white. And to see these white magic snowflakes, I was rubbing my woollen cap against the glass now and then. But invisible breaths become visible and fill it back in; just as every day I call her... despite training the thoughts each night never to see Rita again.

I wasn't stable, neither in life nor in my dreams. They swung right to left, just as did my intentions and actions. No actions ended in zero reactions.

I was looking deep inside my head, my eyes were fixed on the frozen glass, when she repeated herself.

"My dad was gay,"

This one sentence melted the quietness of the barren desert in my ears. Sounds vanished, leaving a vacuum, spinning me, thoughtless... frozen. I couldn't move, my hands, arms, limbs, breaths... All were powerless.

"My dad was gay. My mom knew it. Societal pressures led him to marry, and my mother protected his sexual identity like a silent shield. Back then Europe wasn't so open. But time changes. Yes! Time changed and people change too," Rita's accent was flat.

"My dad left my mom when I was six and my brother Tim was two. One day, on an evening like this, he went out to buy a packet of cigarettes and never came back. Later we found a letter addressed to my mother. I don't know what was written inside, but I remember my mom cried, for the first and last time… all night. I was just right there… now too… I'm right there when I close my eyes. I am right there."

"I don't know why, but I didn't go near her, not even close enough to put my little hand on her back. I regret that. I was afraid, and I wasn't sure what had happened and I… I kept looking for my father. Daddy, daddy, mummy is crying… daddy!! Tim was too young, and I was responsible for taking care of him… I guess I still am."

Rita's eyes were static on the table, her thoughts wandering back to her childhood, nightmares gathering around the table. Sowing tears from the pain of the past, the past from where we often return sad, silent in heavy breaths.

And I wanted to hold her hand, wrap my arms around her, comfort her, and say…

"I'm here with you… I'm here for you." But I just couldn't, just like little Rita… hesitant and afraid of the unknown.

"Meer, I never understood. Why in love do we become so blind that we cannot see the affection and concerns of others? Why is that...? Why does love makes us so selfish?"

"Why!!" She almost punched the table.

"Exactly eleven years later, I ran away from my home with my boyfriend, James. He was two years older, and my mother hated him. She was blind in her love, and I was blind in mine. I did the very same thing as my dad; I went out one evening and then never went back." Rita took a deep breath and emptied her pint.

"James was a drug addict. Okay, let me be honest… we were both drug addicts. Thank God I didn't get pregnant when I was with him, but life was miserable. We were living together in James' council flat, often hungry as our benefit money was spent on drugs. One day James told me that his mate got me a job, that a sex shop in Soho want a young English blonde behind their counter. Come to find out, there was no job but there was an empty bed at a brothel in West London. I told James to fuck off and to be ashamed of turning his sweetheart into a sweet-slut of the city. How could he even think of that! This made him angry, so he beat me and left me half dead in his flat for his friends."

"I was raped."

Rita stopped, and the rollercoaster of my emotions halted. I was speechless, save for the noise of the monster inside me.

"I went back to my mother's place. She said nothing. We didn't talk to each other. I was in emotional shock. I couldn't talk. I couldn't go out. I couldn't express how I felt, my anger... my fear disabled my mind in a way that I couldn't differentiate between where the thin line of anger started and where the boundaries of my fears ended. I was on the verge of insanity. I'm not sure if my mom knew what happened. She never asked me directly. She asked Tim. Tim... my only saviour."

"I said nothing to him either. But after a few weeks, I realised that I was not getting my period. I was feeling sick all the time. Meer, I was pregnant. My mom didn't say a word; she just took me for an abortion. Though I wanted to shout aloud that this is my kid, this is my kid! But I knew that keeping that child wasn't possible. What would I tell this new soul? That I didn't even know his father? On that day, I understood that destiny puts us in situations where we want to do something different. But time, the world, and our very own self will stand between us and our decision. And in the end, we do as destiny instructs."

"That child never came to this planet...but I can tell you Meer where he is now..."

Rita was quiet.

There were no words anymore, yet there was a story... but no sentences... maybe sentences, but no voice... no sound... nothing.

The night was deepening, and the pub had to close. It was dreadfully cold and everybody wanted to be safe before the snowstorm started as the wind was freezing everything, even with its gentlest touch.

On that night, we said nothing else to each other. Rita's hand was on my arm, and her head was on my shoulder. We kept walking through the night, under the dimly lit sky. Facing the chilly winds, twisters from the past froze our words in the burning desert of our memories.
On that night she didn't have to wait for the cue from my shoes, as those boots crossed the threshold of that studio flat with her. I opened the door and took her furry coat away from her warm, soft shoulders. Gave her a hug... to melt breath frosted in grief. Kissed her checks. Wiped away the crystal tears on the edges of her eyes. Put her to the bed, tucked her in, and then looked deeply into her big blue watchful eyes... my palm was on her burning forehead.
"Sleep well, Rita."
I felt her hand on mine and I stood silent for seconds. But before my saintly self-departed, I was out on the cold, lonely road with the snow... Lightly lit saffron sky... And under my feet was the way towards my illusions.

Practical Decisions

My days were full of stress, my nights sleepless. A constant pressure was building inside since I had stopped contacting Rita... deliberately. I couldn't give my best at work, though there were no complaints. I was doing well, but... I was damn fucked. A void within... hollow emptiness was sucking hard, and I felt drained and constantly lonely; life seemed as pointless and directionless as a stray bullet.

Leaving Rita wasn't my first practical decision. I was aware of life. Life had happened to me before.

What is a practical decision? A decision that hurts you, kills you, breaks you and tear you in halves. A sacrifice made to avoid much bigger pain later. A temporary loss that brings uncertain prosperity to the ambiguous future and brings stability to current life.

It's not that I have made no cruel, heart-breaking, or tough decisions in my life. Ending up in this dirty business was a nightmare. But I didn't have any option before. But now... do I have an option?

Yes.

And yes, this affirmation dissects me every time. The option of changing my lifestyle, moving away from this. I felt... after meeting Rita; that this was it. Way too much money had already floated into my life, beyond one's imagination. I don't have any bank account, so I must stack the bills at my flat. I can see small piles of money lying under my bed; I sleep on the comfort of banknotes. Now do you understand how much money I have?

But the question was if she truly loved me too? Or if she only loved this majestic Meer, who sits and charmingly talks with her, is wise, very respectful, very kind, seems like an honest guy with some slightly off-track ideas about life, things, and situations. Someone who isn't trying to use her for sex, someone who knows how to treat a woman, someone who listens to her and responds smartly...

But is it my act she's in love with? Or is it me? She doesn't know who I am really.

Rita also doesn't know what I think about love or how I react when I'm besotted. For me, love means crushing every little joy of the beloved. I can't even stand the idea of anyone else trying to make her happy. Getting attached to something or someone is out of the question in my presence. I want to snatch every bit of affection, admiration and fondness that keep Rita's heart warm for others.

And that is crazy, I know that, but that's me. This is my reality. I want Rita to break all her emotional ties; I want her to be completely dependent on me. When she smiles, she smiles for me... because of me. When she laughs, when she cries, when she's sad, when she is crazy, I should be the reason… I should be the centrepiece of her life. And if not, then I'll destroy and damage everything she keeps close to her heart. That's me.

And when she loves me the way I worship her, the way I wish to be loved, then she'll realise who is the actual hero and what he does in her life. She will see how crazy I am for her, how mad I am... to see her happy, to see her peaceful, in the comfort of swinging joys. I'll take away her tears, I'll end everything and everyone who would try to hurt her, make her feel bad, make her feel sad... That's me.
I am sure you'll think that's bullshit. And I'm a fucking psycho. Some insane motherfucker, who doesn't need a human being, but some plastic, emotionless robot, who will dance on the fingertips of a ruthless master for his pleasure. Love is not slavery. Love is the fruit of heaven. Love is the bond that binds God and humanity. Love is the power that runs the universe. All is the shadow of affection. Everything is coloured in shades of love.
And you are right; I agree with you, what I think is sick. But this is true too that love means making someone a slave of your wishes, binding them with your likes and dislikes, caging them emotionally, confining them and then controlling them… changing them.
Jealousy is just another word for love. You are jealous of everything, from every person who you couldn't be, who brings a smile, a laugh, a breeze of happiness to your beloved and takes her attention away from you.

And yes! Rita displeases me that she loves and worries so much about her daughter, who's not mine. I'm uncomfortable even with the idea of Amelia being around us... disturbing our privacy, bothering our intimacy. The thought of her presence annoys the hell out of me, regardless of how good I think I am with kids. I just can't help it. I have this constant thought of devising a plan to eliminate her, to make Amelia disappear. And I don't want to become so evil, such a monstrous villain who takes the child from its mother... but that's me.

And that was just about Rita's daughter. What about her mother and brother? What about her best friends and band players? Friends? Colleagues? I am not so strong that I can ignore so much, and... What about the child, our child? How can I let her... let her attention be divided among people when she becomes the mother of my child? I am sick, over-sensitive, an idiot who doesn't understand the system of society or family life. You can say anything... Probably no one will understand. So, what can I do... this is me.

I think about those eyes... men seeking her curves, when she sits, when she walks? Her curvy body doesn't invite them, but I recognize that longing, the lust for Rita in their eyes. I can read their minds and I can't help finding myself fighting against them. Maybe I'm insecure, exaggerating. Maybe I'm scared and unconfident, but... what should I do? That's me.

But please, believe me, I'm a very normal guy, believe me, I am... I'm a balanced, intelligent, ordinary guy. But in the last few weeks, I had understood how and why under what psychological circumstances people murder their lovers when they cheat. Why people kill someone who is standing between them and their undoubtedly better half. Rita said rightly. Love is what makes us blind. We act as selfish bastards when in deep love. I am one... I could become one... that's me.... maybe I was one?

Do you understand me now, just a bit? That's why I stopped contacting her. But what I haven't told you is...

First Blood

"When was the last time you had sex?"
Sipping her smooth beer, Rita smoothly tossed the question. Her foot was tapping on the wooden floor as she looked inquisitively at me.
"When did you last have sex Meer?"
I'm a guy who strips off his clothes for almost anyone who can afford me... but still... that question came as a bit of surprise. We were close; I knew that she adores me or saw some future together, but regardless of whatever she thought, her current manoeuvre was alarming, on the scale of time.
When was the last time I had sex? Bingo! How could I reply? I didn't expect this question; I didn't see it coming... She caught me off guard while I was looking at a crossword puzzle and left my conscious motionless. I was tangled between the words and lies, shuffling the new puzzle at hand.
"If you don't want to answer my question that's fine with me." Rita tried to peek at the newspaper to get my attention, and she succeeded.
"No, No, I thought I misheard you." I smiled, or at least... I tried.
"Then tell me." She giggled.
I was trying to compose myself when another comment came.

"Oh God, I never thought a man could be so hesitant in talking about sex. Look at you blush like a young, shy boy." She mocked me and I was laughing with her... at myself, enjoying how life and time had made a situational comedy out of me.
I was taunting myself.
When, shy boy? Less than six hours ago? And you rang her desperately for a date as soon as you cleaned the last drop with the towel, motherfucking small shameless man. And now you're sitting with her, little fuck boy, spending your well-earned money straight from the handbag of some fucked up weird bitch. Isn't it true, you gigolo?"
"Hello Meer? I am here with you in the Palladium in your favourite Lebanese cafe near Florence station. Where are you?" Rita pretended to have a conversation over the phone.
"I'm here, and it's not that I am shy. I was just thinking, where I should start the monologue about my vast bedroom experience." I winked at her.
She laughed, and some snow slipped from the rooftop. Her laughter was echoing inside me.
"Ooh, so… ok… *Pany* (Mr.) Hercules, start your verbal *kamasutra*."
"What would you like to know?" I blinked my eyes with innocence.
"Oh, so cute." She burst with laughter again. "Babe, tell me everything; what you did, how you did it, where and how many times you did it." She winked and clapped with excitement. A naughty smile covered her face.
"Well, my experiences aren't as extensive as yours."

"Excuse me, I slept with only five men in last 39 years including 3 one-night stands and I can tell you, that's nothing," She got somehow defensive.
"And who was the youngest?" I winked.
"Shut up!" She giggled.
"He was... Hey wait! I'm asking the questions; I was the one who asked you first. I will tell you all, no problem, but … 'ladies first.'" Rita burst into laughter, stretching back her neck, face-up, arms in the air. And I was looking at her, laughing... but within the friction of seconds I looked at her gleeful face, wishing to capture the laugh; I wanted to memorize the beauty of this very second of joy so I could recall this moment in the low times of my life. Where life isn't offering what you want but offering you only a lesson.
That moment came and passed... to never come back.
"Hey Meer, what are you thinking? Looking so deeply at me while smiling," She asked curiously with a radiant beam.
"I was just noting how beautiful your laugh is, how... beautiful your lips are ...when you smile. And your eyes, how they shine with happiness when we are together. I just wanted to capture you in my mind. So, you can't run away, even if you want to."
I said those things in a flow of emotions, but Rita wrote them deep in her heart. She recorded them in her memory so she could recall them when no one was around and she could re-play these secret lines, remembering the time when a guy 12 year's younger said, "Let me capture your smile in my mind, so you can't run away, even if you want to..."

For a few seconds, we heard only dinner knives and forks playing on plates.

"Sir, would you like anything else?" A waiter arrived, and the moment departed.

"Yeah, can I have a latté and..." I looked at Rita.

"I will take one too."

There was silence, hopeful about the future, sparking the light between the darkness of uncertainty around us.

"You never talk about sex, Meer?" Rita smiled softly.

"I just don't want you to think I'm meeting you with the wrong intention."

"So, what are your intentions?" She looked deep into my eyes.

"My intentions are..."

"Sir, may I..." A respectful waiter was ready to serve the warm drinks.

"Yes, please." I moved my arms from the table.

Rita stared at the waiter, planning to punch the poor thing out of annoyance.

"We will let you know if we need anything else. Thank you very much." She couldn't hold herself back and told him off with a stern smile.

Rita took a deep breath to normalise herself. She looked a bit stressed, a little uncomfortable.

"Just say it, whatever it is," I said confidently and detached, as distant as I could be in that moment.

"What do you want from me, Meer? Why you are taking me out for beers, coffees, dinners? What are your intentions?"

I don't know why but I heard a plea, a powerless shout, like someone was drowning and calling for help, with such low hope knowing that now the next breath is death.

"Why are you doing all this Meer?" Rita tried to sound impartial, but an emotional burst rose in her voice.

"Like what?" I said plainly.

"You are playing this moral guy act with me, which you are not!" Her expression changed to dismissal.

For a second, I felt like she knew about me, who I am. I started sweating in my boots.

"Meer..."

"Listen, Rita, I don't know what you are talking about but... I am just being myself with you, all the time... I take you out because I like you. Talking to you, staying next to you, these all calm me down... I feel cherished around you. I haven't talked about sex because I didn't want you to take me wrong." To cover myself up, I took charge of the conversation.

"So then tell me, when was the last time you had sex?" She smiled a player's smile and winked, back to being playful.

"It was on my birthday, in Feb, over six months ago." I had to say something. Six months or 6 hours, what was the difference between lies?

"Why don't you find yourself a hot young girl Meer? I can tell you, girls like guys like you. Honestly." Rita nodded.

What could I say? How many there are? But girls? Definitely not.

"Let's go home; it's been a long day. And I'll call you a taxi." I smiled at her; a smile learned through hard work of years was at work. My plan was about to charge; the devil was dancing inside me.
"Ok! I won't ask you anything anymore! Thanks for the dinner and the coffee," Rita picked her bag and stood, completely confident that I would stop her. And I didn't.
"Come on… We will talk about it on the way." I walked with her. "Listen to me."
The taxi was slowing down in the mist…
The way was full of fog. Snowflakes were dancing alive under the rays of road lamps; strong winds scattering them, making them weak. And the folds of thick fog… powerless. So was I… drunk! In love. With her.
Rita's lips were on my face and forehead. Her hands were trying to hold and play with everything. Mad wildness ran through her blood. Her tongue was licking my throat and moving towards the neckline. Heavy breaths loaded the windows with mist and moisture…
Moist was there too where she tried to put my hands. The taxi was slowing down… the driver had his own reasons.
"Take me." I felt Rita's breath on my chest.
Broken buttons hanging helplessly on my open shirt were telling the tale of the night. She slipped her fingers along my hairy chest.
"Tear me up Meer."
And before I could say anything, a kiss sealed my lips. Saliva mingled with the juices of the wild one. I saw the eyes of the driver in the rear-view; surely that was not his first time… mine neither.

This wasn't the first time I was taming a passionate woman in a car. I have been licked, kissed, bitten, chewed, sucked, fucked and beaten twice by some savage women in four-wheeled vehicles. But I was prepared, ready for any type of situation. I have to be alert and sensitive to accept and get accepted, almost like a pet dog... wagging its tail, trying to be cute. There is no shame. Also, I get paid cash to get the service done. Wishes must be fulfilled as demanded by the clients. Isn't this the same as your boss expects of you?

Rita had already opened my zipper and was now undoing my belt. She wasn't drunk but was intoxicated by her overflowing juices mixed with the Prosecco we shared earlier.

"So, you can't run away, even if you want to." She mumbled and tried to sit on my lap, moving her hands on my neck to push it closer to her neckline. I kissed her gently and what I sniffed wasn't perfume but the sweet sweat of her.

"Love me as you want. Do what you like. Feel me. Love me." Rita whispered in a poetic, sensual breath.

It wasn't wild, totally crazy, or utterly raw.

It was what I was seeking... seeking throughout my life. Words are too simple, and sentences are too complicated. How did I touch her, how did I make love to her, how did we kiss, how did she love? I can't explain... but nothing else intoxicated me but her blue sparkling eyes, her reddish cheeks, her beautifully outlined lips, her smile, her breath, her body scent, her feet... I don't remember the last time when I put my head over someone's feet and kissed them. Rubbed them with my facial hair and tickle them with my nose. Gathered their legs and put my head on them... I don't remember... I kept my head in Rita's lap, and she kept her healing palm on my forehead, our eyes closed. I don't know where we were and who we were, but I know it wasn't the orgasm. Wasn't the passionate lovemaking that breaks a sweat; it wasn't our exhaustion. It was our souls which made love to each other somewhere, somehow, for some time... Emotions arrayed; the spectrum as calmingly diverse as the peaceful waves of the ocean. You just stand there on the edge of the water, allowing every layer of water to sway you away. You self-immerse into an ocean of memories of magical moments, to feel the relaxing waters of some lagoon where you can re-write your blissful past. And I have nothing in my hands as I drown in my mind. Words are too simple; sentences are too complicated. All that I know now is that I loved her, more than anyone else I ever loved.

"Rita, you might find many men who will love you, but you wouldn't find anyone who loves you truly, deeply, and madly. And I might find someone who would be crazy for me, but I won't find another you anywhere else..." But I couldn't say that to her aloud. The pain spilled from the corners of my closed eyes...
I wish I could say that to you.
You asked me plenty of times, later, why I was crying that night.
I wish I could tell you why I was crying... for what I was crying... But I can't just open the door behind which I am suffocating.
I wish I could hold you in my arms.
I wish I had never lied to you. I wish... I was brave. I wish... I was honest with myself.
Life doesn't stifle me to death, and I won't give up the battle I am fighting to inhale life out of the poisonous truth of reality. Though now I know that my departure won't be heroic and pious, as the guilt of dark circled life is cancerous. I will die eventually ... and painful death is what I'm afraid of. So I want my journey to end now or later in a way... my way. You take a gun in your hand and hold me tight as you hold me pushing inside you... I kiss you... hard. The motion of final joy begins the final journey... You push me harder, hold me tighter... climbing the last mount of climax and I will be reaching the summit. And before I taste the high pleasures, while my eyes are closed in euphoria, you hold my hair... and pull me away. You keep your eyes closed too in red fanatic fantasy, overloaded in alcohol, and you pull the trigger straight at my head... THUD!!!... And the smoke leaves the barrel as my soul fades away from life...

I wish…
I wish I could say…
I wish…

Oceans Apart

"Who is he, who the hell is he... And what the fuck you were talking about? Who is that motherfucker!! AAAHHHH..."
I shouted exactly that loudly in the prison of my mind.
"Hey, Rita, a new friend in Prague?"
I hope I smiled as I delivered the sentence, keeping my eyes on his typical Czech face. He was younger... more than me, in his late teens.
I had just entered our favourite coffee house near Wenceslas Square, where the Soviet tanks crushed the independence of Czechoslovakia in 1968. Spring didn't bloom that year, as the flowers already knew about the deaths of Czech protestors who gathered around the tanks, asking the soldiers to leave. And when nothing made any difference, they knocked punches against the iron elephants. Till... human blood spillage. And the blood is everywhere, on every page of bloody history. Blood was boiling from my feet and bursting like a geyser in my head.
"Hey... Yeah, when you are not around for so many days, then I have to make some other friends, right?" Rita said it wickedly, exactly what she had promised herself not to say... at least not in her first sentence.

I smirked, noticing the proximity of her fingers to his hand. I felt that boy's hands were on Rita's and still... But I tried to explain myself... that how can I be so narrow-minded when I'm fucking others every day!!!... Though not by choice. Or maybe by choice? I never really tried to leave this circle till now, did I?
"You don't have to be so jealous, boy. Calm down," I told myself.
"Badass, you believe in independence and equality, so why can't she fuck another toy boy in your absence? Come on, don't be so angry, play it cool moron... Accept it! You are just a replaceable gigolo." I stood against myself to shatter my poise. "What happened to your broad-mindedness? Don't piss so quickly on our ideas Meer... Man, as a teenager you never came so quickly so don't...don't you lick your balls in guilt right now." The "I against me" conversation knocked me out.
"This is my student, Jan... He wants to be a writer and is looking for some guidance. I thought you could answer some of his questions and possibly direct him a little?" Rita smiled and put her arm around me as I sat next to her. I felt her cheek against my shoulder and... I can't explain just how good that felt. Relieved... relaxed... are incapable words to explain the gigantic feeling of soothing calmness that entered me.
"Oh, baby Meer, you are so screwed." Someone inside me wasn't at peace yet.

"Shithole! How fucked are you…? Think about it, how much crap is inside you that within seconds you were ready to murder both. Shame on you, dirty gigolo, you have no faith in her. Pisshead, just because you sleep with anyone doesn't mean that she'd do the same. Fuck you!"

"Fuck you too!" I shook my head in negation as I tried to shut the mouth of my conscience.

"Hi! I am Jan, sir." A reluctant, confused boy smiled awkwardly at me. He wasn't sure how to introduce himself to a stranger in a foreign language he had learned only at school.

"Sir?" I looked at Rita and then I looked back to his unsure face.

"I'm not a sir. Call me Meer. How can I help?" I tried to bring frankness to my voice, as it wasn't habitual for me to befriend men or boys. My face was expressionless. I wasn't happy about this kid spoiling my evening, an evening Rita and I found after two weeks.

"What can I do for you, Jan?"

"I want to write. I tried to… but I cannot translate my thoughts. And when I can, it's not the same as what I want to write." I heard a deep sadness and hopelessness in his voice. Maybe that's why Rita had brought him to me.

"How old are you?"

"I am 19". He kept his eyes on the floor.

"And do you read, Jan?"

"Yes... Meer sir." I felt he was about to cry.

"What do you like to read my friend?" Finally, a friendly word came out of me with a smile.

"I read romance, philosophy, fantasy." Now I was sure literature reacted with unsettled hormones, possibly resulting in some one-sided love affair.
"Tell me what you have read lately."
"Brokeback Mountain, the short story" He answered me feebly without raising his eyes.
I looked at Rita; she was in a trance and wasn't listening to our conversation. She was far away… somewhere in another universe.
Now this was new to me. I had never faced this kind of situation before. I had no idea what I should say to this kid… I heard about the short story when I was at university but knew nothing more about it.
Rita stood abruptly, the squeaking chair almost shouting in the cafe.
"Meer, I have to go; I have to go now!" she was hysterical, panicking.
"What happened?" I wasn't sure why she was suddenly almost in tears.
"I have to go. I will tell you later. I will ring you in the morning." She was talking fast while putting on her coat.
"I will ring you in a few hours." And before I could ask questions to understand what was happening, she kissed my lips and rushed towards the exit in tears.
"Is everything ok? I can come with you… I am free, why you are crying? What happened?" I chased after her…worried, anxious, haunted by the thoughts of wrong deeds, sensing pending Karma knocking at my door.

"No, no, I will take a taxi, you talk to Jan, he needs you, he needs you, I'm sorry he needs you." She behaved like a crazed woman, running away from a madhouse. I genuinely was frightened of Rita, just for a second. I was shocked to see her like this. She was shattered.
Jan watched the scene.
I saw Rita hailing a taxi and rushing madly inside with a face soaked in tears.
The taxi drove off ... but I kept looking up the busy road blankly. I felt I had lost something... something intangible, something unexplainable but of massive value. I was spinning, hollow within emptiness, as I sat back in my chair.
"I don't understand what happened." Jan said.
"Me neither." I kept looking at the door where she had left many unanswered questions, expecting her to return.
"Would you like to drink something?" I looked at his soft eyes.
"Maybe… a small beer."
I ordered Tuzemák for myself and a beer for him as Jan played with his fingers and I lit a cigarette.
I was quiet, and I wanted to stay quiet. I couldn't comprehend the situation and my mind was reversing the timeline and playing it back till Rita's departure. I tried to think about my actions and words. I couldn't find a clue to her strange exit. I tried to call her, but her phone was switched off. Jan sat opposite me and was completely silent, breathing carefully to avoid any disturbance to my melancholic brainstorming.

"Sorry, we didn't finish our conversation." I tried to divert my mind by resuming my chat with him before I go demented with stress and fear. I took a rough sip which burned my conscious slowly and lured me to the lighter side of the world.

Jan looked at me with familiarity. For a split second, I saw someone else in him; his eyes were another's, as was his style. I felt I knew him in that instant. He was... someone I remembered?

I was silent, unsure what to tell Jan. He nudged me to visit the part of memory lane where I never go to, not even when I'm alone. Some memories are so different, so out of the box from the life experiences that we never want to revisit them; we never elevate to the point where we can truly understand them. They stay enigmas, holding their secrets... never revealing themselves to us. And whenever we return to the past, the magic is so real that we lose the sense of "who we are". I'm not so sure about everyone else. But I can assure you that 'righteous' people like me don't discuss those darkest mysteries with anyone and we even keep them hidden from ourselves too, never confronting them. We hide them somewhere in our heads, where the hands of our consciousness can't reach them. We keep the scissors of curiosity away from that Pandora's Box as we never know what might come out and change everything... forever.

I was 18 and in college with someone who shared my name. He wasn't an ordinary-looking guy, nor was he a heartthrob. A bit on the chubby side, 5 feet 9, black hair, square jaw with shiny light brown naughty eyes. His thighs were an eye magnet when he sat in his fitted jeans... I stared at them, lustful. I looked in his eyes and felt butterflies in my stomach every time he smiled back, noticing my gaze. He was a friendly guy, and I was drawn to him from the very first day I saw him. I never figured out till now that why I yearned for his presence. Why did I have feelings for him? A male?? The arousal was the same, emotionally charged like the one for the female servant I had taken. I never said anything to him, and he said nothing either... but surely there was an understanding, a connection... the same string on two different ends.

Back in those days, things were way complicated for us. We were living far away from our villages in a boarding house in Lahore. I wasn't able to translate his smile that came whenever I touched his thighs while sitting together in a classroom or sitting on the beds. I was afraid, and so was he. But what were we afraid of? Of a society that's sexually deprived of satisfaction, sexual awareness and education, and pushes people to compromise on more animalistic ways to quench their sexual needs? Or were we just afraid of each other? Our presence and "friendship" shook our moral grounds. Eventually, we couldn't keep our morals clean anymore. My hands were never off from his thighs for long when we were together.... I remember whenever I hugged him, it was too long... or sometimes too short... but never enough!

I constantly had this wish to kiss him hard and move my hands on his body. As a child, I had been taught that these actions are immoral, inappropriate and religiously wrong. The same was taught to him by his parents. But no one explained to us what to do when we are in a situation where we want to be with a person of the same gender all the time and always feel like hugging and kissing them.

He wasn't brave, nor was I. Very quietly we kept hugging each other whenever we had the chance… behind closed doors. And every time we separated; we didn't look into each other's eyes. We were always quiet. Was it a sin? Maybe it was. So as punishment we stop sitting together or meeting each other as the guilt was just too high, till… the day I knocked on his door.

I met him for the last time on our last day at the boarding house. And I only remember this much… that as he closed the door and turned towards me. I threw my arms around his neck and before he could react, my lips were on his… And my hands were all over his body, making love to him.

That was like a dream… dream within a dream.

And when we woke up, the sun was setting… giving way to a long cold night.

After six months, he wrote me a letter with an invitation to his marriage. I couldn't write back.

I wish I could see him again and could tell him that…

Love and life is not a monologue. It's a dialogue.

Time drifts us apart and away we go… quietly.

Back to Business

I was on my way going to Reichenberg in the great Austrian Empire, now Liberec in the Czech Republic, to meet the main reason for the bed of money on which I slept every day…Babel Bergman.
After Rita's bizarre departure, I had heard nothing from her. Her mobile phone was usually off and even when it was ringing there was no one who could press the green button. I left voice messages, texted, wrote her thousand times, but no news arrived. A couple of times I went to her place, but it seemed like no one was inside. I pressed the buzzer forcefully for so long that I nearly cracked my forefinger. But who was there who could open the door? The music school where she worked was trying to reach her too, but all in vain. I had no contact to ask about her whereabouts. I had so many fears, but none of them had any solid grounds on which they could stand. There was no logic… no sense… and that's what exactly makes the fear stronger.
Her absence devastated me. Stupid thoughts and foolish ideas were haunting my mind. I felt lonely… I felt bad… and at the end of my depression, I was walking numb in the silence of death. There was nothing that could bother me, or take my attention, or switch the life back towards worldly pleasures to make me feel normal.

I wasn't picking up any calls or replying to the messages I received. After many days, when I finally looked in the mirror, I couldn't recognize myself. My eyes were puffy, and the rosy face was now pale. I wasn't eating much either, and it showed. Jailing myself in my flat made me think about all the misery that life had forced on me. I hated myself so much that I thought very seriously about taking my own life.

Elevation and depression... Having all in life and still feeling a sense of nothingness... having no hopes about tomorrow. Gloomy, dark feelings about the limited dirty circle of life where I had no freedom. I had money, but nothing to spend the money on. I was still young, powerful, passionate, but there was no one by my side to enjoy 'the life' with. I had no sense of belonging. I felt like an outcast. My glory was doomed, and I felt destined to fail in the game of Karma. I will be poisoned by my own hands and will be the one slicing my throat.

Once the son of a most powerful man, an elected member of the National Assembly, an influential landlord of Punjab, and now... a gigolo.

What did life want me to understand? I was trying to figure that out before crossing the borders of sanity. I tried to comprehend my life: Rita, my feelings, past, present, future, my habits, my attitude, life... But everything was just one colossal mess. Nothing seemed to be right. All sat in a state of chaos and confusion. Several factors dominated, directed by millions of other reasons that were then overshadowed by some unknown forces of life and time.

Everything has a boundary, and all seems good only in limits. After crossing the threshold, either you end up in jail, a madhouse, or hospital. And no option is desirable for any over-stayer. So, I find my balance in just the right amount of alcohol, a necessity to survive another day or night. Last night, almost a bottle of vodka and a few beers were enough for self-realisation.

I was sick. What went in was erupting out. I was puking, throwing up every single drop. Waves of pain pulled out the colourless vodka and some blood. The body was shaking and hurting, paining my soul. Marking me with a hot iron of hurt as I jerked and shivered with my hands on the washbasin. I was trying to pull myself together before the next episode drained what was left inside me. I turned my head up… and there I was, in the mirror… the mirror which shows you who you are, what you want to be… and I was there ugly, dirty, with lips covered in filth. That was me, the real me… is this me? I asked myself. That question cleared it all. The thought, the deepened depression, the negativity, pessimism, sadness and the pain of division between love and self-love. That question was the end of all. It was the alarm that awoke the sleeping egoistic Meer. That was the final trigger.

"This bitch is behaving like a spoiled whore, and you are acting like a mother-fucking Romeo from the 16th century. You could and have fucked better. You can find someone more reliable and better than her. She's trying to hurt you because she doesn't love you. She wants you to look bad, so bad that you couldn't be with any other woman. Boy, you don't know these bitches. She's playing big time with you. She wants all of you for herself my prince. Enough now! Enough!!! Get back to life before you cut your cock and hand it over to her and she runs you like a spineless peasant. You need no one, you need you! You need only you! Remember, the hand that is going to help you at the end of the day is the one at the end of your arm. Just don't forget that."
I guess that was it. My self-love ended the spell of Rita. I could sacrifice my world for her, but I couldn't spill the blood of my ego on the altar of any Goddess or God.
In that second, I bounced back. I tried to behave soberly. I shaved, trimmed my nails, took a shower, dressed up and put on my favourite cologne. I looked at myself with a smile in the mirror. I looked fresh and handsome. This longing for Rita had left a touch of gracefulness and something soft within my eyes.
"My husband is going for three days to Berlin. I told you 3 months ago; I want to see you."
"Are you coming? Where are you?"
"*Ach* Meer, I am waiting for your reply."
"Can you please book the hotel room?"
"I am planning for a hot night after so many months… Oh Gott! Why are you not replying?"

"Don't make the appointment with another woman on those days, I told you. I hate when you ignore me. Reply me before I get angry." I had several messages of the same sort on my phone and who else could it be... crazy, deeply in love with a gigolo? Frau Bergman.
"Why do you love me so much? You know who I am... I mean, I have nothing to offer you in this relationship." I moved my fingers on her 58-year-old slim back, playing with the dark hair lying over her shoulders as she fixed her bright jet-black eyes on my face to read my forever calculating mind, listening very carefully to decide the right response. But she was quiet, very unlike the Frau Bergman I know... dominantly demanding, intelligent, and full of energy. She looked a peculiar Central European mix with dark features, not like any German I had ever seen. Maybe that was a result of blood she inherited from her Hungarian father. Regardless of her age, power and looks, she was in love with me, but I never took unfair advantage of her vulnerability. In fact, I hated the way she wanted to sniff out every detail about me, my life, my past. She chased me to know where I was, with whom and what I was doing. At the end of every month, I receive a courier with a fake name and address in which some practical household things would be packed with money and a short, typed letter.

"I know your taste and I know that you don't like my parcels, but I know you live alone, and I can't be with you. On my shopping day, I saw this frying pan, and I thought of you and bought it. I know you are lazy when it comes to shopping. I know you so well. I would like to see you again. It's not easy for me to look into the eyes of my husband after our meetings, but I don't know how to run away from you and where to go. Hey Meer, I need a little bit from your side too. I wish I was never introduced to you. But it's too late. In my heart, there are three chairs... And I do not know who is on chair number one... I want Bergman to be there... but? I want to see you soon."

That was six months ago, when I asked her, "Why do you love me so much? My fingers were slipping down her back, down.... down... down till her small cheek touched the edge of my finger.

"I love it Meer...that I can make you so hard. I think of your penis every day, oh Gott! Meer... You know I think of you all day with Venus balls inside me. And all day I just think how hard you get when I give you a *blasen*. I stay wet all day, I never cum so quick with my husband but with you.... *Das ist so gut*, I cum in seconds... I don't know what you do to me!" She turned like a little girl who is full of action and energy and speaks non-stop. She could bring all topics of the world in one breath. I hated her youthfulness; in fact, there is a complete list that make her impossible. But it was the money that kept me near her… with a smiling face. But everything has limits. "How's your dad doing?" Frau Bergman asked me millionth time.

"He was shot a couple of years ago; four 9mm bullets tore his chest - And you know that!! Can't we just stop this never-ending interview every time we meet? I mean, why ask me the same questions all the time? Do you think I lied to you, and I will tell you something different and then you will be proud that you found an unknown fact about my past life?" I was fuming!
"Yes, because you lie to me all the time." She said.
"I don't lie. I just don't like to tell the truth to everyone. You know everything. I'm illegal, my dad is dead, I am not an American citizen, the rent of my flat is 15,000 Czech Koruna, my collar size is large, my shoe size is 43, and my brother was a drug addict slash sex worker in Stockholm and now he is in a rehabilitation centre in Karachi. My mom died, likely killed by my dad immediately after my birth. And I do not have any serious girlfriend because I am a gigolo. But why is it so important for you to piss me off every time I see you? What's the pleasure behind fucking hurting me and pushing me towards the dark corners of my life? What do you think? I'll get mad, lose my mind, and will fuck you insanely? Is that the reason? *Du bist ein schlampe! hure!*" I swore at her.
"*Ach* Meer, I just wanted to know more about you, that you are ok. I want to see you happy. You are a very good boy, I just wanted to know a bit more, but you are a boy with few words." She sounded enthusiastic as always, even after her insult.

"I told you I have this kind of personality, that I cannot open myself to anyone. The more you try to know me, try to go deep inside me, the more a web of lies I will knit. This is my defensive mechanism. Why don't you understand? You love me? This is how you love me?"
"Don't be angry, please, *Ich bitte dich*." She hugged me. "I want to see you happy. Why don't you marry some Czech girl?" Her lips were on my face.
"Who will marry me? You are telling me to find a girlfriend? I can tell you *schatzi*, you would be the first person who would try to destroy our life."
"You have no confidence in me Meer?" She was shattered in tears.
"Listen, let me go, I don't want to be here anymore. I am not here to listen to your ideas about my life, and now after all this "lovely time," I am not in the mood to stay. You have my address; you have all the details that you need to give to the immigration department. Do it! I will never contact your rich broker husband. You can make arrangements to kick me out of Europe." I threw the blanket aside and started to dress when she shouted.
"They'll kill you in Pakistan too if you go back! Who do you think I am? If I wanted to throw you out, I could do it. You forget I was working with a lawyer when I was young! You never understood me!!!" She was yelling.
"Then do it… Fick *dich*!!!" I slammed the door and left. That was six months ago. Now, I am going to Reichenberg to meet her again… Babel Bergman…

Delusions

I spat at the sky, and it spat back.
I was in the same hotel... exhausting the same conversation, answering the tiresome questions and indulging the same unexciting woman.
I was licking what I had spat.
"I live a happy life, my husband loves me, my three kids, my two grandkids all of them love me. I have everyone's heart."
"Except mine... right?" I completed her thought.
"Yes! And that hurts. I need more from you Meer. I wish I never knew you, never had so much pain in life... you hurt me so much." She was so emotional after an orgasm.
"I'm definitely your Karma then." I felt her nose on my chest, breathing slowly.
"I never understood why Gott sent you to me."
"I don't know why God sent me your way either, but I do know that Mrs. Kolarova arranged this meeting so she could fuck your husband in peace."
"*Das ist nichts wahr.*" I heard the confidence of the German race. She simply rejected the fact.
"*Meine mann* will never do that, I believe on him very much, every man is not like you."
"No, everyone is not like me, and that's why you have been sleeping with me for almost two and half years." There was revenge in my voice.

"I have much confidence on my husband, and I don't want to talk about it!" She commanded me with the authority of a blindly believing wife.
"Where have you been in the last few months? You never answer my phone calls and messages. And something is... changed inside you when I saw you coming today, you look different." Babel looked closely at my face.
I closed my eyes to keep my secret. She could read eyes easily.
"Are you in love Meer?" She was so psychic, damn it! Now I had to keep my mouth shut at all costs.
"I asked you something, are you listening to me?" There was hope in her tone.
I felt like a thief, caught red-handed.
"You are not answering my question, I know there is something."
"I don't answer nonsense questions." I closed my eyes and held all expression.
"Why are you not looking at me?" She tried to trick me with a complaint.
I opened my eyes.
"I love only one person in this world, myself!" I answered in finality.
"*Ach* Meer, I know you hide things from me... I had lived much life and I know about things. It's written all over your face." She was trying to dig deeper.
"You know, after knowing you I have learned that a badass woman is worse than a detective. If there is something, you will find it." I smiled at her.
"So, you will not tell me anything?" She rubbed her hands against my thighs, scratching gently with her long nails.

"Is there something to say.... even now?" I winked and moved her hands to my erection, as that was my best trick to quiet her.

The evening was spreading shadows over the town hall. Darkness surrounded the city and high in the mountains, the last ray of sun was about to die. Quietness gathered in the streets and streetlamps weren't enough to lighten the depression of silence. Everything was dampened by the dark.

Babel left just before the sunset, to be home before her husband's arrival. I slept throughout the evening after the day's exhausting work. Emotionally and psychologically drained, gloomy and heavy inside when I woke up in the middle of the night. I was alone in a pitch-dark room with emptiness filling my ears. Night muted everything, and shadows masked every face. The stillness in the room was so dreadful that it peaked into a depression. I wanted to shout against the frightening, grave-like darkness. My heartbeat was loud, and breaths were louder… sweating. I felt the bed shaking when I saw Rita... on the edge of a cliff, still as a statue, running towards her, but under my feet were snakes spitting their poison on every step. I tried hard to reach her, but my feet were in the whirlpool of snakes that melted me with toxicity. I ran for my life. I ran for suicide. She was still there... I was... I was... drowning, turning bluish-green under the rattlesnakes' whispers. Promising a rebirth free from sins and pain, a fresh start full of power and sex, hidden wealth, if I accepted my death.

"That's an initiation, the price you pay for immortality. You lose her, you lose yourself. We break you from the pain and misery you inflict on yourself. You love no one; you love 'only' you. All are immaterial. Leave yourself, die now, and we'll carry you on our bodies to the gate of heaven. You'll see the master. You won't die, and you won't cry. Come to us… come now. You are us, and we are you now. You don't know who you are. You belong somewhere very far."
The snakes hissed at me and the next morning I found my mouth full of blood. My wrists were black and green, and my eyes turned midnight black. I heard strange sounds.... like wind hitting glass, trying to enter my room. I looked outside and saw Rita, in the sky, still as a statue with open, inviting arms. I prepared to run to see what this sorcery was when the hotel's phone rang.
"Fuck!"
I shouted and ran back. Pulling the phone next to the window.
"Hello!"
"Sir, there's an envelope for you. Room 205."
I hung up the phone. Rita had disappeared in front of my eyes as I had answered the call. I ran outside, my eyes desperately seeking. And in the street, I noticed a blond, taking quick steps to disappear into an adjacent alley."
"I must be losing my mind." I told myself as I picked envelope from reception.
"No news is good news." The sentence was scribbled on a blank sheet of paper inside the envelope.
"Who left this for me?" I asked the receptionist.

"I don't know. I found this on the counter and.... I called you. Apologies for any inconvenience." And before I could respond, he left the counter and hurried to his back office.

I was going back to Prague.

"No news is good news." Who left that message for me, I kept asking myself. I spoke with Babel and she confirmed she hadn't left anything for me at reception.

"No news... is good... news, good news, good news..." echoed within my worried thoughts while Rita looked down from the sky with a blank face.

News from My Life

Fog settled between the twigs, and snow frosted the roots. There was no single leaf left on the branches to announce life; the bare tree was fighting for its survival that winter.
So was I.
"No news is good news." An unknown messenger whispered inside me as I told myself "Give time to time" countless times that morning to satisfy the discontentment. "Not before time nor without destiny. No one can snatch what's yours. Faith is fate." I recalled esoteric sayings from the past to support my current failure.
I looked out the window to my companion tree; he is always there for me whenever I need him. Recently I had realised that there is not so much different between us. He stands there always, alone, regardless of good or bad times. So do I... fighting against the odds for my survival. We looked at each other through this window like good neighbours, saying "hello" every day with smiles. He is a kind and friendly tree. I can tell you if I have a genuine friendship in this city with anyone, it's with my tree. Last summer when I was sitting under his cool shadow, he asked me if I was happy. I couldn't really answer his question, but like a good friend I asked him the same question, and he replied.

"You know Meer... have you ever noticed that you visit me only in summers?" He paused. "You like my leaves; you like the fresh fragrance of the grass under my shade. You enjoy the chirping birds on my branches. You sit with me, and we share our stories. But you never come to me in winters... when I am cold and frozen. When I'm alone and need a little hug and the warmth of your body... You stand there in your window and wave your hand like a distant acquaintance and never come down." He was silent for a moment.

"Happiness is the care and concern we get in the frozen winters of our life. Today it's sunny and you are here... even if you are not here. I wear a lush green dress. I have stories from these birds. The sun shines on me. But it's only a matter of sunshine. In good times, we are happy, we would be... even if no one cares about us. There is not so much difference between us Meer. We were both born to be alone. Someone planted me here far away from my family where the weather is so bad and I don't have enough sunshine. You are planted here too, just that I have roots and you are holding the roots of your destiny. You live far away; your own home is now a distant foreign land. We are alike... I hope I answered your question."

He was so polite and such a deep thinker.

"So, you mean... we can't be happy anytime in our life?" I touched his trunk to feel his breath.

"We should ask this question of ourselves. Life is what else other than perception?" He was silent for a moment. "Or ask God, if you have one. Ask him why he planted us here? What is our destiny? What's our purpose and direction? Life is much easier if we know the flow... If we can get a glimpse of the destination."

"I know our destination... I think." I said reluctantly.

"Meer, we are not talking about death here."

"What's the destination, if not death?"

"All paths lead to only one road," he said calmly.

"Yes, all paths lead to only one road." Hopeless, I recalled Rita as I repeated his sentence.

We went silent, and I gently put my head on his trunk, as his too philosophical talk dizzied me. I was already missing Rita. I was tired, and soon fell asleep. God knows which dreams are prophetic, but I had a dream.... maybe that was a sign.

I saw myself standing on a mountain. I am on the summit. I am alone and I'm successful. I am on the top of the world. I am the conqueror. I put my hand up in the air to tell the world loudly.

"I'm here, the winner, the conqueror... announcing victory over life."

But as I raised my arms, I realized they were empty. I didn't have my ice axe... I didn't have my gear... I had no ropes. But I was there, at the apex... unhappy, worried, stressed... fighting for my survival. Fog and clouds settled around me. My feet were frosted by snow.

"There is no difference between you and me Meer." My tree friend said from outside the windowpane, as I was unravelling the logic, intuition, and hint from the message I received from the unknown sender.

No news is good news.
Unless it wasn't...

Entertainer

I was still looking at my tree when the phone rang. For a thousandth of a second, I was annoyed by the bloody ring and in the next thousandth 'Rita' flashed in my head. I ran in excitement to get the bitter fruit of love. Broken hopes... disappointment.
"Hello?" I gasped.
"Hello, am I speaking with Meer?" A friendly voice failed to cheer me up.
"Yes." My tone was colder than northern lands.
"I... I... Mrs Nováková gave me your number." He fumbled to speak.
I couldn't remember who she was.
"And?" I added.
"And... we would like to invite you.... for... dinner at our home." He was selecting words carefully and delivering them with polite diplomacy.
"May I please ask, who are 'we'?"
I like to be sure of what invitations I accept, after mistakenly accepting an offer from an unusual and odd couple.
"My wife and I. We would like you to come over next Saturday around 6 pm." He was growing comfortable.
"Ok. Do you know about me?"
"Yes, no, it's ok... I know you... you are..." He was looking for a synonym.
"You are an entertainer." He introduced me to myself.

"Entertainer." I repeated "Entertainer… Indeed, I am." For some reason, this new title amused me a lot. 'Entertainer.' A grin came across my face.
"Alright, you can text me your address. In case you change your mind, just let me know a day before." I sounded totally like a booking agent.
"All is confirmed. I will text you in a minute." An old jazz tune was fading out in his background.
"Ok, see you then, bye." I dropped the call before he even replied.
I was disturbed and a bit rude. I couldn't speak the way I usually do. And Nováková, who the hell is she? I juggled the question till bedtime. I checked my phone to see my contacts, but there was no one with this pseudonym. "I didn't even confirm the client's details. How stupid am I!" I told myself. "Well, didn't have much choice either. I'll be free on coming Saturday, so why not? I'm still alive and have bills to pay."

But I was hesitant as some really weird experiences with couples had fucked my brain. And frankly, this was not my type of thing. I avoid doing couples. The whole concept is kind of messed up in my head. What should I say? I know why this happens. But I can't understand the attraction behind watching the "trophy wife" giving head to a strange man or the husband bang another bird, while filming it or watching and enjoying the sight. I mean... what a fetish. When I was in Newcastle, I thought I knew and did everything. I was well informed in Pakistan too. Swaps, gang bangs, orgies, key parties, I had an idea about all of them. But 'cuckolding' and 'cuckquean' lifestyles were eye-openers. I remember one of my 'cougar' clients telling me about how her husband and his friend had "tag team fun" with her and how she deprived him occasionally from 'pleasuring' himself during power play. I just shook my shoulders over the matter and said: "I hope you are not telling me that you will bring your husband for Devil's threesome." She winked vulgarly and said, "Darling, he is dead by the great grace of God."

There was another occasion too. It was over a year ago. I had a similar call, and the caller provided me with the reference of someone I knew well. At that time, I was relatively uneducated in dating "couples."

In my line of business, every day carries millions of hours of crude experience. Sex workers learn things in the speed of light, even when they don't want to and don't have to. Longevity has nothing to do with time, but it has all to do with gaining experience and insight. Once we touch our maximum, we die. Nature limits us from burdening our self with too much emotional and spiritual cognition. But is there round two? As I firmly believe in the saying of Emperor Baber "Baber, relish the pleasures, for the world is never again."

And again, I repeated the same protocol I had made with the previous couple. I kept the call short as you never knew who is on the other side. A lot of questions raised and stayed in my head, but I couldn't ask them over the phone.

On the fixed date and time, I was there... He was very polite, a retired professor of sociology from Charles University. The wife was much younger, probably younger than I. He told me she had been his student. His first wife died a few years before. The professor looked slightly younger than his 62 years but there was old soul sadness in his eyes; when he laughed, there wasn't any joy. He seemed to force himself to be amused.

For over an hour after dinner, we drank. There was a pleasant discussion with him over nature/nurture theory. The professor knew the art of speech. I paid close attention to the wife while he lectured. She was sitting across the sofa, and between me and her was the professor. She showed no interest in me; she was mesmerized by the charm of her husband, spellbound, deep in love. She even forgot to blink, in deep hypnosis of magical love. The professor snapped his fingers to break the spell.
"Class is over now." He laughed looking at her appraisingly and turned towards me.
I do not know what I expected as I was still in my absorbing zone, processing knowledge and facts in silence, when he said "Hey, young man..." He moved his hand to my shoulder and squeezed meaningfully.
"Be gentle to her... *nazdravi*, cheers!" He raised his glass joyfully.
"I can tell you are a gentleman. I do have one request." He was definitely drunk, and his words were no longer in order, the chain of thoughts left his tongue speechless and now he was using his hands to express himself.
"I will follow your directions and meet your expectations," I smiled and patted his shoulder to calm him.
"Maybe this sounds funny. But.... can I watch...?" He lost his words again.
For a second, I felt like an innocent peasant.
"Sorry, once again.... What did you just say? Sorry..." I was trying to come out of my own fabricated world.
"Can... I see my wife... having sex with you?" His drunken eyes were looking crazy.

Blank, within thoughts. My slight pause suddenly stretched the awkward silence in the room.

"See... you are taking so long to answer... this means, no ... Doesn't it?" Drunken bastard snapped.

"No, No... I was just trying to understand..."

"Understand what? Understand why I am impotent? Why I have a wife my daughter's age?" The alcoholic professor's depression screamed out. He started yelling at me, cursing in Czech. His goodness was gone and now he was a complaining asshole, whose wife was trying to calm him down with her warmth and kisses.

I felt like a piece of shit. A punching bag full of sickness that could be kicked, knocked, smacked anytime. I felt sorry for myself. I was abused for nothing.

"You think I am impotent?!" The professor roared again. Fuck my wife for me, I order you!!!"

I had nothing to say... but I was expected to say something.

"Well, sir, I was not thinking about your impotency. But regarding your question, my answer is no. Not now, not ever. I will not have sex with your wife in front of you and I guess you don't want to continue business with me, so this is goodbye." I moved my hand towards him. "And thanks for dinner." I looked in his eyes and waited a few seconds before withdrawing the offered hand when the professor's palm grabbed mine. "Oh... Oh, I am sorry. I got too drunk; I hate myself when I do that... Don't go, don't go anywhere." He dropped to his knees to hold my calves. He was begging and crying for forgiveness. "I am sorry, don't go, don't go... stay here, she is a nice girl... she is nice... very nice. Don't go; don't go, please... if I asked you for the wrong thing, I'm sorry." He was heaped on the floor now, in tears. "But see, how much courage you need to get your beloved into someone else's bed? How much pain I have inside me...? But it's ok... it's ok... I like you... I like you." He stood up on his feet and indicated the bedroom door. "You are already here... and I like you. I like you... you shouldn't go back, and I apologize for my words. I am sorry." He looked at his wife, standing there, next to the bedroom... expressionless, a blank face, detached.
"She is all yours, inside these walls." He put both of his hands on my shoulders as he stood opposite me and kept the open door of the bedroom behind his back where she was standing still.
"But be gentle to her." I saw tears in his eyes.
"Look here..." He stretched his shirt to show the divide of open-heart surgery.
"Now you have all the answers for the unasked question." I felt the weight of his imbalance on me.

"Why are you doing this? Inviting an entertainer when it hurts you so much? You love her and she loves you too, you know that...then, why another man?"

"Because..." He took a deep breath.

"Because, if I can't make her happy, that doesn't mean that I can't buy happiness for her. And I just want to stand in the room and look at her because... I wanted to see that feeling that I can't give to her. I want to feel that pleasure on her face by staying around her. I want to enjoy her happiness... happiness... Do you know what happiness is? Happiness is a wave... It comes, and it goes... away, far away... and we chase it to get it back. Run... till we drown into the misery of losing that wave without noticing the new waves coming to us." He looked at me, turned, and returned to his darling.

"I love you honey... I love you." The professor kissed her passionately on the lips. "No one loves you more than I... no one... no one." The professor murmured as he turned his back and left the room quickly.

"Be gentle to her... be gentle," I saw the tears floating in his eyes again...

What I should, if I could

The wounds weren't healed yet. Spring was far, and the life was in a storm, there was no one who could rescue me. I closed all the doors from the inside and sat in a corner of the prison of my mind. Loneliness was the result. Life was a dark frozen night, and I couldn't see my North Star. I kept my eyes closed and kept thinking and dreaming about Rita. After two years I pulled out the pages of my partly autobiographical diary/novel written about my life in northeast of England. I looked at the notes, which I added to the tops of the pages. Weird thoughts... weird stories ... really.

I read a few pages, and I realised that there was a character with blue eyes and blonde hair. Was it just a coincidence? Or was I attracted to someone with a similar appearance? Or maybe I was in a spiritual trance where I drew a picture from the future; an appearance or... Was I trying to level the difference between the master and the slave? Or was I obsessed by blondes with coloured eyes? Meanwhile, I was juggling my philosophy. I kept my almost 'had' blonde with blue eyes in my mind as background, the time spent with her. My memories are the fresh stories of the lost protagonist.

I pulled out a new sheet and looked at the empty page, blank, laying silent, waiting to be brought to life. I stared at the tip of my pen as a mad magician looks at the end of his wand, thinking of his power and pain, wondering what barmy he can force to reality by unleashing the reality of his mind. I was looking deep into the soul of the ink thinking how life might reveal itself on this dead page. Will birds sing? Will rainbows flow? Will the sunshine? While I sit in the dark silence of loneliness thinking of the unimaginable madness of life, wondering who fills pens with words, with stories, with signatures? How that would be if we could see the hidden gems concealed in our pens? The blue one with white strips for fantasy fairy tales, the red cap for passionate romantics, yellow with glitter for tomorrow's painter, drawing pictures on walls with her little hands, writing the truth of the world for someone who could see, for someone who could read, for someone who wants to know. And the pen here in this hand is... for Meer, who would blow on the tip of his pen and make the words fall from the tip, just like the dandelions floating in the air listening to the rhythm of nature. Dancing under enchanting spells to find the rainbow words for the master, wild in the air, he captures them in silence to colour the canvas of life, choosing shades of non-existence to beautify unknown worlds by playing with words. Writing stories of others from the words and sentences of another...coming to his blank page to make a difference in the lives of living dead.

I was playing with the pen and thoughts, was trying to translate myself into sentences as they were slipping from my hands again and again. I wanted to blow on the tip of the pen to see if there are really any words hidden inside or not. But I guess I loved these words so much that I lost them. One never keeps for long what one loves. Time takes it back. Time or God or both... or just us, our overprotective, possessive actions just take the life away from what we love the most. In our actions are reactions... equal and opposite, a way towards destruction and demise.

Someone gently knocked on the door.

"Aaah, now who could that be? *Kurwa!*" I lost my temper.

"Fuck off!" I yelled and marched towards the door to see the face of the unreluctant devil who continued to knock.

"*Dobry den.*" The eternally confused Jan was staring at me.

"Who told you where I live?" I was furious.

"I am sorry. I just... wanted to see... I am sorry," Jan was stuttering, his face turned red in shame.

"She told me... you live here."

"She who?" I shouted.

"*Pani* Rita.... I will come back later... I am sorry!" Jan was about to cry.

I realised that I had overreacted for no reason. And strangely felt sorry for him.

"Why are you here, what do you want?" I asked, still annoyed.

"No, I...." He struggled to speak. His mouth turned dry and dried his self-confidence. The poor boy was in the gutter psychologically.

"Hey Jan. Just give me one minute; we can go for a drink. Don't go anywhere... I am sorry." I apologized while wondering what I was sorry for.
"Give me a minute, I will be with you." I went back inside feeling awful for shouting at the man-child.
The trouble was that I don't tell anyone where I live, ever. I never invited anyone inside. Not even Rita. She wanted to have a sneak peek, but I made excuses about the mess. So what was the secret inside the flat? Absolutely nothing! Just me and my loneliness, money, and books, that's all.
Jan was there, standing still, waiting for a command from me.
"Let's go." I marched him away from my door and towards the nearest pub.
"Hey, don't be so sad. I know I was rude. It's just that I like my privacy. I'm sorry. Now relax, please."
"I would like to ask you something," Jan said, emotionless.
"Yeah, yeah sure, but let's order something first," I said as we sat.
The first thought that came to me was that he had a crush on me. But it's ok; I will clear it with him that I am not gay. I can handle this.
"What were you saying?" I smiled placing beers in front of him, trying to make him comfortable.
"Do you know her?" Jan put a picture in front of me, watching my face silently and with expectation.
I looked at him carefully then glanced at the photo. A flash... an alarm triggered.
"How do you know her, Jan?" I didn't look in his eyes. I was puzzled.

"She is my mother." He smiled cunningly.
His mother was a customer whom I had met twice over a year ago, maybe more. She was a sexually frigid woman, cold as ice. Nothing worked on her, no trick, no magic... nothing. The first meeting took place at her house when her husband was abroad. The whole evening, we just talked. She said she hadn't had had an orgasm for years. When she was young someone tried to rape her. From that day onwards she had issues in getting comfortable during sex. The fortunate part was that her husband was a guy with a low sex drive. After having his son, her sexual appetite decreased to zero.
So what could I do for her?
She told me that something had changed in the last year, and she now had cravings for sex. But her brain interrupted her solo attempts, and her husband's appetites had ended years ago. So now she slept alone, turning restlessly in the big bed at night.
She sought advice and an orgasm. I bought her different sex toys, and played with them together, results were satisfactory. And I filled her hunger both times too. After that, she never contacted me again. I wasn't bothered. I knew she was almost a God-fearing woman who would turn back to unfulfilling monogamy after failing to manage her new physiological change. I later thought she probably contacted me only to buy sex toys for her, but I didn't care. Whatever mission I was hired for was accomplished.
"What can I do for you, Jan?" I was totally shocked and somehow lost.
"I will be straight." He sipped his beer.

"I want you to help get my mother a divorce. Don't even think about saying no. You remember you came to my house once and my mother thought I was not at home. Well, I wasn't, but my spy cam was." I felt him enjoying my discomfort and confusion the way a pervert relishes a lap dance.

"It was my good fortune that I met you through my teacher."

"What do you mean?" I could barely stop myself from slamming him against the wall.

"Don't interrupt me, again. Soon enough, you will understand." His smile and confidence hinted that he had a plan. He wasn't the same guy I had met not so long ago.

"I want you to help my mother divorce my dad. The story you started; you have to end that. I know who you are, and I know what you do. But I have never said anything to my 'favourite' teacher. I know you are deeply in love with her."

This child was racing my blood pressure and staying quiet wasn't helping either.

"She loved you too; I love her too..." He was slowing his conversation on purpose with a perfect script.

"If you want me to keep your secret with *Pani* Rita and also if you want me to get out of her life after…" He took a meaningful pause to suspend my breath as I looked powerlessly at him.

"But let me tell you something first that will interest you." A player's smile sat on his face.

"What?" I felt trapped.

"Her new address and work location. She is back in Prague, two weeks ago, with her daughter. All is possible if you get my mother out of our house and later... divorced."

I wanted to beat this child. I would probably have killed him... but he had planned it all so wonderfully, that I couldn't afford to do anything against this incestuous bastard.

"So, we are all clear now, right?" He stood up to end the torture session.

"But Jan, why do you want me to get your mother a divorce? She is an adult, not a child that I can convince." I asked out of my numbness.

"The pictures in the envelope will explain all." He slipped an envelope towards me.

"For your pleasure only." He looked deep inside my eyes.

"I want to see her happy, doing things that she likes. She doesn't deserve a man like my father, who's never been there for her." Jan said these last words and left swiftly.

My head was spinning, my brain was fucked, and I wasn't able to think about what had just happened. What to do, what not to, and what would be the plan. I didn't believe in his reasoning. He was lying. I was sure the reality was different, but that didn't bother me. I was partly sure it had something to do money and nothing to do with his mom's happiness.

"Rita... Meer is a gigolo!" In my head I saw Jan telling Rita.

What Rita would think?

I asked this question of myself before. What will happen if Rita discovers my reality?

I'm not sure if I'm brave enough to commit suicide. And if she comes to know I am gigolo then what's the big deal? We are not associated, not in an officially approved relationship. Her family doesn't know about me, and her child doesn't either. So what if I'm a gigolo? Anyway, I am one! Fuck it!!! The painful part is that I will lose her forever, not because I am a sex worker but because I lied. She will not believe in anyone anymore. Maybe that's not my problem. Then what is my problem?
I didn't want to lose Rita, but I didn't want to hurt her either. And I can't leave this business. I can't change my past. I can't leave the Czech Republic. I can't kill anyone. What should I do? I couldn't understand a thing between the clashing thoughts and Jan's admissions. "She loved you too! She loved you too!"
I went back to the flat completely wasted and started hitting my head against the wall. Depression took over me, and out of my frustrated anger, I rang Jan.
"OOY! OOY! OOY!! asshole Jan! Tell me why you said she loved me too; don't she love me anymore? Shit face, son of a bitch!" I kept yelling at the unanswered phone. I smashed the phone against the sofa. Felt shit for a brief moment of consciousness which came as enlightenment. I'm a zero; once again, I was standing on a ZERO... Rita... Jan... Babel Bergmann...
Rolling on the bed in a deep depression of alcohol, drowning, when Jan's name flashed on my phone.
"Why are you calling me in the middle of the night asshole?" Jan swore in deep sleep.
"I just wanted to ask... Why did you say she loved me too, she still loves me right?" Surprisingly I was suddenly cool, sober, and calm.

"Fuck you! You will find out all, once my mother leaves the hellhole - goodbye!"

Fragment of Demise

The silent phone was blinking in the dark...
Like a neon sign, switching itself ON and OFF... ON and OFF in the jet-black hollowness. And it continued... the phone didn't stop, neither did the stress of the caller. The irregular glow of the phone hit hard against the walls, seeking to convey the message of the ringer... "Pick up the phone! ... I said, pick up the PHONE!" The flickering illumination begged to be answered.
I kept watching the blinking phone with my dead dry eyes. I was silent... my mother, my daughter, my house... everything seemed to be out of life, powerless... As if there were no more words left to say, no more sounds to be played.
I'm Rita. You know me. But do you know about death? That it has its own odour? I didn't realise this until I smelled it myself. I sensed it for the first time on that day, when Meer was talking with Jan...
"Rita," My mom was on the phone.
"Rita... it's more than two weeks and Tim hasn't contacted us. I tried to reach him through the army base, but they always tell me... 'He is not here now. He's out.'" My mother's voice was full of tears.
"Mom, everything will be fine... I am sure he is there. He is just busy, you know, he will be ok... he will be." I tried to comfort her, but for the last few days, my heart was feeling low too.
"No news is the best news mom. All will be ok. He will ring you..."

"Rita, please come back. Amelia is missing you and I cannot..." She started sobbing and the receiver slipped from her hands onto the floor.
"Granny, don't cry, granny..." I heard Amelia's sweet voice. She was far away from me, but I saw her wiping my mother's tears.
"Hello mama," I heard my angel.
"Hello Amelia. How are you, little darling?" I asked excitedly.
"Mama? Please come back."
I can't explain how it feels to be a mother of a child who loves you, to hear her voice full of concern. A warm-hearted mother never has the words to express herself. And they tell us about heaven in the holy books... But I can tell you, that a mother feels the gentlest cool breeze from heaven when she hears her child from miles and miles away. Even when the mother moves back to heaven, she can still listen to her child. She still can...
"Mama, come back... please." My angel pleaded with me.
"Darling, I will be there tomorrow, I promise, before evening. Tell granny and you know granny is old, so please just be with her darling, ok?"
"I promise you, mama." I knew she had tears in her eyes. No Meer, no love, no reasoning can stop a mother and a daughter from being together.
I was both.
So, I must go... to come back again.

For many days, the Army said nothing. Tim was missing. That's what we were told a fortnight ago. I don't know everything... but one day the army officers came to our house.

The Ministry of Defence said, "It is with great regret that we can confirm that a member of the Armed Forces has been killed in action during ongoing operations against insurgent positions in Helmand Province, Southern Afghanistan."
That was my brother, that's what I know… My mother just lost her only son, that's what I know. That's what our reality is…
My heart has been feeling low since the war…
The war against terrorism: Taliban, Afghans, Muslims, Osama… I did not know what it meant till my brother went to Afghanistan. War changed him; it made him an unfamiliar person. Whenever I talked to him, he either felt tired or unwell. He never talked openly about his feelings towards the situation and was always in a rush. I used to play the harp for him, and he pretended to be an opera singer. We used to share jokes and laughed together… a lot. My mother had nothing in her life, except the two of us. And now, after having the shock of my brother's death, she is in the hospital.
I don't understand how, by wrapping up a coffin in the national flag, indicating respect, offering money, or splashing a name in the media, anyone can rightly console the family who has lost a family member to war.

I never believed in the bullshit they said about Muslims in the news and newspapers. I had always arguments with my brother. I tried to explain different aspects to him. But he was blind... He lost his job due to the economic recession. The cities were full of immigrants and students; job market was saturated. He was angry about the immigrants, though as 'Kiwis' we were immigrants as well, but we moved here 20 years ago. Finally, he decided to join the Army. He was a big, active, intelligent lad, so they selected him... to be killed. That's how death plays its trick.

He wanted to earn money. He wanted it so he could buy his own house. The Army paid him well, but that cost him his life.

I never believed the media, but now after his death, it seems what they tell us is true... Muslims are terrorist; they beat women; they kill people; they are wild and angry as animals. They are brutal, rude, and ignorant. They invade foreign lands, sometimes in the name of religion, sometimes in the name of immigration and asylum. Now, I hate them!!! Whenever I see them on the street, I want to shout at them... get out! Go home!

I told Meer that our love makes us blind and selfish. But now I see more. Our love makes us blind and selfish, but our hatred too... it blinds us and leaves us cruel.

My dead open eyes are watching the blinking phone. Splashing its reflection in the mirror that holds a photo of Meer. My gaze is frozen on his smile as when he laughed. I skipped a heartbeat... That was one of those moments when I clicked my camera to capture his full of life laughter. I kept his picture at my bedside in Prague and before I left, I took it with me and placed it on this mirror on my arrival.
"Who is that mummy?" Amelia asked me.
What should I say to her? Who is he? I didn't want to give any information regarding him to the little girl's curious mind.
"Is he your best friend, mummy?" she came up with another question.
"Mummy!" She sounded authoritative.
"Yes, darling." I sounded so helpless and tired.
"Can we go for ice cream, please?" She sweetened her tone.
"Sure, go change your clothes then." I sent her away before she added another question. But how long I could escape her questions?
I was worried, and now I am lost... The sister of a dead brother, the daughter of a mother on death's bed. And I am not feeling well myself. I feel tired; I feel unwell, annoyed, angry… And yes! My period is late.
"Did you come inside me Meer?" He was all over me, exhausted, after making my neighbours well aware of his intense orgasm.
"Meer..." I pushed him away, but he moved back closer to cuddle me.
"Meer did you come inside me?"
"Yes, I did." He was gasping.

"What if I get pregnant?" I was stressed.
"Then you will choose the name of the boy and I will choose the name of the girl." He wrapped me with himself and slept straight away. He had no trouble, no stress on his face. He looked like an angel and his kind words relaxed my nerves and I fell asleep myself, breathing on his chest.
Now, I really ask myself did he really mean what he said? Or was it a regular punch line to keep peace with hysterical women who are afraid to get pregnant? Was I afraid to get pregnant by him? Not at all, but still, you never know that how and when men will change and show the woman his true colours. Well, all men are the same I guess, when it comes to sex. If they can get it up, they are up for the fun. Bastards. But was he like that too?
I know he's Muslim. He never said anything to me about his religion. Probably that was not his thing. He had firm opinions about everything else, but he never said much about anyone's religion. He was "live and let others live" kind of person. I didn't know much about Islam, anyway. For me he was very normal; consumed alcohol, gambled if he wanted, wasn't fussy about food. He avoided pork but his argument was that it was a cultural thing, and he wasn't keen on trying pork. He was never awkward, never asked me to cover up from head to toe. Did he ever go to a mosque in Prague? Not sure of that either. For me, he was a contemporary human.

I noticed his circumcision the morning after our first night. He felt different inside me; it was wonderful. No complaints, only compliments. But still, I was a bit affected by Islamophobia. I knew him well enough before I jumped into bed with him. I was starving for sex, but I was extra careful. Bad experiences and being the mother of a daughter who's only seven. I don't get opportunities to meet men or invite a man to my place and I can't go with a man to a hotel room easily either. So all I end up with is me and my solo flight.

But I fell for Meer... I wasn't passing time with him to get some good intimate company while I was in Prague. Truly he touched my heart. His charm, his words and his addictive sex were the final blows to my sanity. I decided to speak with my mother, with my daughter and with Tim once he comes back from the war. I wanted to break tradition by asking him for marriage. Religion wasn't a trouble for anyone. He understood me completely and I guess I could bear his bullshit throughout my life. He was younger than I and that did bother me but on a psychological level, we complimented each other perfectly. I was sure once we agreed to marriage, we would find a solution to smooth our sharp edges. I never anticipated anything worse with him. Why would I? He was so much in love with me. I saw his eyes... they were soft and full of love. I was sure he would become a perfect father figure to our kids. Amelia would be absolutely delighted to meet him. His larger-than-life persona can win over everyone, at least that's what I believed. And I was sure that he would love to have a family. That's what I concluded from our conversations, he was very enthusiastic about becoming a father and I hoped that my body still could bear a child.

A week ago, before I left Prague, I reserved a table for two on the cruise restaurant floating on the Vltava. I bought rings and kept the sweet secret surprise.

My heart was beating loud, and I was a bit nervous. I don't know what to expect from my life this time. He wasn't my first man, but I had never felt so good with anyone else. What to say... Tim... I was waiting for Tim to call me, but he was out there hunting death and death hunting him in barren lands of Afghanistan.

"My brother is in Afghanistan Meer." I updated him one evening, though Tim strictly told me not to tell anyone about it. "He is a soldier on duty…" I sounded like a proud Brit kid.

"What the fuck he is doing there, saving the ass of the drug mafia?" He was sarcastic and drunk. "On the name of war on terrorism, they are trying to get rid of the regime that banned the opium production that eventually nearly killed the mafia."

"What are you talking about Meer?"

"Drugs... I am saying it's a business like any other business, and they need to produce a cheap supply. And how many countries will allow opium to grow on their lands?

"Are you nuts?" I got annoyed.

"What the fuck you think the Americans are doing? The idiot Mullah's the one Americans think blew up the twin towers. The ones fighting against the massive, best-equipped military of the world. I wonder where they have been funded from and how the hell, they are so well-armed. And who's selling them the arms? Which arm producing countries are involved in it? When Americans, their allies are dominating the institutions of the world then how come these uneducated Taliban's are dodging? You know what Rita, please don't piss me off with your expressions and fuck off! Your liberalism is shitting in its pants. In the name of war, they killed innocent kids and people. The country and the generation might forgive them, but the time remembers all. Is there a God or not? I won't argue that. But time keeps all frozen in moments of the clock." Then he raised his voice dramatically and spoke.

"Misery, gloom, pain and death, shall and will invite nothing but demise and destruction. An unjust death bleeds and meets the blood chain of unwarranted murders turning the human history into the graveyard of unequal equals,"
"And now!" He clapped the table and stood up from his chair.
"Ciao!"
Meer left without any smiles and kisses, walked straight out of the door into the frozen night.
On that day I understood how strong his beliefs and his humanitarian views were. He didn't even turn back that night when he was leaving. He was hurt over the death and suffering. I saw that in his fearless eyes, and I liked him even more after that. At least he showed me he is a man. But he left a scar of fear unconsciously over my unconscious, that he could leave me for having a different opinion? Does his belief system have priority over me? His sense of justice is stronger than our love? And what it would be when Meer and Tim would sit down on the same table? But... but I know today could never happen...unless Meer dies, too.
Death inflicts death...

His hatred towards my brother's job killed him; he is one of them too! His bright smile, intelligence and kind nature all are fake, I am sure he would enrol himself against the peacekeeping army in Afghanistan if he could. He will kill my brother too if he would see him. And not just my brother, he would kill sons, brothers, husbands, partners of thousands who are on grounds of Afghanistan to protect the world from radicalization and religious Islamic extremism. I had seen hatred in his eyes; I had heard his thoughtful speeches against western society, the society where he lives and appreciates but is not ready to accept what we stand for. We stand united against hate and religious Nazism which is coming towards our lands. Our shores are no longer as safe as they used to be. They infiltrated our lands and there are many here within our borders that share and promote a similar agenda of religious fanaticism. Enough with those who sympathise with the bastards and mourn over their deaths. They should be harmed and punished, thrown out back to the jungles where they came from with their opinions about us, peasants. Meer isn't one of them, but he is one of them! I can't stand the pain of the hatred inside.

And don't mix my emotions with his picture still sitting on my mirror because of my love. Yes, I still love him, but I hate him too... I kept the photo where it is as I don't want to forget who killed my brother with his words... who's hate was it that reached and stirred in Tim's life. I know it's not just one person, but the whole community behind it committing the crime silently. Not all of them are active but all of them are psychologically active and their collective hate against our brothers, sons, partners is murdering them in the battlefield. They want this world to be a Muslim world, hijabbed and bearded. A Muhammadan world! Even at the cost of bloodshed! Forgetting that "Death inflicts death."

Hunt Begins

Meer is *'high'* mates...
That high, where you reach after four shots of rum, one after another, and you end up in a slow spin. Time, fear, and the future all lose their meanings. People appear and disappear; they get naked and show up with instincts they are born with. You can see so clearly who's who, their intensions and minds... and the animals inside.
Do you think I am misleading you? No, I am not... Only those with "righteous minds" can do that. Not drunks.
I am in the zone... a free zone. I never do drugs, but I do drink. And when I drink, I drink till I can't drink anymore. And always alone. Whatever I am drinking, vodka, whisky, rum, or gin, I drink neat. I am lazy when it comes to drinking; I don't like much movement as I like to enjoy the ride of the earth with closed eyes. High in the sky, you fly... and feel the spin of the Earth underneath your feet. Isn't it magic? I'm that little boy inside who likes magic. In my childhood, I loved magic shows... But I had no taste today, to be entertained as Jan screwed me well hard with his trick.
I have this envelope with his mother's photographs in front of me. No nudes, sadly. Shame, there's no skin show for me but there is a telephone number. Maybe a call could draw out those tits?
"Hello, Jan's horny mommy." I laughed vulgarly inside. A drunken call in the early morning is probably the best way to communicate and discuss difficult matters, isn't it?

It was six a.m. I dialled her number.

"*Ano...*" A deep sleepy voice from my phone.

"*Dobry den*. Hello madam, my name is Meer. I am calling from the Only Erotic Market. Is this a good time to talk?"

"Meer?" My name was an eye-opener.

"Darling, your Meer... you remembered!"

"How can I forget you? Are you drunk?" A flat interrogative tone it was.

"No." I said if that was the only word I had ever learned.

"My husband is here; he is in the shower now. Can I call you in a few hours? By the way, I was thinking about you just last week." She whispered.

"Only last week and not every day?" I was drunk, but not so drunk that I would miss the chance to make a woman laugh.

"I will call you." I heard a smile before she hung up the phone.

"Cheers! *Nszdravi! Prost*! Here's another shot, to more sucky sex" I shouted.

"Bottoms up." I raised the shot glass and scorched my pain away with alcohol. But alcohol doesn't take anyone anywhere, we all know that. Yet, we still dip ourselves into drunkenness occasionally because nobody escapes this self-created messy life, nothing changes once we return from our 'delight'. Then why do we drink? Is getting "high" is part of our basic instinct? Is it necessary to get out of our senses to stay levelled and function normally? That's why most of us are addicted to sex, alcohol, drugs, food… because reality sucks and escapism wins in this imperfect world order. For many, it's not about pure pleasure but way to normalise miserable lives, to find an hour of peace before hell breaks again. But where does the money from antidepressants, cigarettes, drugs, alcohol, coffee, tea, sugary and salty things go? We feed the system helplessly as puppets, yet we choose to live in an illusion of freedom… Freedom, liberty? How bogus are these words and the thoughts behind them? East, West, South or North, any continent, any race and any country, any religion. Look around. You will find a perfect system to bring you to your knees. I guess God does the same… limit your options, bind you, control you, remotely watch your psychological manoeuvres to direct life their decided way.

So, I ask myself if this world order is the divine order too. A chain of religious worldly-gods enacted to delude, divide and fail us here and threating to control the life after too!

An afterlife, a day of judgement, heaven and hell. Are they for real or is that another chapter of fiction within fiction to fix a comedy of errors? Promises of bringing little gods to justice for lies and falsify godhood, punishing them for division, hatred, cheating, manipulation and inflicting pain on humanity. To award and reward, one's on 'righteous path'. Well, we all can invite hell now on us and on each other in defining that 'righteous' to prove the truthfulness of our beliefs or non-beliefs. Slicing throats of one another to settle the argument of "what is right". That's just one way how we ruined the world but who we can blame for the total failure of the "might is right" system? Turning the world uglier by each passing day, making it severely odd for the 'unchosen masses', putting them to disadvantage at the hands of cruel moralities, political and social systems...judged and scrutinised, taken advantage of their incapacities. And the poor souls are back in the middle of a vicious circle.... alcohol, drugs, antidepressants, addictive foods, looking for an escape. I was looking for escape too, from an uneven and odd life. What should I say? My life has been at odds since I left Newcastle for Europe. I'm an insomniac, strange dreams and restlessness haunt me. Blood, shouts, noises…often I see myself dying, thrown from a height, stabbed, shot. A few times I watch myself commit suicide, hanging and kicking in the air as the suspension grips my life.
I didn't know what time it was when I finally heard the phone, first far and then gradually closer. The phone was yelling at me.
"Aah..." I reverse kicked the phone towards myself.

"Hello." I felt a headache coming on.
"Where have you been? I called a few times already." It was Norika Hoskova, Jan's mother.
"Oh, darling, where else I would be, except in your heart." I tried to smooth her.
"Are you still drunk?"
"No, not all. I am swinging in joy after listening to your sexy bedroom voice *Zlato*."
"I hope you are not mixing me up with some other woman. And what did you say? *Zlato*? You are getting better at Czech." She admired me.
"*Miláček*, how can I mix you up with anyone else... you are special and the best I ever had." I kept up my flirty mood.
"So, sales agent of sex shop who calls drunk at 6 in the morning, how are you? Did you leave your successful carrier for telesales?" She was all fun now.
"Lonely... very, very, lonely honey, without you." I am sure she saw my wink over the phone.
"You are such a bastard." She laughed.
"Tell me, why did you call me? I saw you once a few months ago near Palladium; you get more handsome with each passing day, cheeky." She giggled.
Wow! This was new, flirts and compliments.
"So tell me, why did you call?" She asked again.
"I have my reasons." I laughed naughtily over the hard-core truth.
"Oh, I see... your reasons! But I can't afford you right now. I am sorry." She was suddenly serious.

"Ok, I will be honest, I am going to London in a few weeks, and I wanted to see you before I left. I know we crossed each other's paths only briefly, but I always liked you. But as you know, I was a professional. Didn't want to mix pleasure with business, so I never rang earlier. But before I leave, I would like to see you for a coffee, if you feel comfortable." I created a pile of lies on the spot.
"*Londýn*, wow! And now I can hear the Meer I knew." She laughed vulgarly.
"And this morning, you said that you were thinking about me a week or so ago?" I tested the waters.
"Well, my memory and body are easily manipulated." She giggled. "And by the way, if you have your hidden motives then I have some hidden secrets too. I will give you a call later this evening. I have to get back to work; my lunch break is over. When we will meet, I will tell you what I was thinking." The naughtiness in her voice and the games she was trying to play over the phone made me smile. "Well, let me keep you waiting then. And yes! I was thinking about you *Zlata*. Ok, I have to go now... *ciao*." Before the line disconnected, I heard her laugh like a schoolgirl.
What was she going on about? But fuck, at least give some credit to my luck! What a lucky devil am I? A drunken phone call! And it worked, wow! Probably the magic of the right person at the right time in the right place? But who arranges that kind of coincidence?
And she had been thinking about me? That's not a new line to me. And I think I knew the reason too, just as you... why do women say things like that? Yes! It's not just men who hunt women. Women hunt too, in subtler ways.

I had a game plan, produced as a by-product of my lies. I could see my moves and if all went by calculation, I needed nearly three months to cut through her.

"Today is simply a lucky day," I thought as I got up, slowly recalculating the expected psychological response of Norika.

Yesterday, I couldn't handle the situation. I was missing Rita and scared by Jan's threat and the task of divorcing this frozen woman, who isn't so frozen anymore looked like an impossible task. All these thoughts screwed me. And before my brain burst by the stress, I started drinking and convincing myself that Jan's a bastard who bullshit scared me. He tried to play with my feelings. He lied to me because he wants Rita too. He's blackmailing me to push me towards Norika. Rita isn't in the city, and he is a LIAR... LIAR... LIAR... LIAR!!! I hammered the sentence the whole night in my head to bring my confidence back... And it bounced back.

Around 6 pm, Norika rang back.

"What are you doing tomorrow? I have taken a day off for you. What are you doing, are you cooking, Meer?" She sounded like a lover. I felt her tone implied dual meanings.

"Yes, I am cooking. I am free. Where would you like to meet?" I added oil to the frying pan.

"What are you cooking? Maybe I could taste your cooking tomorrow?" I heard the vulgarity.

"Oh wow, where did that one come from?" I laughed.

"Sure, I will save a "meal" for you."

"I will text you the address. We can meet at my friend's place. Enjoy your cooking and see you tomorrow at 10...bye."

I didn't understand her attitude, but she was way more confident and bolder in her sentences now.

I was keen about tomorrow and for the day after tomorrow too. I was curious and fresh, sipping a cup of homemade Irish coffee with Jan's envelope on my table. The first set of pictures came out from the envelope. And what was there for my pleasure? A slim, pale woman, fearful, woman, standing with her son at some party. The make-up on her face was an epic failure and that party dress she was wearing looked flat dead, hanging on her shoulder bones. The picture was from 1997, a long time ago, before I met her. But her youth seemed to be dried up and the drops of energy and power squeezed out of her body.

That was the first picture.

The last sips of Irish coffee raved me with astonishment as I flipped the last picture from the collection. I was witnessing the biggest professional success of my life. This picture was taken just a few months ago. This square image made me wonder how it could be that the face of human psychology fakes someone else for so long then suddenly become another. Takes over the control of life… changing all, challenging all.

This last picture of Norika is a miracle of transformations.

She was standing and hugging a tall, over-sized, fully tattooed guy with biker boots in front of a Harley Davidson. Norika had her hair done in pink and purple with a piercing at the edge of her left eyebrow & another under her lower lip. Later I found out that her lower lips were pierced too. She had a medium-sized cigar in her slim fingers, a curvaceous figure, and the cherry on the top was her "Silicon Valley". And in there, where the valley goes deeper, was a Christian cross, trying to breathe. Definitely she's a God-fearing woman, giving an opportunity to the ones struggling to tame her wildness, to remember Jesus and their sins in the storm of her exhausting breaths turning them deaf. And surely the one's accepted the challenge was often calling God, even the ones who forgot him ages ago, strayed by the ease of comfortable lives.

The cross was testing its strength...

So was I.... against destiny, throwing curveballs towards me.

"Should I seek forgiveness?" I asked myself.

Should I bow down my head in front of God's oneness? Surrender to his power that can change the course of anyone's life? With valid and invalid reasons, he could turn a gold crown into thorns and thorns into diamonds. That's what he does... But is God so helpless, after all, that he needs us in trouble to attract our attention? Does he want to be the God of poor, needy, and suffering, and not of the happy and satisfied?

And yes! God exists in the world of the deprived and unfortunate ones more than in the cosy lives of satisfied humans. So, does the business of God run on the excess of unsettled ones?

Maybe I shouldn't ask these questions. My brain stops me from asking such horrific questions, making me stand in my own eyes in the line of nonbelievers.
Is it the colour of my skin interfering with my thoughts? My cultural background is holding me in a circle, a circle of expected and accepted behavioural guidelines. I'm sure that the trouble in my thinking process is my nationality.
Am I suffering from self-hate, from some form of inferiority complex?
Is "the word of God" active only for coloured nations, who follow him and suffer as a whole? Is it?
Beautiful cruelty of mind strays me from Norika's picture to the pictures that are shouting inside my head. Like the elevations of Norika's body, the wildness which doesn't come under any grip. The friction in her eyes, the thirst of her posture, the arm around the biker, the cigar in her carefree fingers, the manicure, piercing, tattoos, hair, clothes, bra, boots all became the signature of a fearless state of mind. She rebelled against her own fears, driving her forward in the game called life. In her careless posture, there was opposition to everything and anything that might try to stop her. FUCK YOU! Was written on her ripped jeans. She was all there in lioness attitude with burning wild eyes, wilder than the red mountains of Sedona, where the snapshot was taken.
"Norika..." I moved a finger over the picture.

"You are my job, once again... Or I should say for the first time. As these nights that shadow the city into darkness played all their magic on you. You were another person when I first stepped into your life, and I was another man. Now, waters and matters are deeper, thickened by the plot of life. And what awaits us in this dream after dream after...the dream?"

One Conscious Dream

I know now that the warmth of every second is too much for reality. It burns away time and turns all into ashes of memories. If I had known this truth before, I might have let time and people fade away more easily. But I also kept another truth in my mind, allowing it to haunt me. That this beautiful time, this "emperor moment" that we're enjoying, won't come back and will die in the beginning of forthcoming sensation. All is temporary. And what's not loses its pleasure quickly. So the pain of loss was so unbearable and inevitable that it spoiled the golden moments of my life.

Life is a dream...

A dream. A set of audio-visual, arranged or unarranged scenes that creates sensations and leave us with experiences, some memorable and some blurry.

Real life? A set of arranged or unarranged shots creating a sensation, leaving us with an experience which is sometimes more memorable, more recallable, depending on the emotional intensity. It's like a conscious dream where we manipulate simulated reality, though nothing changes, and we fade regardless with a stronger impression.

Life is a dream: a dream is this life. On a one-way timeline, no fast forwards, no reverse, no U-turns.

And If I had one chance to rewind, I might return just to the day I met Norika.

I was anxious about tomorrow and the day after, too. I guess all of us are curious about the unfolding of the future. But I'm keen about yesterday too, the day already experienced. I would like to understand the 'importance' of that day... that would be the beginning of the future. But does it matter?

Does anything matter in a dream? Life is a dream as a whole. What has passed and what's forthcoming, that too is a dream. You can't touch it; you can't live it. It's just a series of dreams after dreams.

And that's the dream which I wanted to rewind.

I was there, where she wanted me to be...in bed.

"How was it, after so long... with me again?" I moved my fingers in her hair.

"You are the same, great in bed," she smiled. "This is what I have missed with the other men I slept with, the sense, this feeling what you leave inside me, the sensation... with every touch, you make my soul shiver and your eyes... The way you look at me, when you touch me, when you are inside me, when you are getting me there, when we come, when you breathe on my neck after you can't breathe anymore."

I smiled.

"Yes, that's why I wanted to see you. With you, it's not the money, and our first time and this time, the feeling is the same, the intensity, the pleasure, though time has changed you." I looked at her silicones and bit a nipple gently as I lied.

"You like them?" She winked.

"Yes, if you think they add to your personality." I moved my hands on her thigh and calf to continue my worship.

"You helped me realise that I am a woman with all that pleasure locked inside me. You told me, you showed me the way. Thank you." Norika moved her fingers to comb my hairy chest.

"Would you do me another favour? Would you please pass me the cigarettes Meer?" Norika stretched her arm towards the side table.

"Would you like to smoke?" I asked.

"Yes." Norika smiled, embarrassed.

"You can smoke something 'harder' honey. What about an Asian cigar?" I placed her hands on my crotch with a naughty wink.

She laughed, and I laughed, listening to her laughter. We laughed and laughed at the stupid joke, louder and louder, till he heard. The one who's famous for attending the poor & needy...when they aren't poor or needy anymore.

"Why are you going to London... leaving *Praha*?" She puffed.

"My brother's buying some property, so I might move there for a while. You are welcome anytime."

"When is your flight?" She looked deep in my eyes.

"The end of next month." I tried to smile.

"Can you meet me every day till then?" She kept her eyes on my face.

"If you like," I replied so quietly that I didn't even hear myself. Something suddenly switched off inside me as my heart sunk like a stone.

I heard her talking.

"Can I see you every day, Meer? I'm not well; I just want to talk to you every day because I would like to share how this all happened. This change…" she moved my hand to her inked thigh. "I am sure you are busy, but I can pay you if you like. I know you might have some other clients, but I can pay."
Norika continued, and I felt worse inside. Instead of enjoying the surprise gift from destiny, I felt wrong, very wrong about me, about my life. The inner silence accused me silently: "A cheater, a liar, a dirty man, who isn't honest to himself, to his own happiness, to anyone."
God was hearing us...
"Can we meet daily? Please?" I heard something crack inside of her.
"What could I say?" I thought to myself, and just kept looking powerlessly at her. She was a simple task now, but I felt trapped, felt unwell and unhappy like I lost the meaning of life. Something was changing. Was I feeling guilty? Unsure of my emotions?
"Why are you looking at me this way? I asked you for a very simple thing. If you don't want to, then say no to me and I will understand." Norika touched my check.
And I didn't know what to say… to her, to myself. So I just hide, once again, behind my crazy sex drive.
I stretched my arm to grab her hair, to pull her closer. I moved my lips from her petals to her neck.
Slowly...taking deep breaths to inhale what calms me or ignites, moving my hands on the silicones, kissing, rubbing, grabbing, pushing, pulling, biting...
And in the end, she claimed victory with her legs.
I had no answers… I had only actions.
Actions speak louder than words.

I ended up meeting her every day.

"Show me your fingers." That was just another day after sex when she asked me.

"Show me your palm, show me your phalanges." I passed her my hand.

"I want to see what it is in there that takes my breath away, when you move them in my hair, touch my head? Where does that magic come from? And these whirls, loops, like Yin and Yang on your tips? Do you know what they mean?" She sat up like a *queen* on my top and took both of my hands in hers, forcing them down to the mattress. "Do you know Meer?" she bowed to rub her nose with mine. "That means you are an unsure and complicated person, the way you analyse things. Are you so complicated? I am sure you are, that's why you are so silent after our first reunion date. You are always thinking something… always. You are never alone with me anymore, absorbed in self, and I hate that." She was watching me for a response.

And what should I say? Why am I so quiet?

I was seeing Norika for last one week, a few hours every day after her work. Conversations were getting shorter and sex dirtier. I try to keep my eyes and mouth shut apart from the busy moments. But I felt worse every day. I was unsure. What was so bad? Memories. Rita? Am I finding Rita in her? Or was she becoming another version of Rita? Was I unconsciously swapping Rita with Norika, remorse was saddening my soul because of the guilt, failure, pain of loss?

I was losing myself in pleasing her.

And what the fuck is wrong with me? Maybe I'm just afraid of Norika's emotional attachment? But I handle and have handled this type of occasion well. I know some women are more vulnerable and older women do become very sensitive. They often forget that I am a gigolo and not their boyfriend.

But am I afraid of myself then? Am I worried about Jan's complete disappearance after the last visit? Was I stressed out by no news from him and Rita? I wanted to ask Norika about Jan, but neither the time nor my position was right. All was confusing. I was debating questions that I couldn't ask, wondering what to do next. Time was shortening.

"Hey, where are you, I am here." She whispered in my ear and kissed my earlobe to get my attention.

"I'm here, with you," I smiled.

"Yes, you are here but not with me, but you will see, you'll be nowhere else, but with me. This scares you now and your heartbeat pumps and see…" She placed her right palm on my heart. "It's beating hard, just as you exhaust yourself three times in a row." I saw madness in her eyes.

She was already a queen, a "queen" in charge. Swinging in joy, back and forth…

I heard her asking, "Meer, can you meet me every day, please? Life is once and once is the moment you live. Once is the breath you inhale. Just once. Then why do I keep waiting for joy and not accept pleasures? Meer, please don't go away. Meet me every day. I don't want this money. You can have it all. I just want your time. I know you can find someone better, but you wouldn't find me… I don't ask for much, I just ask for your time. Can you see me tomorrow? I can see you just want to run away from this room, but please… This isn't love; it's me. And I am nothing but a dream. A dream… Let me be in this sweet dream where we are together, living and breathing dream after dream."

In Between Halves

So, what's it like, wishing not to be loved?
I wasn't sure where to start.
I know sharing helps. But very hesitantly, I am requesting... can I share my mind with you? I need some enlightenment over a complicated emotional affair. So... can I ask you to step into my dirty shoes, just for a while, please?
Please. I can't handle rejection... so please!
If you are a gentleman, then it's a simple question. And for a woman... its bit tricky, things are always a bit unusual when it comes to love, anyway.
But here's the situation.
What would you do, if someone who loves you deeply decides to be with you forever, putting the well-paid job on hold to spend the day with you? Trying to sell property to move in with you or buy a new place jointly in a different city to start a new life? Spending money on you, for you, or with you? Holding your feet in their laps, massaging them, kissing them, moving lips to your ankles. Trying, always, to please you, never saying "no" to anything. Never complaining, regardless of what you do. Tireless efforts to comfort you, sorting your troubles, supporting you to get you where you want to be. Talking about you, with you, for you, and subtracting themselves from conversations. And in return, asking for nothing, absolutely nothing except your time, touch, gaze, and smile.

Here I am, stuck in that scenario... but I'm not done yet. There is more for your understanding.
Someone loves you truly, deeply, madly and honestly, while you are actually in love with someone else.
Someone bewitched you exactly the way you charmed your lover.
You are there... sleeping with one and thinking about the other. Since you are in bed with this lover who's gone mad for you, absolutely crazy, you started missing the previous one more strongly. Becoming emotional over tiny matters. Shedding tears everywhere. Finding the lost one in the face of a new one. Spotting the similarities, merging both, or embossing one on another subconsciously so you can live in peace. You are trying to fake harmony but at the back of your mind you're still yearning intimacy with your true love, who isn't getting back to you, never replying to you, never trying to be with you. What would you do?
What's it like, wishing I weren't loved?
Have you ever wished the same?
I want to run away from all the attention and care Norika is giving me. I'm growing tired of her wishes and listening to talks about "our future." Norika was planning to find a flat for us once I return from London. I was super suspicious, growing more scared. I was running out of lies. How regularly can you lie about everything? You must remember the lies, too, and adjust them accordingly. But for how long?

Since I started (let's say) dating Norika, I stopped picking up jobs. I had money, so I decided to gamble life and live rationally. Norika had savings, she was in love with me, and according to my assumption, she would marry me. I could keep Jan's mouth shut and get rid of him but also legalise my immigration status in the Czech Republic. The money was a bonus. The evil money.
But there was one problem. Rita. And our unsaid promises, my feelings for her, and what about all that faith she had in me? What about our hopes to be happy in life? What about all those wishes we made when we tossed coins in the Vltava? Our unfulfilled desires, our fantasies, our dreams, what about all of them? I wish I could speak with Rita and tell her all about my misery, without thinking about negative consequences… about my pain, my fears. I am exhausted. I feel like giving up and ending my life and never being reborn again. I understand I am a selfish bastard who disturbs humanity, exploits people, abuses and uses. I am this person. I'm ugly inside, more than one might think. That's why I'm in constant pain due to karmas. The people I fucked emotionally, disturbed psychologically, and left paralysed are still mourning their losses. They aren't at peace yet and there is a God regardless of my opinion about him. He still exists and monitors... to balance.
"I have blood on my hands!" I shouted.
This is another night when I am out of mind with suicidal thoughts. My pain isn't lessening. And I consider my loss greater than anyone else's. I lost Rita, my Rita…
"Why the fuck did you leave?" I was crying in deepened depressions of alcohol.

"Why? Why? Why?" My shouts were shaking the walls. "Why did you have to go? The one person I had; one person who made life beautiful. And she's gone!" I was sobbing.
"I was finally alive! I even asked forgiveness from God. God!!" My tears were running down my face as the infidel inside me shouted for help.
"I know I am not forgiven. I won't ever be forgiven." I was looking at the mirror.
"I need to disgrace myself. I need to hurt myself. I need to be in more pain. In pain forever. But I can't take it anymore. No fucking more!" I roared and smacked my head against the mirror.
The silence of grief was scarred in the darkness. I felt some wetness.
I was bleeding...
The blood was dropping into my eyes as an ecstatic pleasure of powerlessness ran through me.
I saw my cracked smile in the shattered mirror.
"*Nazdravi*. Cheers." My laugh was filled with a quarter bottle of vodka, which I smashed on the floor.
"NAZDRAVI, NAZDRAVI, NAZDRAVI..."
Pieces of glass slid in darkness to the horrified corners. Joys of pain and a wave of immense calm filled my body as my head spun. Tears of blood fell on my face, and I felt them on my lips before I dropped like a stone over the sharp shining crystal diamonds.
"Rita, I will meet you on the other side." I smiled, when I saw her rushing towards me to hold me, to be with me, to love me. I saw her before I was blinded by my frozen blood.

"I am glad you arrived; we will meet on the other side. I am yours; you are mine... You are inside me! And me.... inside you Meer.... forever!"

Three Colours of Love

It's me again. Rita.
I'm sorry. I am extremely sorry. I apologise for my rude words. I never wanted to sound like a right-wing, fanatically racist Caucasian and I feel worse now for what I had said before about Muslims, about Meer... I know damage has been done and there's not much I can do about it. I was in pain, depressed, and last week I lost my mother, too.
Don't really know what to say.
My mom's no more, but she left her echo in this lonely house. I can hear her.
"Rita, don't do it sweetie...Rita."
I looked outside from the kitchen window and spotted her running in the garden, chasing 2-year-old mischievous Rita.
Mothers die. And a sudden, premature death of a child is too much for any mum. It wouldn't be justice to keep a mother alive with such an unbearable pain in her heart. That's why her heart failed.
But I'm her child too! I am not complaining. I wasn't as important as Tim. Yeah, I recall that I ran away. So that's why...that's why... I understand now.
Don't remember what I wanted to say...
Pain is in every inch of my soul, and I had gone through so much in the last six weeks. I attended two funerals of two beloveds and Amelia isn't doing very well either.
I seem to have lost control over life once again...
Chain of events...

Two days ago, I fainted.
I came back from the graveyard after the burial. I was shattered, weeping over the loss. My grief had no end and for the first time I missed Meer a lot. I cried over my selfishness and the pain I must have inflicted over his poor soul because of my foolish ignorance. I have no friends or family I can speak to. Everyone is busy in his own life.
One of my neighbours took care of Amelia for a night and I ended up with a bottle of wine in the darkness. It was the second sip when I smelled something. Death? And the breath I inhaled was Meer's.
"MEER!" The wine glass dropped from my hand as the last sip entered my windpipe. My eyes were soaked in tears as I ran blindly, coughing badly, to get my phone to dial Meer. I was choking, inhaling roughly. Every time I breathed in, I sensed him strongly. I was sure I saw him a second ago covered in blood on his floor, looking at me with hope. He was raising his hand, asking me to hold him. His forehead was bleeding with pieces of glass reflecting through droplets. I saw his tears, the unbearable pain on his face when he shouted my name out of his misery… "RITA".
I dialled his number while trying to get some air, but he didn't answer. How could he?
"Meer, Meer…" I was trying to shout his name, but I couldn't hear my own voice.
Fabrication of my fear and guilt were peaking. I didn't know where I was. I felt weak and before I could reach for him in that unexplainable illusion, I was gone.

Amelia wasn't settled at Sarah's and Steve's house. She kept insisting on coming back home. She was crying and yelling and eventually, the couple decided to bring her back. After a lot of knocking, calling, and several shouts, when I didn't answer the door, they decided to call the police. Meanwhile, Amelia jumped the back garden fence and saw me through a window lying unconscious on the floor.

They rushed me to the hospital.

Blood and urine samples were taken. A complete medical check-up was performed, and they discharged me with the second-best news of my life.

"Miss Rita Newman... congratulations, you are pregnant and according to your results, you are in the 9th week of pregnancy. There are no major complications apart from the stress and fatigue. Try to take care of yourself, book yourself the next available appointment with your GP and one of our midwives will be in touch with you next week. Also, you will be contacted for the 10-week scan." I kept looking at the doctor like a zombie.

"I understand you are going through a lot. But this is life, and you have a new soul inside you who needs you more than anyone else at this moment. Eat healthy and sleep plenty. Congratulations again." The doctor shook my hand and left me speechless with a strange sensation in my bones.

"Meer…" I just couldn't think of anyone else.

"You will give the name to the boy, and I will give the name to the girl." I remembered what he said.

"Imagine, Rita, a girl, half you, half me. Blue eyes but dark hair or dark eyes with blonde hair and a round cute nose like yours and lips like mine and she will be a little sweet angel. Wow! That's one exotic child. I can see her now, I can." He was laughing and smiling as we were walking with the tourists over Charles Bridge. I kept looking at him. I just couldn't say anything as I was getting older and wasn't sure if I still wanted to have a child but still... didn't want to break his blessed heart. I was in love, but I never fancied having another child after what happened between me and Amelia's father. But that's another story.
"A cute little girl, a cute little girl we will have." He was holding my hand and swinging it just like a little boy. We were hand in hand…
"Mummy, a new baby is coming... yippie!" Excited Amelia jumped out from nowhere.
"Mummy, what's the name of the baby? Is she girl mummy? I am sure she's a girl. Mummy, mummy…" I hadn't recovered from the news and Amelia was all over the place with her questions. "When's the baby coming mummy, when we will go to buy clothes for the baby mummy?" Jesus Christ, this girl should be my life organiser but regardless of her innocent childish excitement, I ended up giving a good hard stare to Amelia. Her face was another me from the past.
How difficult is to be a daughter and how difficult is then to be a mother? I asked myself.
"Where's the daddy mummy?" Amelia whispered gently as she hugged me tightly without looking into my eyes. She knew that was a tough thing to ask for. I'm sure silent tears floated in her eyes.

What should I say? I kissed her head and hugged her tightly with all the love and warmth left inside me. I had nothing to say to my daughter. I just wished I could comfort her with some bright hope.

For the last two days, I have been trying to reach Meer. I left messages in tears for him to call me back as soon as he can. Voicemails with apologies and request of forgiveness for my stupid behaviour.

"One chance Meer, one chance. Give me please one chance to explain myself to you, MEER, MEER… MEER!" I shouted within as loud as I could to scold myself and broke into tears.

What else I could do? I forced myself to eat healthy but resting plenty is impossible as nights are already sleepless and a few hours nap are haunted by nightmares about Meer. I just simply couldn't think of anything else. Meer and my kids; my mind is just rotating around them.

Amelia is by my side every second now, chasing me always. She's so afraid of what happened that she follows me everywhere. I can't even take a shower or go to the toilet with a locked door. I'm trying to be strong and I'm struggling to understand so many things at the same time. How come I got pregnant so quickly this time? Would he accept this child? Will he be a responsible father? Do I really need this child? Why is he not getting back to me? What should I tell Amelia, how Meer belongs to her new sibling and who is he? I just hope I have not been tricked. I have no desire to raise another child at my own. But the soothing memories of Meer are not leaving me alone either. I am drowning in the past, helplessly thinking that this guy left everything inside me. What's important for a woman to bloom… love, attention, care, passion? His child is inside me, waiting to be discovered by his daddy. He gave me everything and I…? What I have I really given him? Nothing. I just hope he hasn't forgotten me for someone else. With men everything is possible but I'm still hoping he wasn't one randy fucker. But honestly, I feel lonely, so lonely without him now. Since I am back from the hospital, I am so aroused most of the time. I miss him in my bed. I miss my intimacy with him.

Do you want to know a secret?

I was touching myself gently last night as our intimate moments ran in front of my eyes. I felt Meer all over me, kissing and moving his unshy lips on my body while he keeps his firm grip over my thighs, biting me softly before he whisked me into the fields of pleasure, ploughing me, and I let him pet me with his manly passions. He had my waters on his tongue, lustful proud eyes opening every pore, and I broke all of my fences to draw him in. He was shameless in bed and vulgar as fuck. Oops... sorry but he's a badass in bed. Made me do stuff I had never thought of. I felt like a nasty whore with him, one who isn't worried about risking things, and anytime I deviated he grabbed my hair roughly. "Blondie, you aren't saying no to me." He slapped my ass and dominated his bitch. I never thought I would be so submissive. He pushed his fingers into my mouth while licking my nipple and stroking vigorously inside me. When I moaned in pleasure, he choked me gently and dropped his saliva into my mouth, which I received with immense gratitude "Oh Lord..." I screamed as I jerked involuntarily. Love bites on my body as he told me to call him my husband "Will you be a good wife, *Haan*?" I was too breathless to answer, "Talk to me slut!" He pulled my hair as he roared "Tell me, tell me what I asked." He was squashing my breasts brutally and I felt pleasure running through me, wanting more of it as the pain was unveiling my real self. I kept pushing his limits. I wanted his animal out on the bed scratching and marking me with his desires; I wanted that moment so badly when he growls before he completes the circle and shiver in the ecstasy of losing his identity into mine.

"I know, I know exactly what you want from me Blondie." He pulled my hair as he pulled his fully erected cock out to direct me, "Bend over..." he ordered, "BEND OVER!" His reckless instinct smacked a powerful slap to sign my ass.
"That's it horny, that's it, now you know all the game. But you can't predict me, honey." And before I understood the meaning of his strong hands on my buttocks, his face was between the split, he was breathing hard to inhale the lust and lick the love out of my body.
He wasn't reluctant where his senses have taken him, he offered his worship in a trance "I need the love of you, and I need all of it. Tell me I am your husband. All of you is mine, Rita." His voice got emotional when he called my name, biting me right by the darker hole and entrusted himself for a unique joy of pleasuring where all is one and one is all.
Passionate red rose love bites turned lavender then yellow. Fading away like autumn.
Three colours of love...
I kept Meer updated about the passionate marks he left and every time he apologised.
"Please forgive me."
I am thinking, how will I forgive him now? While I'm waiting by the phone for his call, looking at a passionate red rose from last night.

Ether Stories

Never thought I would have to do this.
Come out of the shadow.
Most of you have probably never considered that a shadow can be an astral body, a mirror of your real self. Or that your own shadow is actually an independent entity that isn't dependent on any sort of illumination to exist or appear. I'm always there regardless of the situation and time.
Your shadow sees you.
Follows you everywhere and adjusts accordingly.
Perhaps you never observed that your own shadow is waving slowly regardless of how still you are. When you notice it under one of the four pure elements… fire.
I'm alive and will still be even after the physical death of my body.
I want to keep my introduction brief for several reasons, but I don't want you to have doubts, either. I am Meer's dual, his shadow body. I belong to Meer or Meer belongs to me. It's the same thing, as your reflection in the mirror is adjusted conditioned reality. Remember that what you can't touch isn't always unreal.
I was standing in the dark looking at Meer smashing himself into the mirror. Banging his body into the walls, yelling, shouting, swearing. He was bleeding badly when he dropped to the floor, and thick sharp glass pieces wounded him severely. I knew only a few minutes before he broke the bottle that this was coming…

A big chunk of glass sat right by my foot, and I whispered to the poor bottle to hold its anger, not to be aggressive before it tries to slice his life away as it's not time for his departure... not yet.

I saw him falling... and I knew something unexpected was coming. His pain disperses me among the conscious of his beloveds, and they receive the sign of his misery according to their perceptibility. I have to make sure that he stays alive with a perfectly logical reason that could be defined afterwards. Miracles don't happen often. It's all supernatural reality surrounding humans all the time. In simple words, life is a miracle in its own self from rebirth to birth to rebirth regardless of time and space.

Meer crashed over the glass bottle, and I splashed myself in four directions, reaching for the loved ones to alert them that he's in need. I was everywhere in a fraction of a second, making my way through the ether... Norika, Babel, Rita, who else I could come across?

Norika was looking for the properties in Český Krumlov, thinking about Meer already, planning to buy an old house to renovate and open as a guest house. I signalled Meer's blood and pain to discomfort her, to get her attention. I even froze her laptop, but she got agitated and lit a cigarette. She was hopelessly in love. Though she thought to call Meer, but as she was told off by him for calling late at night very recently, she stopped herself to avoid the same mistake.

I reached to Babel Bergmann. She was sitting with her husband, bored, and looking at semi-erotic film with empty eyes. There was no Eros or lust of the flesh in the room. I sent my message about Meer to Mrs Bergmann. I pushed her to think about him. But my efforts ended up as sexual arousal in her. Goosebumps, virginal discharge, and erect nipples through her nightgown became visible to Mr Bergmann. He hadn't been able to delight Mrs Bergmann for months now, and this semi-nude scene was doing the magic for him. Before Mrs Bergmann could get comfortable, *Herr* Bergmann was between her legs.

Rita's dual met me as she was anticipating my arrival. She held my hand and tranced herself to project suffering Meer to breathless Rita. Rita wasn't doing very well, and eventually collapsed as she enhanced her experience by sharing Meer's pain physically. Rita's dual rushed to Amelia to get help and before I left, I saw the reason for my anticipation. A bit of me and a bit of her was moving inside Rita...

I remember when Meer and Rita were making passionate love. We duals used to sit together and watch them till they fell asleep so we could be free for a while and go for our astral flight.

The next morning, following their romantic night, I heard Rita.

"Can you imagine Meer…?"

"I don't have to imagine anymore; I saw it all last night." He laughed, butt naked, as he fried eggs.

"Jesus, let me complete…"

"You are complete, we tested it." Meer turned and threw her a wink.

"I guess you wish your balls frying and not eggs, innit?" Rita pulled cockney slang.
Amused, Meer burst into laughter.
"Hey, serious now, listen, I saw you in my dream last night, how strange." Rita sounded melted in love.
"Do you want to know something more mysterious Rita?" Meer fixed his eyes on her. "But let me ask you something, were we walking over a green path, a lot of lush greenery around us?"
Rita's jaw dropped...
It was us, duals, having a stroll together, and the dream was shared by our physical bodies.
I gave a last look to Rita's belly before I stared at Meer; he was nearly unconscious because of the heavy bleeding.
"Kumari... Kumari…" I heard him mumbling the name of the most enigmatic relationship he had in Prague, a genuine friend, an old soul... a karmic bond.

Seeds of Past

Kumari's real name was Razia Begum; she was one of those thousands of war kids born in the aftermath of Bangladesh's liberation war in 1971. Orphan at the age of 16 she moved to Dhaka, but the imperfection of fortune landed her in a local brothel. After three years in hell, she charmed one Bengali-Italian man to help her escape and eventually take her to Milan. Her black eyes, charisma, and silky hair won the hearts of many, but she stayed loyal and faithful to Emran until he could no longer quench her sexual thirst. Disappointed by her sexuality and the husband's lack of interest in having a family, Kumari had many secret hourly affairs, till she met Czech tourist Petr Miroslav, who left her with a beautiful poem and his telephone number after a deep conversation about life.
"Come to Prague, I will show you beauty and life... together."
She was speechless.
Three years later, 26-year-old divorced Kumari moved to Prague, in search of her inner equilibrium.
Years after, while conducting a city tour for Italians, she spotted a tall dark south-Asian man with sad eyes looking a bit lost over a tourist map.

That was Meer, on his first day in Prague as a tourist. She noted he tried to speak with a couple of people, but they shook their heads and moved on. English wasn't widely spoken back then. She saw an opportunity, and she grabbed it, leaving the Italians with their unplanned photo stop. She approached Meer, who looked stressed, decoding miniature map of Prague Centrum.
"Maybe I could help you with something." She smiled with well-kept charm.
Meer looked and fell silent, breathless, and stunned. She was his first South Asian face in years, which left him speechless.
"Hey! Hi... yeah, sure, please. Please, can you direct me where's the National Museum?" Meer was trying to maintain eye contact with the goddess who was standing close enough that he could smell her perfume.
"Are you good with directions?" She kept smiling, hiding her melting confidence. Kumari didn't want to throw away this chance as she knew her nervousness would be over in the next few minutes. If she could hang around with him, she could possibly get him to a dining table.
"Why don't you join me? I am running a tour for Italian people, but if you are interested you can walk with us. I would be able to show you Prague for free." She smiled. "You won't get lost, plus the bonus is I know one really nice south Asian restaurant in Prague 5 that you can't find in any travel guide." She held her breath to see if she had caught her fish.
"I can pay you for the tour. Nothing is free in life."
He looked unimpressed by the offer and Kumari felt it clear that the gentleman didn't seem to be very amused by her selection of words.

"You can pay for my dinner then." She felt the depth of his eyes over her skin. He wasn't as easy as she thought. His accent and clothes weren't of someone who just got off a boat. His perfume, the way he talks, his impressions weren't cheap and most importantly he wasn't looking at her breasts as South Asian men usually do. Women aren't humans but objects of pleasure for most.

"That's a deal." He finally smiled.

Kumari was curious to know his background, but he seemed distant and snobbish in his attitude. He didn't force himself to smile to be accepted by the Italians. In fact, he didn't seem to be bothered by them at all. His eyes were continuously looking around and observing his surroundings. Kumari's running Italian commentary was useless to him and every time the rest of the tourists scattered, she went to Meer and told him briefly about the history and the significance of the place, or she tried to crack jokes to make him friendly. Meer seemed impressed by her grasp over the history and historical facts.

Finally, Kumari's hard work paid off at her favourite time of the day when she was smiling and shaking her silky hair like a doll. *"Grazie... Bonasera... Grazie, Grazie..."* She was receiving tips from merry tourists who were disappearing into local pubs for the toilets and then for some famous Czech beer.

"So…" Meer was the last in the queue as he knew that it wasn't done for him yet. He took out a 500 Czech Koruna note and held it in his two fingers with a meaningful smile.

"That's…. not for you." He paused and looked for the first time deep into her jet-black eyes.

"This 500 Koruna note is for something that you like, and I will get that for you, Kumari B." He read her name loud from the name badge as he joked with her.

"I like you; can I get you instead of the note?" That was what she really wanted to say but she smiled and said instead, "I might eat you; I am so hungry now. Look at me. I have been talking all day. My jaws are painful from smiling and you are making me laugh more with silly jokes. I am angry." She mocked Meer as he laughed loudly.

"That isn't funny. Let's go. We have to take the metro and then a tram and that will take 40 minutes. To wait for the nice spicy food is another half an hour." Kumari said. That evening Meer was honest for probably the last time in Prague.

"I'm studying at Northumberland University in the northeast of England, and I am living in Newcastle. My business degree is almost finished, and I am on a small Euro trip for three weeks. Took a ferry from Dover to France and then a train to overrated Paris. From there I was off to taste Belgian waffles and chocolate… Brussels, Antwerp, then the red-light district of Amsterdam."

"So, you have been a bad boy?" Kumari winked at him.

"No. I was very curious about all what I heard so I wanted to see for myself and frankly I was not very impressed." He paused, and Kumari's keen and judgmental eyes tried to measure his honesty.

"From the country of windmills, I made my way to Berlin, then Dresden and from there, I made my way to your mesmerizing Prague." Meer openly flirted as he sipped his juice.

"And you didn't tell me, from where did you get these handsome features from?" Flirt shall breed flirt, Meer thought.
"I am from Pakistan. I am Pakistani." Meer smiled at Kumari, but his smile froze when he saw the hell of hate boiling in her eyes.
"PAKISTAN?" She chewed her lips.
"Yeah…" Meer was confused. He expected hostility from other races but not from someone very south Asian looking, well-learned and settled in Europe. He didn't expect that the backward approach of judging the people according to their nationality would follow his trails in Europe. And Kumari was an Indian name; maybe she was a conservative Hindu who didn't accept Pakistan or Pakistanis.
"Why, what's the matter Kumari, are you ok?" He was concerned.
"I am from Bangladesh, which your people called East Pakistan," Kumari almost shouted.
"I was born much later, and I know nothing about Bangladesh apart from what I learned at school." Meer had innocence in his eyes.
"Then you don't know about the Bangladesh genocide that started with the launch of Operation Search Light. Over 200,000 Muslim sisters were raped by our Muslim brothers and fatwas were given to justify the guilty actions. Fuck you bloody Punjabi Paki!!!" Kumari took a long sip of her red wine.
"Learn fucking history before you talk to any more Bengalis and offer your apologies to them every time you see them for what your ancestors did!"
In shock, Meer was speechless.

Holding his breathe he watched Kumari exiting, leaving him stunned.

Meer paid the bill, went straight back to his hotel to checkout, and made his way to the central railway station to catch the next train to Bratislava.

Prague was deepening in the dark while Meer wept, reading about the horrors of 1971 Bangladesh Liberation war. Meer was shivering when he got off at the unbelievably small central railway station of Slovakia. Sweating under his clothes, he dragged himself out of the train station and located the nearest accommodation where he could dump his body.

Terrible weather, sickness and depression were probably enough to make a city look ugly. There wasn't much to see in Bratislava compared to the Czech capital. After a couple of days of self-medication, Meer was able to push himself around the city half-heartedly. He forced himself to smile at every tourist, but his cheerful fake smile didn't last long. Kumari's insult degraded him in his own eyes, though he was already ashamed of himself as Pakistani and Muslim. Media bashing of Muslims was one thing but his own self-doubt over political, cultural and divisive religious practices damaged his self-worth over the years and Kumari's hostility was just a trigger. Though he was considered more powerful than his own father, a member of National Assembly with several villages in southern Punjab under his thumb. He was a rigid, autocratic and ruthless landlord. Meer was his second son, and Raees was the first. At the age of 20, Raees was sent to Stockholm University in hopes that a degree in agricultural sciences would help him in win a provincial assembly seat. Unfortunately, Meer's father's hopes were dashed when Rees failed badly in his first year due to heroin addiction. It didn't take very long for him to get caught and deported back to Lahore, where his father's right-hand man greeted him cheerfully at the airport and flew with him straight to a private rehabilitation centre in Karachi. Elections were coming soon, and father didn't want to any controversy that could affect the campaign.

Meer became his father's favourite and grew strong just like his dad had in his late teens. His charisma was visible in his sharp eyes and diplomatic words; his only problem was womanising, though that trait was accepted proudly by his father. "You are my real son, Meer." Drunk Sikandar patted his shoulder with joy as he got up and pulled the arm of a provocative, semi-nude dancing girl towards him boldly in a private party held in a religiously orthodox area of Punjab.

The next couple of years were full of sexual volatility. Meer went crazy for the opposite gender after he returned from college. No women, young or old, were spared. Twenty-year-old Meer was out in his Jeep every evening to hunt. Tall, short, curvy, ugly, fair, dark, brunette, it didn't matter. The only thing that interested him was disinterest; women with attitude, women who looked away and didn't bother to take notice of him. He was after those who made him feel small and unimportant; the ones who ignored him. Often by force or by fear and rarely by charm, he was getting them in bed. Resisting ones were given ultimatums involving disappearance of family members and lack of response by local police was all part of his little plan. And later in the night, when women appear in his bedroom full of hate, eyes filled with sadness and thoughts of evil, he often responded by pulling cash from his pocket and letting them go with that prize money they earned by showing up. Weird. But when he was in the mood, he played very differently. After finding a desired woman in his room, Meer would direct her to take wash in his luxurious Jacuzzi-style bathroom. Meanwhile, he ordered his kitchen to prepare a special three-course dinner. One of his female servants would rush to bathe the lady with scented water infused with herbs and flowers. After thirty minutes, the new queen appeared in a see-through nightgown, fragranced in Meer's favourite perfume...sitting opposite him at the dining table. A posh dinner was served in a private dining area with beautiful paintings and classic Asian music wafting the soothing vibes. With a smile, Meer greeted that night's special guest and fed her with his own hands, "Is the food, ok? I hope it's according to your taste. Let's try another dish now." Gestures like these were unreal for a woman born in a village of a third world country. Life couldn't surprise her more. A man from a higher class treating her like a queen in his palace.

After the dinner, Meer made sure that the desert was served on the bed, on the fragranced beauty's navel.

High on the locally made alcohol, distilled by outcasts, Meer brewed pleasure for both in romantic intercourse. She wouldn't know what "oral receiving" meant but the fountain splashing and the idea of a man going down and using his tongue was unknown. No one cared about her orgasm; she was used to being used. After that night she was an addition to the list of Meer's admirers, who wanted to roll at his feet.

Only once did everything go wrong, so wrong that it changed the course of his life.

Lust Arrived

Mishki was a 34-year-old cleaner, a divorced mother of 2 kids with different fathers. A curvy woman with a big, loud, dirty-mouth known in local men for her sexual addictive pleasures in bed. She was a nymphomaniac who spotted her talent of milking favours from men at a young age in return of milking her.
Different men, different bodies, different emotions, different stories and at the end all was lust, the desire of a warm body and dopamine. She taught herself that pain can be lessened only when it's shared and when it splits, each partner gets only half. This helps the sufferer. She had a passion for pleasing through inflicting and receiving pain and once her ex-husband figured that out, local forms of bondage, choking, submission, spanking and humiliation were practised together. Mishki was finally sated. But since the birth of her first child, she had not been satisfied. Men mostly jizzed within seconds that turned her violent, she muscled on dicks for better lasting erection, going deep throat to hurt the partner and suffocate herself to gag.

Meer came across Mishki when he was about 16 and she was already a mother. Breasts are the unchallengeable favourite of straight growing boys. Meer wasn't any different. As a young teen, he had a first-hand opportunity to see Raees fondling Mishki's boobs while he tried to get his pants off and he noticed that Raees began jerking immediately as she grabbed his cock. He never forgot their facial expressions and what Mishki told to Raees in Saraiki.

"Prince, I think you need some medicine."

Raees was so ashamed that he said nothing and escaped before Mishki openly insulted him again. Mishki noted timid Meer peeking inside the room, both afraid and excited.

"Little prince. Come in. Don't be afraid of life." She was all sweet and sugar to him.

"Don't become like your brother. Be a man, a real man who doesn't release before his woman reaches the sky of pleasure. Treat her like a goddess and find pleasure in pleasing her. Do you understand?" She told a stunned Meer, who nodded his head as he kept his hungry eyes on her massive breasts.

"Do you like them? Do you want to touch them?" And before Meer could say anything, she took his hands and slipped them on her. Meer grabbed and held them strong; his palm had that grip which could ignite fire. He was a virgin, but Mishki's intuition told her that he was the one, the one she saw repeatedly in her dreams... the eyes were the same.

"My prince, I promise you myself but not today, not now. You are not ready." Meer was melting with heat when Raees shouted angrily from a roaring Pajero.

"Meer, motherfucker, are you staying in filth now?"
And he knew that he had to go, regardless.
"Go my prince, go, your brother is calling. Mishki will keep her promise." She kissed Meer's clutched hand.
After that, Mishki disappeared from the area for the next year and a half. No one knew where, why or for what she had left the village, but it was widely suspected that she left with some secret lover from the city. After around eighteen months, Mishki came back with a second child clenching her breast.
Meanwhile, Meer had some first-hand experience in understanding female sexual anatomy. Mature female servants came very handy in practising pornographic guidelines. The time he spent in Lahore with the lads of other political and bureaucratic elites for his studies was pure fun. But all this time at the back of his mind was Mishki and her golden advice, which revealed its true essence in nights and intimate moments he had with the opposite gender. He was young, so sexual arousal wasn't any trouble of any kind, but he noticed that he went mad after thinking about Mishki. The lust and the thirst of that woman drove him nuts. He tried to find her, but all efforts ended in smoke.
Summer holidays of 98 brought Meer back to the village and on his way, he spotted Mishki.

His black four-by-four pulled next to her; the black tinted windows released a puff of air-conditioned freshness over the anticipating face. Right away she knew who it was. Him. And now she was ready. His face was unveiling slowly, full of excitement from the expected pleasures of the flesh. She noticed his eyes were burning and eyebrows were questioning. There was a smile on his face, happy or sad she could not tell. He was mature in his features, and she loved his long, slightly curly hair. "Mishki..." Meer wanted to say something more, but there was nothing untold between them. She knew exactly what he was thinking.

"*Hoon*..." The absurd sound and smile on Mishki's face were an agreement between them.

Lust, sex, benefit, pleasure, love, and darkness...

Who knew that the prince would fall for the pleasures of a self-styled prostitute and that the secret affair would end up with Mishki pregnant with Meer's illegitimate child? And that would never be revealed by Mishki that who's the father of her third kid. Insistence of immature Meer lead Mishki stubborn and bitter. She demanded to live in Lahore, not in the village anymore. She was concerned and scared about Meer's status. His position in society was a wall between them, a wall she couldn't jump, a wall which he couldn't break. The distance between them made her unsure about the acceptance of their child by him and society.

The child was delivered in Lahore in autumn of 1999 and in winter of 2000 Mishki was pregnant again by Meer, and this time he couldn't hold his anger. After an intense argument, Meer choked her during sex. His hate pumped his arms and while he was sexually thrashing her in the dark, he couldn't see her face turning white.

Mishki was in heaven that night. Her dream was fulfilled. She knew years ago that this day was coming and for that she prepared Meer, asking him to promise to take care of her kids, provide them with an education and a house to live, an opportunity to grow that she never had.

Unintentional murder couldn't be justified and escaped from...unless one holds the power. And blood is never cheap unless it is of the poor.

Later in the night, one phone call from Meer's father removed the dead body from the property quietly in a private ambulance and, despite plans and promises, the three kids were sent to an orphanage.

"You are a fucking bastard! Get lost from my eyes. Don't come back or contact me!" Meer was slapped for the first and last time by his father.

In the morning Meer flew to Peshawar to stay with some unknown uncle, who was responsible for his safety, security and mental health. One week after, scared and depressed, Meer travelled back to his village with the same uncle to see his dad.

"You are flying to England in two days; you will complete your degree in Newcastle and remember one thing... My people will keep a close eye on you. Forget what happened and move on." His father paused to read his son's expression.

"Tomorrow you are getting engaged to Raheela. You know her already, she is the daughter of my friend and political ally and no, you can't say no!"
"I thought she was promised to Raees." Meer murmured.
"Don't speak the name of that bastard in front of me; he's dead to us now." His father roared with anger.
And Meer knew he made a mistake of mentioning the wrong person.
Raees escaped from the rehabilitation centre after a few months and was under the protection of opposition political party who used him as a political tool. One insider updated them that Raees would stand against his father in the next election. After a few months, Raees arranged a press conference in which he revealed spiced up, untold truths about his father's assets, hidden businesses and corruption that damaged Sikander Bakht's political position and health. But he wasn't ready to lose his power and accept defeat because of Raees. Sikandar was a master of conjunctions and oppositions of politics. Meer's engagement was part of his plan to eradicate political opponents and come out even stronger from the political mess.
He handed the final judgement to Meer regarding the engagement. Both knew it was about power, politics, land and money. Meer and Raheela were pawns, showcasing political somersaults of their fathers on their engagement party, held privately with a dozen other politicians and dancing girls sipping alcohol in a five-star hotel near Lahore.

The new couple was retired after an early dinner. And Meer thanked God for this and made his way straight to a separate bedroom to celebrate the evening with the Russian blonde given as an engagement present from Sikandar. Ready to fly him high in pleasure before the long flight to England.

Turning Tides

Newcastle upon Tyne was cold, windy and mostly wet. Meer didn't fit in well the first few months. He was living awkwardly with the family of some distant relative. After three months of suffocation and cultural exhaustion, he finally convinced his father to live on his own. In mood of celebration, he tried every sort of alcohol and women. He held house parties and invited all international and local students to his place except Pakistanis, Indians and Bangladeshis to avoid any political or religious arguments. He started writing stories, reading a lot of international literature, listening to different genres of music and ate whatever he wanted. He wasn't fussy with Halal, kosher or non-Halal food. And Meer's new favourite pastime was to listen to his petite South Korean girlfriend Ji-Su during sex.
Life was good for him and regardless of some racist incidents after 9/11, he was absolutely fine. Meer never considered himself a strict Muslim; he was drinking openly, gambling frequently, eating bacon and sausages for Sunday breakfasts and never even drove near a mosque.
But he felt things changing. Something was in the air, even in a small city like Newcastle. Something was changing in the eyes of the people who looked at him, the way they observed him, the way they kept the conversations short.
They were infected.
Once he was stopped late at night by two police officers.

That had never happened before.

Immigration police were looking actively for illegal immigrants. Muslims from third world countries were their favourite. Poor Asians working in chicken shops, restaurants, corner stores... the lowest of the low were their targets, already exploited by the British-Asian community. Underpaid, cash-in-hand jobs in local off-licences, restaurants, and takeaways were all staffed with illegals or students who were not allowed to work more than a certain number of hours. They were brutally used by their own people with the excuse "who else will give a job to these poor people? After all, they are our own." Meer wasn't a British-Pakistani, but he was not different in his attitude from brown-whites of Britain. He spotted a few illegal Pakistanis in local takeaways and chip shops. One of them hesitantly approached Meer and asked about renting a room in his flat. Though he generally kept Pakistanis at arm's length, after 9/11 his attitude was much more polite.

"There are two of us. We share a room now, but our landlord is insisting we leave." He took a brief pause to look at Meer, deciding... if he could tell him something forbidden or not. "I came here three years ago on a visitor's visa. I have two kids back home and life wasn't easy. I am Christian, and you know how we are treated. We are discriminated against, sir *jee*. My close friend was burned to death by a Muslim mob." He sighed. "Somebody falsely made up a story about him trying to tear up the Quran and burn it." He had sadness but no tears in his eyes. "We are not even Muslim, but because of our face and skin colour people look down on us. I don't know how long I will have this job and what's my future. If you don't have a room for us, it's no problem. But maybe you know someone who can help us." Meer saw hope in his eyes.

"What's your name?" Meer looked at him closely.

"Babar, sir *jee*."

"Babar I will meet you here tomorrow evening. Let me see what I can do for you." Meer smiled, as this illegal immigrant had given him an unexpected, excellent opportunity. Money wasn't his trouble, but he wanted to earn something by himself.

The next morning, Meer went to the local estate agent to see a four-bedroom property. In the afternoon, Meer paid the deposit, signed the contract, and officially rented the property under his name. The keys were with him when he went to see Babar.

"One of my friends has a house in Gateshead, I can get you a room under my name, but I don't want any trouble from you. Rent is £300 bills all included with one month's advance, good?" Meer watched him.

"Very good sir-*jee*, very good, thank you sir-*jee*. I didn't expect that. You are a good man. I don't know what I can do for you to thank you enough." Babar's head was shaking in sheer gratitude.

"Don't worry. When I will start my takeaway, you will be the manager and I will sort your visa out as well. I have an excellent lawyer." He smiled diplomatically.

"Thank you, sir *jee*! Thank you. God bless you. The world needs the people like you, sir-*jee,* I don't have words to praise you. My family will always be servants to your kids even, thank you!" While Babar was bowing with gratitude in front of Meer, praising his kind heart, Meer was already planning his next move. The university's student notice board got him three more students in the next couple of days, and Babar got him one more tenant too. The four-bedroom house contained 6 people, 3 illegal and 3 university students on two separate floors. A handsome amount of money started pouring into his bank account.

In the next six months, Meer was able to rent a dying takeaway and the right person for the job was in his pocket, Babar Gulzar. Underappreciated, underpaid and underestimated by his previous bosses, Babar was used to his maximum by sweet words, respect and just with a little bit better money and authority to motivate him. Babar was an honest and a hardworking man who thanked the Lord Jesus Christ that he finally got such a wonderful boss who was genuinely interested in his wellbeing, finding him a good immigration solicitor.

Time was running out fast, and Meer was about to finish his degree. There was pressure building up from his father to return to Lahore. The political sphere wasn't stable. This idea was not warmly welcomed by Meer as he wasn't sure about going back so quickly. Income from the renters was handsome, though subletting was a criminal offence. Furthermore, as a student, he wasn't allowed to engage in any business activities. But everything was well hidden. Life was smooth without any stress or extreme effort for stability. Books, music, alcohol, Ji-Su, parties, Saturday nights out, dine-outs and no pollution around him, inside him, gave much clarity about life. Things he admired or strongly disliked were rediscovered. His hidden self was unveiled through the power of literature. Gradually he realised the value of inner peace and serenity that could strike the inner equilibrium. His need to rush and dominate was balancing, and one quote from Rumi changed his perspective.

"Let yourself be silently drawn by the stronger pull of what you really love."

And the question was... what did he really loved? An easy life, full of comforts without the warmth of family bonding left him emotionally cold and damaged him with the idea that everything could be bought by money or achieved by power. Meer was totally unaware of love. His mom was died at his birth, and Meer was ignored throughout his childhood. For him, father meant nothing more than a serious face which he irregularly saw during the week. He was raised by a team of servants whom he ordered around. The older he grew, the slimmer the wish to be loved became. He learned quickly that his words have the power to get him what he wants, when he wants it, and how he wants it. He detached himself from people and focused his mind on psychologically subordinating them, making them accept him with his stubborn, angry attitude. Money wasn't short and the money bought him all that could comfort him physically, sometimes emotionally too, but temporarily. He couldn't develop genuine friendships and when he did, he often was betrayed. That eventually led him to be an introverted, sarcastic, secretive person. From the ages of 5 to 13 he played alone, read books, watched television in his room and made plans to win the love of his father, who preferred Raees. So, from the beginning, there was child jealousy between the boys. Raees was older, stronger, and legitimate. Meer's thirst to prove himself made him a sharp student but his lust to show superiority and get unconditionally accepted by all got worse with time.

Back then, romance wasn't his strong suit and Meer's need to unwind emotionally was snubbed long enough that he couldn't harmonise with the opposite gender. No wonder he gelled well with wiser and experienced Mishki who undoubtedly stirred some sweetness of love in Meer's heart. But the relationship that opened him as a person was the magic of shy and hesitant but curious South Korean Ji-Su, an exchange student from the Busan University of Foreign Studies.

"I have a wish... That I take you to the Haedong Yonggung temple, you just sit next to me, and I will do that one prayer for which I waited long; one wish is always granted on the first visit. Do you have something to wish for?"

Ji-Su's quiet personality helped her to understand Meer. She observed that he's a reserved person who doesn't say at all what's in his heart. His socialising was for the sake of understanding foreign cultures and learning the differences; otherwise, his mingling was shallow and unimpressive. During conversations, whenever he realised that he was talking unnecessarily, or someone was trying to look inside him or ask complicated questions about his past, he was fully capable of walking away. He held parties in which people came for free alcohol, free snacks and the bad host just sat in a corner with his whiskey on the rocks to observe people. One Friday night Ji-Su came as an uninvited guest in Meer's party. She was dragged along by Portuguese Rosa, who knew Meer from the management class.

"You have to come with me please, please, please!" Landed her in Meer's flat with a Japanese *sake* for the host whom she noted wasn't very loud, welcoming, or caring. When she handed him the *sake*, a dry and smile-free "thank you" was all he said before vanishing into his kitchen. She felt that the host was crude, and she spent hardly an hour there. After an hour, she walked out of his flat with a perfect reason not to come back again. A couple of weeks later she was waiting for a taxi in Chinatown with her weekly groceries when Meer appeared in his Smart car, beeping the horn to get her attention."

"Jump in." He shouted.

"No, I am waiting for a taxi, thank you."

"I am your taxi, hop on, before I get a ticket." He was loud and people were looking at them.

"Ok" Ji-Su shook her head slightly.

On the way to Sunderland, she came to understand that he was handicapped in expressing his emotions; he doesn't know how to reply in kindness or with love and every time he tried to say something he struggled with his words.

"I like your hair." Meer kept his eyes on the road but couldn't get much friendliness in his voice.

"Thank you." Ji-Su smiled over the compliment as she saw on his face that Meer was trying to communicate, but he couldn't gather his sentences.

"I like your jawline and high cheekbones."

"Thank you" Ji-Su didn't really know what she could possibly say. There was reluctance, a slight language barrier and the unpleasant history.

Meer was driving very carefully but didn't have enough courage to steal a look at her. She wasn't really his type either; all skin and bones... but her silence, shy behaviour and her vibe moved him emotionally. He regretted not being friendlier with her at the party.

He beat himself silently as Ji-Su wondered about the real motivation behind the compliments, their conversation halting after a few sentences within the 25-minute drive. But Ji-Su quickly reached to the core of Meer without knowing anything about his past.

After that day, they both gave up on each other. Ji-Su was interested, but she curbed her feelings and Meer didn't bother to reach out to her. He was partly sure that Ji-Su was in a relationship. Otherwise, why wouldn't she give him any hint to meet again or ask him up for a cup of tea?

The end of semester hustle, exams, projects, presentations wiped away the feelings between them. They were students of two different universities and lived in neighbouring cities. There was nothing in common that could bring them together, until Ji-Su had a gas leak in her building late one night. Luckily, the dorm was mostly empty as most of the students were travelling within the UK or Europe. In fact, Ji-Su herself was flying to Florence in two days. Unsure who to call, Ji-Su rang Rosa for advice.

"Wait, I'll contact Meer. I'm sure he'd be able to help." And before Ji-Su could reply Rosa was adding him on the call. Busy in watching Al-Pacino starrer crime drama when his mobile rang. He knew instantly she needed his help, but he wasn't eager to do any good deeds at 1 a.m. He rejected the incoming call but then within a couple of minutes with remorse he called back.

"What the fuck has gone wrong this time? Aren't you in London visiting your sister?"

"Smart-ass, I'm. But do you remember Ji-Su...."

In the next 30 minutes, Meer was returning to his flat with Ji-Su in flip-flops.

"I'm sure you are hungry. Let's get you a snack." Meer turned the steering wheel cheerfully toward the local chicken shop, famous for its 5:00 am closure in locals. While engineers worked to fix the trouble, Meer and Ji-Su shared a meal and watched "Before Sunrise" while sipping their beers at his flat.

"Engineers would take few hours more; we have closed the main switch for the security of the residents. You are welcome to stay in the building but there's no hot water or heating in the building for now." Security informed her on the call.

"I think its best you stay tonight here Ji-Su." Around 5 a.m., Meer offered his bedroom, which was accepted reluctantly after she asked certain questions.

"Are you still sure, this is a good idea?" Ji-Su inquired on her return from the toilet.

Exhausted, Meer was already snoring on the sofa.

The next afternoon they were laughing over the brunch in the town centre, sharing omelette and jokes together, and pouring coffee for each other. Meer drove her to the dorm to get her changed while he waited outside the building. They planned to spend the rest of the day at Whitley Bay. A short drive out of the city and they were walking next to seafront holding hot chocolates.

Hearts melted and emotions flowed freely in their conversation. The thoughts were overlapping topics that kept them talking. They both just talked, talked, talked and talked as if they wouldn't have another chance. And the chances were slim, as the next day was Ji-Su's flight. With a long face, Meer drove her to the airport. But he knew the trip was for just three days.

Three days could change anything, he thought.

Ji-Su wasn't very excited either. She even thought about cancelling her trip, but she knew that she would regret not seeing Michelangelo's 'David'. She wanted a break too, to re-evaluate her feelings, to make sure she wasn't part of any illusion. Even if she was, she thought, it's better to lose herself and ruin her life to catch this dream rather than not dreaming at all. Life lived in fear of consequences isn't life. Pain is life, too, when you hurt yourself and learn that life isn't the name of continues joy or seeking pain but a quest for internal and external balance. Life is also that dream to live in happiness, to catch that sand slipping through your fingers. Life is in the air; every breath can light you up and every second lost is another step toward decay. Life is a blessing. Life lies somewhere within the clash of our reluctance, our passion, our smile and tears, the joys within sorrow and sorrows inside the pleasures. That's all life.

The next day, with this thought in mind, she addressed a postcard to Newcastle upon Tyne.
"I wish you were here, your hand would be in my hand, and I keep my eyes close, I would feel the warmth of your palm. Meer, Buddha had revealed life over me and it's you... unveiling me."
Ji-Su.
Night was falling as Meer read the postcard for the hundredth time. He loved the poetic feeling of being admired as his name was written next to Buddha.
"Maybe she knows something about me, which I don't." Meer was sure that Ji-Su could untangle him, and they would complement each other at every stage of life. Meer was fond of her company; her eyes, her face, the silky dark hair that bounced unintentional with every affirmed head shake, with innocent blinks. They all touched his heart. Sex was just ok, but Meer weighed the quality time out of bed more than the time spent in. But the most important detail was that he took her virginity. Meer was Ji-Su's first lover, and she enjoyed the sexually experienced Meer very much, which in return he enjoyed more than anything else. He was happy to see her contented and pleased.

Satisfaction, predictability, and bliss all blended in an easy life and Meer had no plans to go back to Pakistan. Not to inhale dust and live a proud, ignorant life with peasants lingering around, telling him he was the best landlord ever. Meer had no interest in jumping any political mess with his brother. Television channels, print media, and journalists all were hungry for the news, hunting sensational breakthroughs, and Sikandar had enough personal, political opposition that Raees could bank on. The government's unpopularity hit a high as ministers were caught in offshoring and money laundering cases. He asked himself why he should return…money, power, rivalry? He was slowly losing the taste for it. His plan was to finish his degree, get a work permit, and expand his businesses legally. A plan for a Euro trip was on his mind for a long time, but busy routines sucked his ambitious dreams out.

Ji-Su moved in with him, so they were on each other's nerves most of the time, but the things were still solid between them. Ji-Su's opinion regarding the future and other things was much different from his. She wanted Meer to visit South Korea, meet her parents and try to explore some import-export opportunities between the UK and South Korea. Her deepest wish was to convert him, so teaching Meer about the life of Buddha gave her immense satisfaction. Her fondness of the clarity between mind and soul pushed Meer to decide not to hide from his father.

"You must tell your *Appa* what you feel, what you want and what you value in your life. What's the point to sit depressed, doing nothing about it? He's calling you every day and you are not even answering his calls. I understand it's difficult for you to say 'no' to your father but he's your father, Meer. I don't think that you can live a peaceful life in this manner. Let's go to Busan for a week. Lord Buddha will open your inner eye when you seek the liberation from the pain of this world. It's all an illusion, the pain and beyond the pain too."
But Meer couldn't do much about his misery. He was scared of Sikandar and didn't want to break his heart like Raees had. He was sure that his father would be devastated by his decision. To him, political legacy and power were more important than anything else. Politics was his drug, and he wasn't high on it anymore.
To break the momentum of the gripping depression, Meer decided to travel home at the end of his last semester. He told Ji-Su that he was more than happy to visit her parents in Busan after visiting Pakistan. He told his father that he was coming home in three months but before all, he planned a Euro trip for three weeks.
One month later, with his visa, train tickets and some hotel bookings in hand, he made his way to Paris, while Ji-Su headed to see her family in Busan where she expected Meer after two months.

Paris, Brussels, Antwerp, Bruges, Amsterdam, Berlin, Dresden, Prague and Bratislava, where a sick, upset, depressed and suffering Meer realised that his visa was expiring in 4 days. And on his return to England, he had an appointment in the South Korean Embassy in London. His return ticket to London was yet to be purchased but before anything…he wanted to go back to Prague and find Kumari to apologise.

Act Two

Prague was wet and cold that afternoon when he came out of the central station. The Metro took him to Malostranská, from where he walked to Prague Castle with his heavy rucksack. He was sure that he would find Kumari near the castle this time of day. If not, he would try his luck for the last time tomorrow morning near Namesti Republiky.
Prague Castle wasn't busy. Dark clouds gathered around the 9th-century architectural jewel. Meer looked around the courtyards but couldn't find any sign of Kumari. Drizzle was turning into heavy rain and Meer thought that it would be wiser to make his way back.
He felt fatigued on return, starving, and heavy rucksack on his shoulders was killing him. He noticed some missed calls and text about two voicemails as he stepped onto a tram.
"That couldn't be Ji-Su," he thought, and slipped his mobile phone back in his pocket.
Hungry, Meer went straight to the hotel's restaurant to have a large dinner after dumping his rucksack in a room.
"Chicken *schnitzel*, baby potatoes, broccoli with tartar sauce and squeezed orange juice, *Děkuji*." He smiled and took his phone out to listen to the voicemails.
"Sir *jee*, it's me, Babar, can you please call me back? I'm in Newcastle city centre police station. Thank you."
The 15-second voice message turned Meer pale.

"Sir *jee*, it's me Baber Gulzar, I was waiting for your call Sir jee. Immigration raided the takeaway. They detained me and Barkat. They asked for our address, I am sure they will raid there too. They were asking about you a few minutes ago. They are looking for you. The other owner of the takeaway went to Pakistan yesterday. I gave him the money you asked me to pass him. They are looking for him also. Sir *jee* I don't know how much more I can cry but please don't come back here immediately. I will be transferred to Manchester detention centre from here. I wanted to ask for the telephone number of your immigration lawyer or if you can call him for me, thank you Sir *jee*." Babar's voice was husky, and he was breathing heavily, in pauses.

His food was served, but Meer's hands were incapable of holding the knife and fork. He was shivering. He couldn't understand what had happened and what he should do. Meer's mind was blank. He knew no immigration lawyer. His brain was completely shut. What to do? What not to? It wasn't the loss of money, it was the loss of his dreams to live in peace, live in harmony. He couldn't think clearly about how he could go back to England. What excuse he could make on his arrival that wouldn't end him in a detention centre? What were his options? He was sure that the immigration police would go to his sublet property, where they would find belongings of all three illegal immigrants. Several cases would be opened against him, for running business on a student visa, housing illegal immigrants, and subletting a house without the owner's permission.

"Shit!" Meer cursed himself.

"I'm screwed and nothing can be done about it now. What could save me from going to the jail? God, why didn't I think about the consequences of the worst-case scenario before?" He shook his head.

"Better I go back to Pakistan, live a sick life, ask Ji-Su to come and see me and take our relationship from there. Maybe later, we can go to South Korea." He thought.

Meer left his cold dinner on the plate and made his way to his room. He was exhausted, numb, and powerless. Things got fucked up badly, but a few shots of vodka from the mini bar helped the broken man sleep.

The next morning, he popped in quickly to one travel agent's office to check the prices for Prague-Islamabad flights. From there he made his way to the Náměstí Republiky where he hoped to find Kumari B holding an Italian flag umbrella.

It was a glorious day, a day on which flocks of tourists are running everywhere in excitement, looking for good food, beautiful photographs, drinks, and a wonderful time to remember forever.

Meer strolled between people, running his eyes around, hoping that he would catch site of Kumari somewhere. He wanted to end the disgusting feeling of inferiority and self-hate by accepting the irreversible sins of his fucked-up nation. Though the separation of East Pakistan is an old tale of bad politics, a power grab from all sides, Meer wanted to ask where the people were who claimed to be brothers and sisters under the single flag of one religion. Now they were divided poorly into so many sects. The division goes further to cultural values, as languages, race, cast and colour of skin seem to have more priority. No wonder they could not condemn the injustice. The lives of dark-skinned Bengalis were alien to West Pakistan.

Meer couldn't find any hint of Kumari. He was standing in old town square planning to go further down to the Jewish quarter when he noticed that his mobile was vibrating madly in his jacket's side pocket.

"That could be Babar again." He thought.

Meer really wanted to speak to him, to advise Babar to look for some lawyer for whom Meer would pay.

The phone kept ringing in Meer's hand... Dad, Dad, Dad kept blinking on his phone's screen.

"Not again." Meer shook his head hopelessly with a half-smile.

"I am going to Pakistan anyway." He told himself. "So, let me give him the good news now."

"Hellooooooo Daddy!" Meer tried to cheer up his voice.

"Meer, I'm Mumtaz, your dad's secretary." The man was sobbing.

"Yeah, is everything ok?" Meer immediately tensed.

"Your father is no more Meer, Raees shot your dad yesterday at home."
The world went still, lifeless. Colours faded away. Everything was blurry. Suddenly weightless, Meer couldn't understand if what he heard was true. How? How come? His head was spinning slowly in numbness.
"Meer, are you with me son?" Mumtaz was breathless.
"I don't know... Is daddy ok, is he well?" Meer tried to retrieve his voice.
"Son, he's no more. Raees came yesterday and shot your dad at home. Please don't come back for revenge. It's pointless. Police were looking for Raees but late last night, another man represented himself at the police station as your father's killer. Please stay in England. I am sure Raees is after you now. He's gone mad for power. Try to take care of yourself. Try to accept it as the will of God." He paused and said hesitantly,
"Please avoid coming here. Everything is toxic. Please be careful." Mumtaz bit his lip with regret for what he said.
"I don't... understand... anything." Meer was trying to come out of his blankness. His feet were burning with frozen tears in his eyes. He tried to breathe harder, but something was holding the air. He moved his hand roughly in his hair and looked pointlessly around not knowing where he was, what he should do, or what was happening.
"Meer... son, I will call you back later, ok?" Mumtaz felt he wasn't very effective in melting Meer's wall of grief. The call was dropped but Meer kept his phone to his ear. He wasn't there. A wave from the past reeled him in.

"You are my real son Meer, a real man." Watching his father patting his back, cheering him up with bright eyes, Meer smelled his scent, his breath. He was there.
People were moving away from him when a soft hand at his back stroked him and a sweet, concerned voice called his name.
"Meer…"
It was Kumari, patting him soothingly.
"Meer, what happened? Come here, let me get you somewhere to sit." Kumari looked around and escorted him to a nearby coffee shop.
"What happened to you? Where were you? I tried to find you in different hotels. Look I am sorry I was so mean to you, sorry. Why are you crying? Take this." she offered him a tissue paper and then reluctantly she wiped off his face. Meer was crying like a baby, his nose running, and she doubted that he was even aware of her presence.
"Meer, Meer, are you ok?" Kumari's voice reached him at last.
"Yes, yes I am, I am ok." His eyes were red as he came out of the trance. He was surprised to see Kumari.
"Is this a dream?" He asked himself.
"Are you ok, what happened?" Kumari rubbed his hand and scanned him with her eyes.
"Nothing happened."
"Don't lie to me. No one cries buckets without reason, especially in the middle of the city centre." She was infuriated.
"My dad was murdered." Meer looked at his shoes.
"*Cristo*, oh *Dio!*" Kumari was shocked.
"By my brother." His dry, red eyes were on Kumari.

She was speechless, in a state of shock, clueless what to say that could comfort his crying heart.
"Was it because of money?" she asked quietly.
"Money, power, I don't know... my... mind can't accept this." Meer shook his head in denial.
"Are you going home?"
"I don't know, I have been advised not to go there otherwise I might also be killed." Meer tried to smile.
"What?"
"I don't know. I can't think very clearly. I am not sure what can I do. What are my options?" He was thinking about calling Ji- Su to discuss everything.
"When's your flight back to London?"
"Don't know." Meer was getting irritated by her questions.
"Ok, let me take you for dinner at my flat. Today is my day off. I came to the office to drop off something when I saw you. Come on... come with me, I cooked my favourite dish today, deep-fried capsicum with chicken, you will like it, come on."

Kumari was living in Prague 8, not very far from the Ladvi station in a two-bedroom property, alone. Petr Miroslav left her a year ago with a flat full of books and memories. Forty-one-year-old Kumari was struggling after Petr's sudden departure; his death left her unsure, vulnerable, and scared from life in general. She couldn't get herself together to go out and look for a date. Times changed, and so had she, preferring loneliness over any tiring relationship. Also, Kumari found most Czech men cold and selfish. Her colour of the skin was a hurdle too, but she was also very dominant type with an active working brain. Usually, women of that sort end up lonely, heartbroken and misunderstood in this man's world. She had no kids but since Petr's death, she was wishing every day to be a mother. Time was running faster than ever, leaving her with fears of ending alone, childless, without family, without anyone who would care for her. A few times she thought about moving back to Bangladesh, but who was there? Who would welcome her with open arms?
While serving the food, Kumari reluctantly asked lost-in-thoughts Meer about his commitments. He looked tired and very sad.
"I am engaged." Meer noticed her luscious cleavage as she served.
It's all about satisfying the hunger, psychological, physical, sexual, emotional and the cure of grief is hidden somewhere between intense intimacy and intoxication. That evening Meer was melting his sorrow with *'Becherovka'* as he entered Kumari's den, where she was waiting for him.

"Sleep, just sleep…" She gently stroked fingers in his hair, fading consciousness.

It was midnight.

In the darkness, his strength was powered by her lips as she moved her hands slowly over his stretched softness, mastering the madness forever.

Fluids flow, nectar pour, as amazement reveals in the moment's truth that everything is just steam and we are evaporating dreams, disappearing clouds.

"Aaaaaaaa……hhhhhhhhhhhhh……" Meer was quivering before Kumari could put her hand on his mouth.

 The night's silence was getting louder when Kumari whispered.

"I need someone." She was moving her hands on Meer's throat, breathing in skies of indecent pleasure.

"I need you; I need to feel the life. Help me, Meer." She could hear his exhausted breath, but Meer's body was no match for Kumari's lust.

Sinking slowly, down, deeper, he heard… "I would take your erection as a sign that you agree with me." The Bengali goddess moved closer to her target. Meer flooded her twice and fell asleep on the comfort of her silky skin and fragranced breasts were lavender pillows.

"Let me tell you something Meer," she combed her fingers in his floppy hair. "Let me tell you that the decisions which we make with the heart bring happiness, brief but strong. And the decisions made from by the brain are stable, though hollow, leaving us empty and mad in peace. And with the death of each dream Meer, we die a bit too. We die and no one comes to say a prayer at our grave. I am not ready yet to lay myself in a graveyard of people with no hopes. I can't live in self-inflicted grief and knowingly not doing something about this pain when life is that only second when I am breathing. I don't have that power to live a miserable life."

She breathed gently on sleeping Meer, looking at his forehead, his eyebrows, his lashes, listening to the rhythm of his breath.

"You won't stay with me, but I've decided to be happy. Trying it again, knowing that I could fall, but I will try... regardless."

The next morning, after dawn, Meer awoke fresh with remorse.

"I shouldn't cheat on Ji-Su like this." He thought.

"It's too late to change what I did. I should leave now." Meer looked outside but his gaze returned to Kumari.

"What the fuck I am doing, again?" He thought, as his hand unintentionally moved onto sleeping Kumari's plump breast.

"They look nice." He pinched a nipple and rubbed his thumb to arouse the latent pleasure evoking him and her.

"Mmmmmmmmmm..." Kumari smiled in deep sleep.

"Why am I doing this?" He asked his unsatisfied self.

"And what was she saying, she needs me?" He looked at Kumari's well-formed lips.

"I really should get out and run away, call Ji-Su and talk to her. England is a big no-no and Pakistan is a burning hell." Meer rubbed his fingers on his forehead. Meer closed his eyes to look deep into the situation, exploring some options for the future. He couldn't gamble on his life, but his visa was expiring in two days.

"Maybe I ask her to marry me." Meer looked at Kumari.

"No, I think I am screwed enough. No more fuck ups and I am not living with her either. I have seen enough already that how she can treat a Pakistani. I'm not sure what she would do to me next time if she's in her 'hate mode."

Half-covered by a blanket. Her breasts were luring him, and he could feel enticement in his bones, the pleasure flowing like alcohol in his blood.

Meer was inside her, just as a dream slide into a sleep.

"Who are you?"

"Who am I?"

"Meer?"

"Meer... Meer... Are you ok?" Kumari was trying to wake him up. He was talking in his sleep, grinding his teeth, sweating, breathing awkwardly.

"I am sorry. I got scared. I woke you up because you were screaming in your sleep; I was frightened. Are you ok?" Kumari turned a bit pale.

Meer felt some stickiness on his thighs, his head was dizzy, and he noticed a love bite on his left shoulder.

"10:05..." He checked the time and tried to recall the last few hours.

"Let me pee..." Meer jumped out of the bed, ignoring Kumari's concerned face and went to the toilet where he noticed the ova, residue on his penis.

"We were so wild." He noticed another love mark hidden in the hair on his chest.

A quick shower, a light breakfast, and an empty kiss without any discussion about the previous night, Meer was ready to leave. He wanted his space to make a few telephone calls. He hadn't spoken with Ji-Su since he left Dresden.

"Can we meet for dinner tonight?" Kumari asked hesitantly as Meer slipped his foot into his boot.

"I will catch up with you. I know where you are now, don't I?" Meer faked a smile.

"Hey, I don't know what's wrong, but we had a beautiful time. Come back to me...I promise no strings attached. You can be here as long as you want." Meer felt the depth of her truthfulness.

"When's your flight to England?" Kumari reached for him.

"It's today at 4. It was lovely to see you. I am sorry but I can't be here anymore." He didn't have the courage to look into her eyes.

And before Kumari replied, Meer was gone with the wind.

Time played the same old hand with Meer again. He didn't know that he turned Kumari's secrete dream, a reality that night. It was about a year later when she saw Meer again near Muzeum station with rich, middle-aged German, loud and drunk in his arms. Kumari saw him almost bowing when he opened the taxi's door for that bucket mouth, swearing in a Bavarian accent.

She couldn't believe that it was Meer. But it was him. He looked tired, nervous, and something was wrong with his body language. He walked with a limp.
"What he's doing in Prague?" Kumari thought.
She hadn't been able to contact him at all since his departure. His mobile number which she managed to get from his hotel with his address was constantly off, and her letters to Meer about the pregnancy and the baby girl were never returned. But Kumari had no regrets. Having a child was her dream, and Meer was not part of that. He gave her no false hopes, never promised anything to her. Still, she thought, maybe he would be interested in keeping in touch with his daughter. Once Kumari even thought to fly to Newcastle and knock on his door. Kumari wanted to forget him completely after what she sighted... but she couldn't. She wasn't at peace and her mind was full of questions and doubts.
"Could that be his girlfriend?" She thought.
"But that ugly loud woman!" She shook her head helplessly.
"Maybe I was mistaken. It wasn't Meer. He got married? He told me he was engaged." Meer was glued to her mind.
The next day, Kumari was near the same spot pushing the buggy around Wenceslas Square but couldn't find any sign of Meer.
"I must have gone mad, silly cow! Why I am chasing someone, whom I don't even know properly? He never existed in my life, didn't bother to contact me even once and..." She looked at little Sahanara Begum.

"Sahanara has got me, her mother. I am fully capable of raising a daughter without anyone's help. She doesn't need a father. You don't miss what you never had. I am sure I will find a perfect answer to her curious questions about her dad. She doesn't need to know everything." Kumari reassured herself as she headed back home.
The evening was getting cold, and darkness was filling the emptiness of fall. Autumn leaves crinkled under Kumari's feet, sounding like broken hopes, bleak thoughts, patchy memories.
It took her 10 minutes to walk from the station back to her flat. As Kumari turned onto her quiet street, irregular footsteps chased her, trying to maintain a distance but slowly getting closer.
"Should I call the police?" She thought. But as she took her phone out a shadow crossed her path quickly. A man stood opposite her.
"Kumari?" Destiny was calling her name, recognizing her face...
"Meer?" Kumari froze.
"I have been waiting here for the last hour. I knocked on the door of your flat, but I saw the lights were off." His voice was a bit dry.
Kumari was wordless.
"I saw you yesterday in the centre. I was at work, so I couldn't say hello." Meer looked at Sahanara in the buggy.
"She's, our daughter." Kumari wanted to say but stayed quiet.
"It's cold, I think we should take the baby inside." Meer looked closely at Sahanara. Her face looked a bit familiar.

"Is she... mine?" He thought reluctantly.

"Come inside. What are you doing in Prague?" Kumari unlocked the building's door as Meer pushed the pram inside.

"You don't have to do that." Kumari smiled.

"No, no, it's ok, I got it now." Meer kept his eyes on the little one.

Room was silent, filled with unasked questions. Sahanara was crawling on the carpet. The sounds of her tapping hands and knees moistened Kumari's eyes. Meer's heavy breaths blotted the silence. He was curiously observing the baby girl crawling around him, trying to stand up and grabbing his jeans in her little fist to pull herself up. Smiling, Meer gave her his pinky. She looked proud of her efforts and her smile was so familiar to him. Her eyes were deep jet black like her mom's, so were the hair and olive skin. He was trying to find his traces in her facial features.

"Her father is Indian. Don't worry. She's not your responsibility." Kumari broke the silence rudely as she added sugar to his tea.

Something smashed inside him.

"You didn't tell me, what are you doing in Prague?" Meer felt the arrows of bitterness in Kumari's voice.

"Nothing. Doing nothing." He realised it was a terrible idea to appear uninvited.

"What do you mean by nothing? You just told me that you were at work when you saw me yesterday." There was a threatening challenge in her tone.

"No, nothing, it was a bad idea... my bad, I am sorry; you won't see me again." Meer smiled at little Sahanara. Kumari felt she messed it all up again.

"So that's it then." Meer stood up.
"I'm sorry and... take care. Please ignore me if you see me in the city again. I am here for a while, fixing some personal business." Meer smiled robotically and left quickly without saying anything he had in mind.
Struggling with a limp in chilly October, breathing hard, his last departure from Kumari's ground-floor flat was playing in front of him, when he lied about his flight to England but actually had nowhere to go. All he wanted to do was to speak with Ji-Su. He tried to call her several times... but, "The person you're trying to reach is unavailable, please try again later." Meer couldn't think straight. He had only two days to leave the Czech Republic. His travel cheques were exhausted. Prague suddenly seemed to be an expensive city for him now. After settling his bill with the hotel, Meer decided to visit Liberec, a small town an hour away from Prague and famous for its Ještěd tower.
There was no reason for him to jump on a bus and go to an unknown city surrounded by Izera Mountains. But he wanted a quiet place, away from everything. He had no plans, no schedule to follow, nothing to do purposely till he spoke with Ji-Su.
A bus from Černý Most took him to Liberec bus station from where he made his way to the tourist information centre, helpful enough to get him the addresses of a few local hotels. Asking directions in English, getting lost and pronouncing incorrectly Czech addresses, locals looked at him at first as an alien. He hardly reached Penzion, a guesthouse whose Czech owner's daughter was conversational in English.

"I need a single room for two nights." Meer tried to smile.
"With breakfast?" Her eyes were reading Meer's features.
"Is it free?" He inquired politely.
"You are... a student?" she blinked her blue eyes.
"Yes. Not here, but in England." Meer looked helplessly towards her.
"Moment..." She went to speak with her father.
"My father says, if you say your friend come to Liberec and live here, we give you breakfast free. You promise?" She made a serious business proposition.
"I promise." Meer smiled.
The room was small but clean, with the basics. A little restaurant with a bar was on the ground floor where some old Czech songs played.
Meer was observing his surroundings when the busy waitress, serving hot plates to tables, reached him with a smile. She was the same girl from the hotel reception.
"Hello, you eat? My mamma makes good food." She pointed smilingly towards a happy customer.
"Do you have fish?" Meer flipped through the Czech-German menu.
"Yes, yes with potato chips and *salat*, you like?" she noticed his tired eyes.
"What's your name?" He knew that the girl was looking curiously at him.
"Marta." Her red cheeks bloomed.
"Yeah Marta, so I will take fish and any Czech beer please." Meer ran his eyes over her curves as she turned towards the kitchen.

She seemed like an oasis in which he wanted to drench himself. Her body was an escape, and pleasure was an illusion where he could hide from reality. There was no news from Ju-Su. And disturbed Meer knew he wouldn't be able to sleep tonight unless he injected himself with morphine. He wanted something to play with. Alcohol would be helpful but not without a Venus in bed, though guilty pleasures of last night seemed enough for a few days but as evening lost into darkness, the depression of grief crept inside him.

Meer sat for two hours in the restaurant playing with his thoughts, observing Marta, understanding her body language. She set him on fire, and the heat was already melting his sorrow.

"What time you are closing?" He followed her as she went for a cigarette break.

"One hour I am here more." She had meaningful eyes.

"Ok, so I'll see you in one hour." Meer looked at his watch before he took a step close to Marta.

"What you want?" Marta looked deeper in his eyes.

Meer silently moved his eyes on her soft neckline, lowering them to a hiding locket in the depths of serenity and moving them back to her eyes.

"Go Centrum, look town-hall and I see you there after one hour."

Half an hour later Meer was standing opposite to the Town hall admiring the Neo-Renaissance architecture. He was under the long shadow of an adjacent building of town hall. The square was empty, and the occasional laughs of drunken teens reached him from neighbouring streets. Still, he had to wait another 30 minutes more for Marta. He slowly walked onto a street taking him out of the square, finding a bank, a hotel with a posh restaurant, a clothing store, a coffee shop with sweets. He was looking to window displays with keen interest when somebody whistled to get his attention.
"Čekáme už 15 minute." She was an ordinary looking, housewife type of woman.
Meer looked around, but nobody else was there.
"Sorry... are you talking to me?" Meer came in the light; she was surely looking for someone else.
"Ježíši Kriste, nikdo mi neřekl ze mluvíš anglicky." She sounded a bit annoyed.
"Sorry, I don't speak Czech," Meer confusedly smile.
"Sex, you make sex?" That regular looking woman whispered secretly with wide hungry eyes, spreading in the excitement of swallowing him.
Surprised Meer couldn't say anything, but his head shook in affirmation without his consent and before he realised it, she dragged him inside a shop. A dark door at the back leading to a lighten room playing low and slow jazz.
"Go, go!" The housewife locked the door.
Meer was sluggish. He was regretting the vodka shot he had had with Marta before he left the restaurant.
"Go, go..." She was waving at Meer from some distance in the dark.

Dizzy headed, fatigued, he looked at the locked door and then followed that short stout woman into an unlit corridor. He wasn't afraid but didn't want to miss seeing Marta.

Meer looked around himself. It was a furniture shop.

"Moment *Zlato*." She said and walked calmly towards the room and called someone... Babel, Babel!"

"It's already time to meet Marta." Meer looked at his watch.

"*Hallo, sprechen sie Deutsch*?" A lady appeared from the room and switched on the lights in the showroom... beds, sofas, recliners appeared.

"*Nine, aber English bitte.*" Meer spoke in German as he looked at her. She was 50 something, skinny with dark curly hair, her smile seemed full of life without any regrets.

"You are an exotic boy; would you like to drink with us?" She switched the lights off again.

"I mean no disrespect, but I should really get going, probably your friend wanted to say something else, and she said something... I don't know, can you please get the door for me?" Meer didn't fancy drinking with a boring skinny grandmother when a darling like Marta, waiting for him outside under the lamp opposite to the town hall looking to tower clock every ten seconds. She was waiting there for 7, 8 minutes and wasn't very comfortable alone.

"You come *hier bitte* for a coffee in the afternoon, I am sorry for Frau Kolarova, she is a little drunk lady today." She smiled as she opened the door.

"*Danke.*" Meer warmly shook Babel's hand as he looked towards the town hall; he was good 12 minutes late.

"Fuck my life!" He ran towards the square, but it was too late, the echo of Marta's heels left the Centrum knocking anger over a can of a beer.

"*Hajzlové!*" She mumbled as she kicked the empty can to another corner of the square.

Meer reached panting near the town hall.

"Where is she now? I hope she didn't leave already." Meer ran his eyes around the square.

The wind was rolling a newspaper on the cobbled street, splashing emptiness around, rattling loose glass windows, whistling...

Meer saw someone with a red coat turning left to the street on left.

"What's happening here, where's she?" Meer heard heels, walking towards the square at his back.

"Handsome boy..." Meer turned around. It was Babel coming towards him with a silly smile.

"What does this gran want from me?" Meer thought.

"It will rain, I come *für* you *mit* umbrella." She smiled.

"Danke, but I am good, I am staying just around the corner." Meer swept his eye again around the square.

"Are you waiting for someone?" She meaningfully smiled.

"Yes!" Meer smiled bitterly on her guess.

"First date?"

"Kind of..."

"Maybe it's me you are waiting for." Babel placed her hand boldly on Meer's chest, pressing it gently, encircling, rubbing the middle finger on his nipple. And in a flash with a spark of shooting pleasure, Meer pulled her wildly for a kiss, squashing Babel's boobs. She moved her long arms around Meer and jumped to wrap her legs around. Meer leaned her against the wall and opened the belt of his trousers, sealing a bite on her jersey, on the poking nipple in excitement.

"Hey, hey, hot boy, *wir habe bet*, let's go, *Zwei minute*." And she pulled his arm on the steep street, following her, running down, giggling. She was slightly drunk, laughing in excitement. Meer grabbed her petite ass as she opened the side door.

"Hey!" Babel shouted as Meer threw her on one of the display beds, as they entered the store, he couldn't hold himself and pulled her leggings, sticky thong shaping the camel-toe off from one hand and kissed her wildly to keep her mouth shut.

"*Nine, Arschloch!*" She shouted helplessly to stop him, but he pulled his pants down and ripped Babel's t-shirt and sucked her tiny juggling tits as Meer pushed his erection between her thin legs.

And Meer's dual was there, standing outside as a window shopper looking through the glass, watching him having sex over a display bed next to a vase with plastic roses covered in the dust. The mattress was getting marked by saliva and ova as Meer continued his exploration of her body. She gave up eventually the fight she put up initially. She knew that she's showcasing her intimate moments as Meer unfolded all her sweet spots magically and who cares if she was being watched or not. She was thrilled if someone would walk through the street and look inside, finding a heterosexual couple getting raunchy, randy in a furniture store's display bed, practically trying it before buying it.

After they boiled down, Babel grabbed Meer's cock with a threat that if he resisted her lead, she would pull the piece out. Babel directed him to a small room at the back of the store where half bottle of Vodka was placed over a jazz CD. Walls were decorated with semi-nude posters, a couple of bulbs with dimmer switch, a stereo joined with a speaker, a double bed and a washbasin with a toilet. Meer looked carefully around.

"Stay here *bitte*." Babel laid him on a bed where drunk Kolarova snoring on one side.

"*Ich Komme...ich komme* later." She moved her hand over Meer's densely haired chest.

"Ok."

Meer took a long sip of vodka and closed his eyes as Babel left the room.

Next afternoon, when he woke up, there was a hand-written note under the empty bottle with 5000 Czech Koruna with a German telephone number.

"A small gift, please accept, call me if you like it... again."

Babel Bergmann.

Demands of Existence

I must admit, I never anticipated my life would be this way...
A war child, an orphan, a prostitute couldn't think of a life of comfort and independence in the third world...
You guessed right. I am Kumari, mother of Sahanara and just because of her I am in this beautiful world with a reason to live. She is three years old, a curious girl now, asking me about things I don't understand myself sometimes. Why is the sky blue? Why is water tasteless? Why some days I am very happy and some days I'm not? Where do the stars go in the morning? Often, I wonder where these questions come from. Is she an indigo child? I wish I could answer her questions tirelessly but it's not possible. I must work and during those hours I have to leave Sahanara with a babysitter and I am very tired by the time I reach home. Initially, my Asian soul wasn't comfortable with the idea of leaving my child with someone I didn't know closely.
Money is evil and unfortunately; money is involved more than compassion in childcare nowadays. I struggled to find a Bangladeshi or South Asian woman who could babysit Sahanara. Here I would like to point out very clearly that I wasn't looking for a Muslim babysitter but for the Asian feminine warmth for my daughter that could compensate for my absence.

An Uzbek girl was my final choice. Sahanara was 7 months when Dilafroz started taking care of her.
Affection grew among all of us with the passage of time and Dilafroz learned some family secrets.
"I really think you should try to find a husband," Dilafroz said yesterday.
"Sahanara was asking if I knew where her daddy is, and I didn't know what to say. She's stubborn and it's very difficult to divert her curious, attentive mind." Dilafroz looked a bit worried.

I'm single, and I stopped seeing men completely after my pregnancy. I directed all my energies to raising Sahanara and giving her good life. I contacted Meer, wrote to him, sent him pictures but when I saw him by chance, bowing and kissing that classless woman, I was hurt. That wasn't something I thought about the father of my daughter; that wasn't the representation in my mind of Meer. And when he came to visit me, he wasn't same man. I felt nothing for him. On the contrary, I was repelled by his presence in my flat. I didn't like that Sahanara was playing with him either. After Meer left that day, I cried a lot for my daughter. She deserves a better life, a father, a provider, a carer, someone who's genuinely concerned, and I couldn't see any goodness in that man. I had no one in my childhood. I am not even sure what childhood means. Loneliness, hunger, fear, violence probably? But yes, I dreamed of having a child and giving her the best of this world, providing opportunities to reach the stars. But nothing is possible without a strong personality, self-belief and faith that someone is there to hold you if you fall. Girls do need a father figure, otherwise often they end up having a relationship with some wise old guy. Look at me, I did the same.

Sahanara asked me a couple of days ago about her father. It's not that I wasn't expecting this question, but I wasn't expecting it so soon.

Sahanara was going with Dilafroz for swimming lessons where she saw fathers coming with their kids. That's where she learnt about the family unit.

A mummy, a daddy and the child, that's one family.

"Where's our *tatinek, maminka*?"

It was a long day for me, and my exhausted self didn't expect a troubled question like that at the end of the day.
"*Maminka...*" Sahanara touched my face in the dark to see if I was sleeping, and I was, nearly...
"*Maminka,*" She snuggled against me.
"I can tell you all about your daddy, but tomorrow. I am super tired today. Let's sleep." And I hugged Sahanara tightly. I was so afraid to tell her anything after what I learnt recently about Meer.
Just four days ago I bumped into Meer at Smíchov shopping mall's food court. It was after work and I went for Middle Eastern fast food, Chicken Shawarma with pickled salad, garlic sauce and chilly dipping. My mouth was watering with heavenly flavours when I saw Meer carrying his tray looking for an empty table.
"Hey, Meer!" I waved at him spontaneously.
He looked at me and his expressions could be easily translated into 'what the fuck'. Some people were looking at me because of my "hey" and I am sure he didn't want to look too awkward, so he waved back at me with an insincere smile.
"So much excitement. I wasn't expecting to see you." He started with the sarcasm straight away.
I giggled like a teenager.
He gave me a good hard look. "Anyway, I can't see Sahanara here, but I'm sure she must be running around somewhere." He ran his eyes around.
"She's at home with her babysitter and I am here treating myself to the tastes of Lebanon." I smilingly stared at his plate like a hungry lunatic, shaking my head.

"That's not real food." He scooped his salad and said, "Now eat before this slightly overcooked meat gets dry." And before I even replied he dug in, using his hands, stuffing his mouth, licking his fingers, dipping his wrap in the garlic-yoghurt base sauce. He was in love with flavours.

I looked at him, having his meal, and recalled what was told to me by one girl at the brothel, "If you want to know how the man is in the bed, look at him when he is having his meal. The more animalistic he is, the greater the passion in bed." And by looking at Meer, I could relate that bedroom wisdom with my experience with him.

"You never told me, what you are doing in Prague?" I failed to stop myself from asking this question.

"Fucking women for cash." He sounded completely cool.

"Sorry?"

"I said, fucking women for cash!" Meer chewed every word of his sentence as he looked in my eyes.

"You are joking, right?" I was startled.

"If life can do something wrong to anyone then what makes you think that time won't seek some legitimate revenge from me?" He wiped his lips.

"I don't believe you."

"You don't have to; I am not here to prove anything." Meer scratched his chin as he looked around for something.

"Look at me, please," I begged him, as I saw some tears in his eyes.

"There's nothing left to see." He bowed his head down.

"But, how? Why... You were in England, and then I saw you in Prague. I don't understand anything, I sent you letters at Newcastle, tried to call you on your English number, you never responded."
"I never went back to England," Meer tapped the table.
"What?"
"Yeah..."
"You never went back to England?" I was in a state of denial.
"Yes."
Meer told me everything that he wanted to say on that night when he visited me years ago. I couldn't believe what he had gone through and what he was going through now. He told me about Rita, Jan... Oh my God, it was too much to understand, too much to digest. I just couldn't get my mind off the thought of what would have happened if I'd told him about Sahanara, about being her father. I thanked God I hadn't. Everything happens for a reason. But I felt very sorry for him, sad to see the father of my child like that and I really wanted to help him, but how? At the same time, I tried to stop myself from getting too emotional as I have no more faith in mankind at all. Try to be nice and then wait what evil comes your way.

Meer is madly in love with Rita. That's the kind of love I had for Petr, love that can drive you insane. All that you want is to be with that person at any cost. Money, friendships, blood relationships, I have seen people sacrificing or do foolish things to be with their true love. Teenagers do this all the time. But the real madness is when a mature person falls for someone younger; that's when things blast. Meer is in his late twenties, but the women he's involved with are sleeping landmines, one wrong step and boom. He's playing with fire and I'm afraid for him. But what you can do for someone who's not in his right mind with such a complicated life.
"So, what's the plan?" I asked Meer.
"I don't know, I'm waiting for Rita, I just want to tell her the truth and then whatever comes my way..." He sounded so tired of life.
Silently he broke my heart.
I extended my hand to touch his fingers...
"Honestly, we should try to meet more often with each other as good friends, please."
Meer looked at me strangely.
"Give me your telephone number and address; we can go out with Sahanara over the weekend Meer." I tried to cheer him.
"Come on, show me a big smile now. You will be fine. I'm sure she will be back."

On that day I offered him a helping hand but in the back of my mind, I also wanted to get Meer to spend time with his daughter, our daughter. Whatever he was or whoever he is was immaterial in relationship to fatherhood. If I keep father and daughter from each other that wouldn't be fair. But I didn't want to rush anything. The last few days I was thinking how to talk about family, parents, and relationships with Sahanara... but my sixth sense told me that something is coming. I was hesitant. I didn't know what to say, how to explain to her without causing confusion and poisoning her innocence.

While juggling these thoughts, I bumped into Meer. And the day after that, Sahanara asked about her father and Dilafroz raised her concerns the following day.

All fell into place, and I understood the sign of the destiny flashing in my eyes. I was barely doing anything as one thing leads to the other, stemming after the concerns borne in my mind.

I exchanged text messages with Meer every day; he seemed ok to me. I decided to pay him a surprise visit before he met Sahanara this time. I was thinking to discuss my pregnancy, childbirth and about challenges of being a single parent, things about Sahanara, her questions...

On my way back home that evening I told Dilafroz that I would be a bit late.

"Going to see Meer?" She asked.

"Yes, how did you know?" I was surprised.

Dilafroz laughed; I heard a kind of loud naughty laughter over the phone that didn't require explanation. But she said, "Get a good drilling girl."

"Right, thank you." I smiled and ended the call.

Frankly, I was a bit stressed, so I went for dinner to prepare mentally for a conversation coming ahead. A glass of red wine with grilled Tilapia, looking over the old town square, listening to different languages around me, thinking a million things at once but concentrating on none. My mind kept drifting towards Meer and the things he told me. I was still trying to comprehend his situation, and nothing seemed to come fully under my grasp.

Suddenly I felt very uncomfortable, my heartbeat escalated, and I had the urge to see Meer immediately. I dialled his number, but no one answered. I was sure he was at his place, as he texted me this afternoon that he would be in tonight. I dialled his number again, but again, it just kept ringing. I got stressed, paid my bill quickly, and rushed to the nearest metro station to make my way to Žižkov, Prague 3. Taking a tram from the station, I called him a few times on my way to his flat, but Meer didn't answer. It took me a while to find his flat. I was exhausted by the time I rang the doorbell. "Trrrrrrrrrrn..." Old-fashioned bell echoed in the silence. There was no movement inside the flat, so I waited for 30 seconds before knocking on the door loudly and then I called his name...

"Meer?"

I tried again to reach him on his mobile. It was around 10 PM and I didn't expect him to go to bed so early. Lights were off, but I could hear his ringing phone.

I was getting frustrated and was about to leave when I jiggled the latch; the door was unlocked.

It was a dark flat that stunk of alcohol. Some unbreathable air filled with an unexplainable odour bubbled my dinner towards my throat. I struggled to find the switch.

"Meer...?"

And the room illuminated to darken my senses...

"MEER!!!" I shouted.

He was on the floor covered in blood; glass pieces crunched under my shoes as I ran towards him.

"Meer! Meer!" I held him in my arms; blood was frozen on his forehead with glass pieces in his skin.

"What happened, Meer?" I shouted his name with tears. Touching his face, shaking him gently, I felt his breath, but he was unconscious...

I didn't know what to do. I wanted to call the emergency service, but he was an illegal immigrant, and I wasn't sure if that was the right thing to do. Instantly I thought about a Canadian doctor, "Jerry," who I knew from a private hospital in Prague.

"Jerry just don't, please just don't ask any questions now. Just come along with all your emergency stuff right away to Křižíkova and I will text you the address. Please, please don't tell anyone about it, please... Yes, I will answer all your questions, please, thank you... Thank you!"

I put the phone down, texted Jerry the address and rushed to look for a first aid kit, with no luck. I cleaned the glass around Meer, used my hand sanitizer over a handkerchief to wipe some blood from his face. I kept his head on my lap, moving my fingers slowly in his hair, holding his hand, when I saw him opening his eyes slowly.

"Kumari..." He said slowly as familiarity sparked in his eyes.
"The doctor is coming, just try to relax." I looked in his eyes with great concern, the eyes of the man who gave me a child, the eyes... whom I remembered from the very first meeting, our date night. He smoothly hypnotized me with them and melted me by his presence. I couldn't say thank you enough to him for that one day we spent together, his concern... that he came back looking for me to apologize, all the way from Bratislava, though I was so rude to him.
I massaged his hand gently, giving him the warmth to stay alive.
"Sorry..." A very quiet apology reached me.
I looked at Meer; a teardrop was slowly absorbing itself in his sideburn. I hugged him gently as the volcano of my stupid love started erupting inside.
I'm fighting a lost battle, I told to myself, and dropped my last tears on his shoulder.
Jerry reached us within minutes and was in action immediately. I already requested him not to ask any unnecessary questions of Meer.
"I think someone tried to break in and broke a bottle on his head and he crashed into the mirror," I told Jerry, though I was not sure if that was the case.
Jerry stitched his wound, took the remaining pieces of glass out of his skin and gave him some strong painkillers for the next two days.

"I think he had a lot of alcohol in his body. Try to keep an eye on him. He needs to sleep and eat healthily. Call me if you need me for anything. Bring him into my clinic in a couple of days for a blood test and wound check." Jerry shook his head.

"It's a police case you know; I think the guy actually tried to kill himself... just don't get yourself in trouble, please." He sighed and left me alone near the doorstep.

Meer was sleeping after the injection, snoring a bit.

I looked at the clock; it was about 11:15 PM and I was sure I wouldn't be able to go home tonight. I was very tired and had no more energy left to deal with anything. I text Dilafroz that I wouldn't be coming back and asked her if she can please stay with Sahanara. She replied...

"Told you, no more drilling girl... always use protection, wink, wink."

I smiled and lay beside Meer, thinking, "What a day." I was completely spent, drained but my mind couldn't fall asleep. I was talking to me inside my head.

What will I say to Sahanara about her father? What will Meer's reaction be when I tell him about Sahanara? Is it the right thing to do? To tell a man about a child with whom he has no emotional connection? Maybe he will think that I just want him for myself, so I am playing up the drama. I wasn't even sure now that Meer is in the right state of his mind.

Believe me, I had gone through enough hardships throughout life, and I thought to commit suicide seriously at least 4 times. I'm doubtful of Meer's strength after today; I thought he must be very strong to fight, after what he had gone through... but maybe he was right? How long one can live like this? I knew he was in love with someone else. That made things much worse for him.

And I probably went beyond the limit to help him sort out his life. But again, I didn't want him to think that he was obliged to me and stay out of gratitude. Honestly, I didn't know what to do. I need someone in my life. I need a man. Dilafroz was right. I need a husband and a father figure for my child. I know, somewhere in my head I am so desperate to be with Meer. Is it sex or his charm or because he is the father of my child? I don't know. But one thing is definite; I'm not going to push this man to do anything for me unless he really wants to do it. Otherwise, there's plenty of fish in the sea.

"Let's see how it is meant to be." I sighed loudly with the last thought of the day looking at Meer, slowly closing my eyes to enter softly into a world of fantasy.

Symphony No.9

Prague Ruzyně International Airport, later named after Václav Havel, first president of Czechoslovakia, was warming up for another busy day. Sleepy travellers approached slowly, dragging luggage trolleys through misty sliding doors, staring at the departure board, looking around for a fresh cup of coffee, listening for announcements and thinking about the long day ahead of them.
Norika joins a slow check-in queue for Toronto's flight, silently wiping her tears, negating her head in pauses, trying to look normal...
A Canadian Chinese man standing next to her in the queue noticed her tears. He could tell she had been crying for a while.
"Are you ok lady?" He looked at Norika with concerned eyes through his thick glasses.
"Yes...Yes, thank you." Norika shivered as she tried to smile. "I'm...ok."
An urgent flight to Canada.
Where her older brother Ivan was fighting for his life at Toronto General Hospital after an accident at his work... collapsed scaffolding at a construction site.
Norika was informed yesterday around 9 PM about the incident when she was nearly done with her search for properties in Český Krumlov.
"Nora, I don't know how much time he has left. His condition isn't good." Her Canadian sister-in-law, Sarah, was in tears.

"Ivan survived the bullets of the bloody communists; I bet he will be fine. And stop crying, be strong. I'm leaving for the airport now, keep me updated." Norika held her breath to stop the falling tears.

The next available flight to Toronto was in the morning. Norika was looking at her watch anxiously. She couldn't wait to fly, an almost 12 hour's flight with a stopover at Frankfurt.

"I really want to talk to Meer." She took out her phone once again and dialled.

"What this man is doing with his phone?" She threw her phone back into her handbag and took out her passport. The airplane was manoeuvring on the runway when Norika took out her mobile phone out for the last time and wrote Meer goodbye. *Khuda Hafiz.*

"*Khuda Hafiz?*" she repeated, "what does that mean?" Norika asked him. She was intrigued when Meer abruptly said something to her in Urdu on his departure one day.

"In the care of God," He smiled.

"In the care of God, Meer." She thought, closing the window shade, sinking into dizziness of a sleeping pill she swallowed before boarding.

Norika didn't know that before her plane would land at Toronto Pearson, somewhere above Iceland, Ivan, a determined Slovak who travelled to Bratislava from Prague without saying goodbye to anyone in autumn of 1968, to cross Czechoslovakian- Austrian border via Jarovce would be dead at Toronto General Hospital. He escaped the fired bullets which chased his death on the night of escape to Kittse, but he couldn't trick death today. His death was keeping him alive throughout for this day.

Ivan survived the initial stage of pain and depression of a refugee, but 21-year-old was not the only Czechoslovakian on the streets of Vienna. He could hear Czech and Slovak languages coming from Viennese shops discussing the current political situation and small Czechoslovakian flags waving everywhere. He received a temporary residence from the Austrian government and temporary accommodation by a local charity. An owner of a coffeehouse offered him a part-time job on the second day of his arrival, though his German only comprised of three sentences:

"Guten Tag, mein name ist Ivan, Ich bin Tschechisch."
Regardless of the local support and a job, Ivan couldn't deepen his roots in Austrian society. His frustration with his mother and Norika's decision not to leave Czechoslovakia exhausted him emotionally. Borders were tighter, the communist regime was getting stronger, the iron curtain was nearly fully closed.

It was middle of September 1969, Ivan heard from someone at work about Canadians taking Czechoslovakian refugees. On that night Ivan spread the world map on the kitchen table of a shared house and moved his finger in a straight line towards the west, crossing the North Atlantic Ocean and then it was there, Canada, a country that could hold complete Czechoslovakia easily in its boundaries with much more snow, longer winters and freezing sun.

Next morning Ivan was standing in front of a modern 8 floors building near river Danube where the Canadian embassy was based. Department of Manpower and Immigration set up a special team in Vienna to fuel the demands of the booming Canadian economy. Doctors, engineers, dentists, students were the gems they were after.

"I... study... a... at... Technical Univerzita in Praha, Civil Engineering, 2nd year, *und... Ich arbiet am cafe hause.*" He took a pause to look in the eyes of the interviewer.

"I want to go to Canada, please." His last sentence was clear with the correct tone and confidence.

Just after 5 days, Ivan was packing a small suitcase with two pairs of pants, three shirts, undergarments, a toothbrush and a record of Beethoven which was gifted to him by one social worker.

"The Symphony No. 9."

Beethoven kept him warm and alive in winter of 1970. Snow, a lot of snow, frozen sky, freezing temperatures nothing was new for him but... nothing was the same. A sense of detachment from society persisted. An overwhelming feeling of loneliness was calmed by the record that played in his head everywhere, on the road, at the factory, at English language school...
"The Symphony No. 9."
And later in life too, his sixth sense attached a string with the symphonies. They played everywhere out of nowhere on all the important occasions of his life: the day he met his future wife, on his son's birthday, the day he bought the house and the day he moved to Toronto from Winnipeg.
Who thought that the autobiography he started to write was titled as 'Symphony No.9 stories.'
Life is so unpredictable... isn't it? And we never realise that till we lose someone in an instant, someone with whom we laughed together... someone who cared for us.
Ivan never went back to Prague, not on his mother's death in '83, not even after the fall of the Soviet Union in '89. How could he? After what was written on the last page of his destiny.
The invisible hand of destiny was ringing someone's phone at Ivan's cremation ceremony...
'Symphony No.9' filled the crematorium as the flame reached his casket.
Silence spread as Sarah walked slowly to the microphone for a eulogy.
"Ivan always talked about Prague with me. I remember the day we met; it was the 3rd of March 1972." Sarah took a pause to compose her trembling voice.

"I was looking for first-hand information about a political situation of central Eastern European countries for my thesis and I…I put a request on student notice board for some volunteers to interview. A few days later I met Ivan at university cafeteria, and he surprised me with a depth of his knowledge on history." Sarah looked at sobbing Norika.

"Ivan's soul always lived in Prague. Wherever we were, he always talked about Prague, Charles Bridge, old town square, Vltava, Prague Castle… he would paint the city in front of the eyes of his listener. We couldn't make it to go back there… he couldn't make it." Silent tears broke on every face.

"Every year we made a plan to visit Prague with the kids after '89. I remember he played the recording of the velvet revolution every November and went into a trance. He jingled keys with rest of them, saying goodbye to communism at Wenceslas Square, he wanted to be one of them. The regret that he wasn't there stayed inside him forever." Sarah took a deep long breath.

"The story of Ivan's emotional struggle is too long. The letters he sent to his family in Prague reached them opened, made unreadable by smudging the ink on the body of the letter. Telephone calls were rare and taped and the communists bothered his family for years after his departure. There was not even one time when he spoke about his family and his homeland without crying. I saw all the sadness in his eyes, but I was helpless, as I am today."

Sarah couldn't keep herself together and started weeping.

"I hope the God, which he argued isn't present for poor and weak, would rest his soul in peace."
Ivan's ashes should go back to Prague as per his will. Norika wanted to go back to Prague as soon as possible, but she wasn't able to leave Sarah alone in this condition, especially after her kids went back to the US to continue their jobs. How long they could be in the state of emotional shock? Their father wasn't alive anymore, but the sharks of debts and instalments were still breathing and chasing them in a merciless economic system. Same sharks wasted their childhood: parents at work, kids with childminders and grandparents resting in graveyards. Norika didn't forget about Meer. She tried every day to speak with him, but his phone was off. She hoped to get a phone call or an anxious text message from him, inquiring where is she. But how would she know that Meer is no more... No more on the pages of her destiny. No more who he used to be.

Depth of Hope

Prague Ruzyně International Airport which later named after Václav Havel, the first and only president of post-Soviet Union Czechoslovakia witnessed another busy day. The last flight from London Heathrow just landed with Rita & Amelia Newman aboard.

Excited travellers collected their hand luggage, walking swiftly through sliding doors, heading towards immigration counters, happy, laughing. Some who came for a stag party were a bit loud and drunk, already tipsy buying duty-free alcohol, tasting *Becherovka* and thinking about the fun night ahead of them. But no one noticed a woman, whose long coat was tightly buttoned over her growing belly, holding firmly to the hand of a young girl and keeping a strong grip on her luggage, leaving the airport.

"Are we going to surprise Meer mama?" Amelia asked Rita excitedly.

"Not today honey, tomorrow, we will visit him tomorrow." Rita smiled nervously.

Rita felt stressed since she landed. Meer seemed to be on her mind all the time now. After her return from the hospital with the good news, Rita was busy in taking care of herself and Amelia. She tried to stay calm, positive, directing her conscious on stability, harmony, utilizing focus to clear the negativity surrounding her wandering mind.

"Fresh start, a fresh start, every day is a fresh start." Rita penned the affirmation thousands of times before she booked her ticket to Prague, though there was absolute silence from Meer's end. But there was something else too, a sign, a dream. She made up her mind to visit Meer regardless of the situation. And that was her choice if she wanted to add another dependent, an additional financial, emotional burden for at least the next 18 years to her life or... maybe not.

She was hesitant.

Reluctant, she came back home after the 1st pregnancy scan at the Royal Victoria Hospital. Rita framed the scan and looked deep into the black and white fluid with the hope that it brought out her maternal instincts... with a small beating heart, making himself known, seeking the attention of his mother.

"I deserve to hold your hand too mama, just as my sister did. I need you. I need you to bring life to me." Rita felt dizzy and lay on the sofa with the framed scan picture lying on her chest that late afternoon, floating unknowingly into a vision enclosed in sleep.

Rita saw Tim and their mom walking smoothly towards her in distance; their feet were just above the sand as if they are walking on a path in the air. Tim was holding a finger of a toddler and their mother was holding an infant, covered in raw silk, walking with a contented face, glowing under a clear blue sky. Beautiful sunshine and a cool breeze blowing green olive trees, freshness in the air.

"Mama... Mama!" Rita calls her mother with excitement, trying to walk quickly but the deep sand bogs her down and three scorpions rise from its depths with stings ready to attack. They move against her in harmony, prepared to poison her. Heartbeat races as heat burns the sand, forcing Rita to run in circles to get away from scorpion tails. The sky gets darker, temperatures rise... Tim and her mother with little children seem to be further than before as the sand flows just like an ocean... pushing Rita back. The scorpions grow bigger and stronger when suddenly someone dashes by her side towards her family. A short figure with black hair and pale skin runs towards Rita's mother, disappearing in a sandstorm. Suddenly the sky turns red, and Meer emerges with an expression of amazement.
"Mama, Mama.... Mama!" Amelia was shaking Rita's shoulder in distress.
 "Aaah, hon, what... What?" stunned, sleepy, gasping Rita tried to locate herself.
"You were shouting mama and yelling, No! No! No! What happened mama?" Amelia hugged Rita tightly.
"Nothing happened sweet. Don't worry. Just a dream." Rita patted Amelia's back "And what's in your hand? Show me." She was trying to divert her attention.
"I was drawing, see..." Amelia stretched her arm with a sketch of a female with two kids standing around her, outside a hut shape residence with a massive square window in the middle and a huge smoking chimney.
"That's you, me and Millie."
"Millie? Who's Millie?"
"My baby sister" Amelia blinked her eyes.

"Oh, I didn't know we have a name for the baby." Rita smiled and moved her hand over her belly.
"What if this is a baby boy?"
"I don't like boys mama." Amelia shook her head in disappointment.
"No, you don't." Rita shook her head in amused negation before she started rubbing her nose against Amelia's, tickling her around her ribs as sunrays crossed the shades, rotating shadows in the room. Slowly brightening the darkened walls. The sun melts gold outside in the waves of English Channel, hypnotising the Sea-World by its threads, floating within the silent motion, dancing layers of water as marine life attending the farewell to the day, witnessing golden aurora underneath the water... gold, golden gold waving inside the rhythm, mesmerising the senses of every unconscious of the conscious, when something opened in Rita on her writing-table while conditioning to positivity.
It's the light within the folds of seconds and you reach to that one moment in the time's travel where your destiny must change for good or bad, depends on conscious, depends on intensions, deeds... But an effort to unlock the potential is crucial, and for her, it's now the right time to move on and be brave. Find Meer, meet him and release the synergy of effort and the destiny.
Night has fallen over Prague.
Tichá noc, svatá noc.
Jala lid v blahý klid.
Dvé jen srdcí tu v Betlémě bdí.
Hvězdy při svitu u jeslí dlí,
V nichž malé děťátko spí,
V nichž malé děťátko spí.

Rita felt the ecstasy of Czech 'Silent Night' inside her as she walked to her hotel.

Rita kept humming, tapping her foot, swinging her head in rhythm with practising choir, her harp strings kept playing in the background from unknown as her fingers move inside her pockets.

"Is this what next Christmas might look like?" A vision floated and beautified her.

"Meer, me, Amelia and Millie," Rita smiled.

Meer was holding the little one and Amelia stood next to her clapping. She squeezed between them with a big smile in a red dress for the Christmas family picture while outside snowflakes paint the glass window.

Silent Night, Holy Night...

Fall in Me

Christmas market in the old town square was packed on Saturday. Praguers floated in from all over the city to see the famous Christmas tree lighting ceremony, to have fun and to enjoy the festivity of tradition. Sweetbreads, mulled wine, sausages, spit roast, jewellery, handicrafts displayed and sold in small beautifully decorated hut shops surrounded by the great architecture. Tourists equipped with cameras captured every moment of their trips. Between them, was Meer carrying Sahanara on his shoulders with a grin on his face as if he won the biggest trophy of the world, while Kumari was shouting at both of them.
"I said it's enough! Put her down!" She yelled from the ground floor.
"*Ne, maminka, ne.*" Sahanara laughed and waved a big no with her arm.
"Meer, aren't you listening to me?"
"What can I do? She isn't coming down." Meer kept his silly clown smile on his face.
"Who's the adult?" Kumari was so annoyed.
"You!" Meer and Sahanara shouted and laughed together.
This was the third day after Meer's stitches were removed and Kumari brought Sahanara to meet Meer. Testing the waters...unwillingly.

She had no faith in Meer's mental stability after what he had done. How could she trust a guy who was in love with someone else? But she gave up. Both asked questions constantly about each other. Kumari felt that Meer was sure he was the girl's father.
"Where's my *tatinek maminka*?" Crying Sahanara asked Kumari the same question for the millionth time and for that, she was scolded badly by her mother just two days ago.
"I told you; he lives in India. Stop asking." Kumari shouted at her.
"I want to see him." Sahanara was sobbing.
"We can go next year." Kumari felt so bad for yelling at Sahanara.
"We can call him..."
"How many times have I told you that his phone isn't working." Kumari shouted. She ran out of patience and used force to shut Sahanara's mouth.
But the girl proved herself Meer's daughter. She was stubborn and doesn't know how to quit. It wasn't her fault... genetics were to blame.
"*Maminka*, I want to see him. I want to see a picture." Sahanara roared aggressively like she never had before, her face and arms red and eyes full of tears due to the slaps but she didn't give up. That's when Kumari lost her first battle with Sahanara.
"Ok, I know one of his friends, who lives in Prague. We can go and meet him, and you can ask him questions about your father, pictures, telephone number, address, all you want." Kumari was exhausted.

She knew something must be done to bring Sahanara back to harmony. So, the next day when she met Meer, Kumari explained to him the situation and requested the "Great Pretender" to pretend something.

"How can I be the best friend of this Indian man?" Meer chewed the words with disgust as he dipped his razor in hot water.

"Oh please, we all are Indians technically." Kumari smiled.

"I have no problems with anyone, but please don't lecture me on history." He looked at Kumari in his mirror.

"And what am I supposed to be saying to Sahanara about her dad? Did you prepare a script for me?"

"You don't need notes; she knows nothing about her father."

"*Subhan Allah*," Meer said ironically.

"Please, just say what you like, but make sure you don't make it too difficult for me to defend anything," Kumari said worryingly.

"We can agree on a few things to keep you out of trouble." Meer pulled his cheek up to stroke the razor.

"We can do that on the phone, but I have another favour to ask you." Kumari looked at his naked back and hairy chest in the mirror. She was trying to ignore since he opened the door wearing boxers.

"Another one and free honey... WOW!" Meer winked vulgarly with the WOW as he moved a hand on his ass just like a pole dancer.

"Seriously, you could have earned well in a gay club Meer."

"Hell yeah!" Meer raised both of his arms and advanced towards Kumari shaking his moobs with shaving foam jiggling on his face.
"Oooouuuu!!!" He shouted.
"Oh, come on, listen to my offer. And don't throw your man boobs at me." Kumari looked at his crotch, which was shattering her confidence.
"So, what do you want to offer me *tonight* hmm?" Meer turned towards her like he was about to give her a lap dance.
"Oh, fuck off man-whore and listen to me." Kumari slapped Meer's ass delightfully.
"I have a Canadian group scheduled next week and I want you to guide that tour for me. I am taking Russians to Karlovy Vary for three days and I can't afford to lose business."
"I have never had a job before." Meer looked seriously at her.
"Only blow jobs." Kumari looked meaningfully to silence Meer and continued.
"It's not difficult, I will explain to you what to do. A script will be provided and then you just entertain, following the wishes of an audience. Not so many people are listening, most of them are busy taking pictures. Sometimes you get a moron who ruins your day by asking questions about history or arguing facts. In this case, just listen to them. Don't disagree. Praise their intellect and make sure that they feel good, so they tip you well."
Meer was comparing the psychological demands of the two jobs, sex worker vs. tour guide.

"Money is honey Meer and most importantly I want my customers to feel good after the tour, to recommend us to others, so..."
"So how would you train me Kumari?"
"Nothing difficult, just join me on Monday for a tour and see how I do it. Then you tailor your own act, make your own character, and play with the facts, stories. History is bunk Meer and you are an entertainer."
"Entertainer? That's what that cuckold professor said." Meer thought.
"I have to go now but... wait, wait, I got something for you." Kumari's hand dived into her massive handbag holding water, snacks, tissue papers, local maps, dictionary, lipstick, makeup, bandages, pain killers, different medicines, hairbrush, matchstick box, tampons, some novel, diary of the year and I think once I saw condoms too.
"Don't you dare peep in my bag!" Kumari shouted.
"Why, have you got something that starts with D in there? Big and round, man!" Meer pulled a Jamaican accent.
"You dirty bastard. Really. I got you a new phone and a sim card." Kumari pulled out a mobile handset.
"I don't need it; my phone is fine and gets service in my area." Meer was checking Kumari's assets which changed the geography in his boxers.
"Meer don't do that, what are you doing, pervert!" Kumari noticed his eyes... not just the eyes though.

"I wasn't doing anything till now." Meer got too close for Kumari's comfort. His nose over her neckline could smell the fading freshness of citrusy perfume, the hint of spice on her skin enveloping with the warmth of her body scent. Meer closed his eyes and felt the combustion inside him, burning him softly. Kumari's heartbeat like a drum, adding motion to the act of silence. She felt a wave of magic cover her over, melting her existence into a surreal body dancing above the Milky Way. Brightness turned her into an illuminating spot that shined through outer worlds and Meer was surrounding her. There wasn't any gravity that could hold them in that air, they were separated but capturing the existence as clouds merge into singularity. No one knows what's what when you move deep into a dark, lightless, pitch-black tunnel leading towards pleasures of heaven. Time spread you into the scattered wilderness; no echoes come back to the hollowness of the ears. Questions drop like stones into an ocean of null and consciousness voids, defies reality of one, nothingness rules over and you find the meaning of all in... fall.

Dad

How does it feel to be a dad? A responsible one?
I used to ask this question all the time when Rita was around, having this overwhelming wish to be the father of a child whose mother I love, emotionally, physically, psychologically. A woman you look at and say, "Thank God, she's in my life", to have a child with someone like that. And today I had similar thoughts when I was on my way to Náměstí Republiky to meet Sahanara. And I was preparing some justifying answers for her questions about her father, the "undocumented Indian man who worked in a kitchen." Yeah, right.
Buttoning my long black coat, tucking the scarf, adjusting the knot, I looked at myself in the glass, making sure that I am presentable as a "Daddy's best friend" to someone's child.
Walking through the station, holding a small stuff toy, smiling towards everyone, looking at the escalator ejecting people on the square, I walked out on the street level where the surprise of my life was waiting for me.
A replica of my childhood, confusingly smiling... a young girl.
I promise you that in my entire life, a moment like that never passed. It's impossible to explain with the unimaginable sensation of happiness.
How it feels to be a dad?

She waved at me, copying her mother, and the entire world went silent for few seconds. Everything was important, what meant a lot to me, my existence, the reason to be alive, my own universe, I saw all of that bowing down to her.
The smile was mine...
I walked towards her or was I drawn like a magnet? I don't remember. But what happened to my voice?
"Hello, Meer." Kumari shook my extended hand nervously.
I couldn't take my eyes away from that "Dot" that created the universe, shining in Sahanara's eyes, turning into a gaze of familiarity.
"I know the smiling face of my dad's best friend but... from where... I never met him." she thought.
Beams of true dreams were brightening on Sahanara's face when she politely said,
"*Dobrý den.*"
"*Dobrý den*, how are you?" I passed her the little teddy with a big smile.
"*Děkuji*" she was looking at me with excitement. She was just a bit shy and a lot more hesitant.
"*Mluvit anglicky zlatíčko?*" I asked her in a very friendly manner if she speaks English and I saw Kumari's head moving in affirmation.
"*Ano.*" Sahanara nodded her head.
"Good... so let's go? Are you ready?" I had the thrill of excitement in my voice when I offered my hand to Sahanara, which she clutched gladly.
Joy was limitless...

Happiness without boundaries and contentment had no ends. I felt that I'm complete today by the touch of this little girl; she perfected and healed me. I was walking on clouds in heaven with the illusion of the Christmas market around, chatting non-stop with Sahanara, asking her questions, telling her jokes. She was laughing, dancing around, clapping with excitement.
I didn't know who I was, until today. I was someone else who's unknown to himself... still.
While I made Sahanara laugh Kumari stayed back, looking stunned and surprised. She hadn't seen Sahanara enjoying herself, so carefree before. Sahanara didn't care if she had the attention of her mother or not.
"I really thought I knew all about this girl," Kumari observed her very closely.
"And she isn't asking anything from Meer either." A strange fear caught her suddenly.
"I hope they don't find each other, not now, not just yet." Kumari gave Meer a look when he raised Sahanara in the air above his head and seated her on his shoulders.
"I am tall, wow, I am tall, I can see far!" Sahanara was excited by the seat with a view.
How long can a woman ignore being ignored? Kumari was following them everywhere, but neither Meer nor her own daughter offered her much attention. She enjoyed seeing them, but she also felt worthless, weak, bored and afraid. Meer was boiling her blood; she hated him, and when he put Sahanara on his shoulders that was it.
"I said enough. Put her down!" She yelled.
"*Ne, maminka, ne.*" Sahanara laughed and waved a big no with her arm.

"Meer, aren't you listening to me?" Kumari threatened him.
"What can I do? She isn't coming down." Meer kept his silly clown smile on his face.
"Who's the adult here?" She was so annoyed.
"You." They both pointed at Kumari and laughed at her.
"PUT HER DOWN, NOW MEER!" Kumari looked fearlessly in his eyes and suddenly the smiles disappeared from their faces. Sahanara slipped herself down to Meer's arms, and the clown left his body leaving him with a blank face.
"What's the problem, what happened?" Meer raised a deep concerning voice.
"What the fuck is wrong with me, honestly," Kumari asked herself.
"You are ok Kumari?" Meer had a comforting hand on her arm, she stayed quiet.
"No, I am not ok!" Kumari changed the tone of her voice.
"What's the matter?" Meer kept his eyes on Kumari's face as Sahanara landed herself to the footpath.
"I want you to carry me."
"What! Sorry?" Meer was sure it isn't what he heard.
"Nothing." Kumari was cursing herself for the slip of the tongue "Bloody, can't even cover up my shit."
"What nothing?" Meer was nearly pumped up, but he behaved. Sahanara was already looking timid, frightened and unsure about the situation.
Kumari looked at Sahanara and smiled. "Can Meer carry me now?" slowly turning her gaze towards him and said, "Please?" very politely with a glossy smile.

Meer could hear a whistling in his ears, storming blood, shaking his body with anger when "Please" brought him down from the peaking madness.

A long deep powerful breath vacated his lungs to balance the negative energies with fresh air following a big smile towards Sahanara.

"Honey, I think your mom is hungry. Let's go for a nice meal. What would you like to eat?" Meer carried the little wonder and started marching towards the nearest restaurant. Kumari joined them swiftly, holding his arm, smiling with a feeling of being won by a charmer who's ready to do anything to win her love, a real man stunning her with charisma, handsome by her side as she entered in another world of pride and joy walking on the cobbled street of the old town.

Kumari didn't want anything else but this, Sahanara, Meer and herself together... living peacefully with an abundance of happiness and harmony. After so long it's just now when her dream found its wings, now flowing in the air with her flying self, care-free in the wind of love without a thought about tomorrow.

"Who sees tomorrow?" she asked herself. "How long would I poison my present with the grudge of the past? Let it be, let me be me again for once this evening. Who knows tomorrow's secrets?"

The evening was carefully crafting fog over the city. High in the sky the bird of Kumari's love looked at Prague and was mesmerised by the view of the majestic capital rising through clouds of fog, red roofs emerging, historical buildings. The setting sun was gathering its last rays from the city and vacating them for the cold winds and the chill, hiding dagger of pain within, slicing the warmth of tranquillity.

Sahanara was asleep in Meer's arms. She was tired and now resting on Meer's broad chest, snoring quietly. Meer's arm was around her, holding Sahanara's back and neck, moving occasionally to caress and pat her in an effort to comfort the sleep. As an attempt to express his love towards her, as an act of apology, an expression of care, concern and reassurance, as a gesture of gratitude for all the love that melted his heart and turned feelings into golden butterfly flakes... dancing, swirling, brightening all the dark corner closed ends. Sahanara proved the grace of God with whom he felt deeply connected on every level, re-breathing life inside him, opening the heavens of peace over his subconscious, setting him on a journey of unknown paternal pleasures and when he looked again at comfortably sleeping Sahanara, dropping all of her weight over him, listening to his heartbeat, butterfly wings and sounds from the mystic heaven where fairies talk to each other and giggle to make her smile. Meer looked at her and a long-awaited answer reached to the finality of revelation.

How it feels to be a dad...

Opposite

The doorbell rang in the emptiness of Meer's flat...
An echo bounced between the walls. Rita pressed the buzzer again and left the bell ringing till neighbours appeared on their balconies looking for the culprit.
"Where's Meer, mama?" Amelia looked confusedly at Rita.
"I think he's not at home darling." Rita looked nervously towards a woman who came out irritated from next door carrying a crying kid.
"Maybe we should go to the city and come back in the evening. I am sure he's at work." Rita tried to smile towards the angry neighbour and pulled the arm of very upset Amelia.
"Come on darling, let's go and don't be sad. I know one super yummy ice cream parlour and then we will go to see a Christmas market. Maybe there's Santa's grotto too?" Rita opened her eyes with excitement.
"Think about Santa's workshop in Prague, yippie!" Rita clapped her hands to cheer Amelia.
"Why did I do this, all of this? For this hassle? To come all this way with a child inside me, dreaming like a lunatic? What's wrong with me? Haven't I learned my lesson yet? I am a mother for God's sake. What sort of example I am setting for her?"

Rita sensed the disappointment when she looked at the flat's door. No one was in, she knew, before she placed her finger on the bell. But life isn't about assumptions and sixth, seventh, eleventh senses. So, she rang the buzzer just to confirm.
The doorbell kept ringing inside the emptiness...
"*Nádraží Florenc*... Florence station," Rita repeated the instructions in English as she stepped into the taxi. Emotionally exhausted, powerless, drained, hungry, annoyed, she didn't feel well at all but couldn't see Amelia with a long face. So, she pretended to be as jovial as possible. If she didn't get hold of Meer today, then she would book return tickets tonight and terminate the pregnancy. She felt she had no power to go through the same crap again. Rita raised Amelia almost alone with a bit of help from her mother. And now, all by herself and not young anymore, she wasn't making the same mistake.
Rita looked at Amelia watching the floating boats over the Vltava. The taxi was crossing the bridge over the river with Prague Castle on right and National theatre in front of them near Národní třída.
"This city is so different mama."
"I know very beautiful, right?" Rita smiled.
"Yeah." Amelia turned to see Prague castle in the distance running away from the sight.
"Can we go to see that castle mama?"
"Sure darling, after lunch today," Rita answered and looked outside to a floating restaurant and a lost dream swimming through the ocean of past reached to the shores of her conscious.
A dream which was about to come true...

An evening cruise over the Vltava with a dance floor on the upper deck, Prosecco bottle on ice, and a jazz band playing old romantics spread love in the air of magical Prague. Meer is holding Rita, both dancing in their best outfits, Ms Newman in a black evening dress and Meer, in a suit with a matching black bow.
"I'll be right back," Meer whispered to Rita as one song ended, and he disappeared swiftly into the crowd.
Rita was waiting for this moment.
She quickly took this opportunity and waved at the band singer, who gave her a thumbs-up.
"*Dámy a pánové*, Ladies and Gents," the jazz singer smiles as he fills his voice in the mic.
"Love is in the air and tonight, two hearts, two beautiful hearts are about to melt together into love forever." Loud whistles, clapping and shouts of "*Bravo, Bravo!*" boosted Rita's confidence as she stepped up to take the microphone in her hand when suddenly Meer appeared, looking around for her. Rita shouts in a shivering voice "*Tum say pyaar kiya hai.*"
Meer immediately laughs out loud in response to a very Bollywood dialogue. Finding Rita near the band amused him.
"That means I love you." She giggled in microphone.
"Good evening to all of you and thank you for your warm welcome. I am very excited but still very nervous and," Rita paused to look at Meer who was coming close to the stage.
"Meer, I just want to say *thank you* for coming into my life and beautifying every second of the journey with your presence. I..." She hesitated for a second.

"I would like to be part of you for the rest of my life." Rita's voice was filled with emotions that couldn't express themselves in words, turned into tears of joy and hope.
"I want to be yours for the rest of my days. Will you marry me, my darling?" And in a great silence, before she took out the ring, Meer ran and jump towards Rita to hold her in his arms and a round of applause with cheerful shouts filled the sky.
"Yeah! Hooray!" Clapping, flying kisses, balloons tossed in the air by an emotional crowd in tears when a passionate kiss shared by the couple as the band played 'You brought a new kind of love to me'.
The taxi stopped at the Florence station, bringing Rita out of her daydreaming. High hopes without ropes won't take anyone too far. She knew it but couldn't help herself from falling. Rita had no option other than to be foolishly positive, listening to her heart who was promising 'All good and all fine' regardless of the situation.
"Take it easy, deep breath." Rita heard her heart talking.
"Yes, Meer's return seems like a delusion now but a bit of belief in the power of love, a little confidence in the destiny of an unborn child. Do remember you ignored him, rejected him because of his faith which he doesn't practice, his political opinions which are just another version of the truth, a different perspective of reality. But do you also remember he was so critical of his own people; I am sure you can recall that bold sentence..."
"We are full of shit-heads and dick-heads, now go figure whose shit and whose dick."

"Race, religion, politics, caste and sectarian systems, he was sick of them and the people who played these cards for power and money; he hated them....Then how do you manage to convince yourself that he's right-wing, when he was opposition to extremism and war, that war which was condemned by many British, European and Americans too. Don't forget those protests you witnessed with your own eyes in London were full of white Brits."
"Dick heads and shit heads are everywhere, and you can't run away from the aftershocks of their foolish, selfish and careless actions in society nowadays. But don't be blind for goodness' sake by the ignorance, negativity, propaganda bubbling fake news and lousy journalism. Don't be so rotten in head to consume media's junk always as unhealthy fast-food." Rita scolded herself.
"Are we going to see the Christmas market mummy?" Amelia was circling her spoon in melted ice-cream.
"Are you done?" Rita looked at her glass bowl with disappointment.
Amelia nodded her head in affirmation and the silky blonde hair covering the forehead dropped over her eyes with the nod.
"Finish it or next time there'll be no ice cream." Rita took her last sip of coffee and turned to look outside.
"Is it snowing mamma?"
"Finish your ice cream Amelia," Rita suddenly wore a stern face.
"I am full."
"Give it to me," Rita growled.

"This is why I cannot lose even a bit of weight, eating your leftovers, always hoovering the food and see how you wasted your ice cream now." Rita grabbed the spoon and slapped it in the glass bowl.
"I should stop treating you."
Amelia kept her eyes on the table, scratching her toe on the floor, looking at her mother in pauses with a long face.
"Don't look at me like this and wipe your face." Rita's mood was sour.
She thought... having a child, a child who became the centre of your life, a child... one awaited long as a mother, a child who melted your heart and opened something spiritually inside as you gave birth to her. When you held her in your arms for the first time, putting her against your warmth, feeding that little angel you cried with feelings of maternal love, hope, determination and fear. Those tears purify you, make you a stronger person. But raising that child is another experience, living with that gift of God every day. Watching them yelling, shouting, crying, screaming, acting stubborn, making continues mistakes, going against your wishes, leaving high hopes in total shambles, shattering dreams of poor parents, leaving them frustrated, which weakens that bond of what was once the most precious... till the kid runs into some trouble and an emotional shock reveals the renewed value of the relationship.
Rita felt bad for her attitude, taking her frustration out on a child. She hated strictly disciplining Amelia; her actions backfired psychologically.

"How can I be so angry with my daughter? I should tell her that I am sorry." She told herself.
"I should take her to see the Christmas market, just to cheer her up. I spoiled her mood and God I feel tired." Rita yawned even just thinking about their journey to Můstek.
Wenceslas Square was alive with a Christmas vibe and with all the magic of festivity and celebration. Christmas decorations on beautiful wooden huts with toys, ceramics, puppets and costumes, traditional sweets, a lot of candies...
Rita and Amelia were walking into a fairy-tale land, filled with happiness around, looking at colourful brightness with amazement in eyes. Rita forgot about Meer for a while in the middle of so much joy and laughter. Amelia was smiling and was excited to see so many different things; this was her first European Christmas market in mainland Europe.
"Mama, look at this, Mama, look at that, and WOW this is wonderful..." Amelia's every sentence carried the surprised innocence of the childhood while Rita smiled and drew happiness by just looking at energised Amelia, but her body was giving up.
"Sweetheart I know you are enjoying yourself but I'm tired. Maybe we can come back later in the evening when we go back to see Meer?" Rita pulled Amelia's arm. She was busy with some other kids looking at puppets.
"Let's take a quick walk up to the Saint Wenceslas monument for a photo and then go back to the hotel; I feel very light-headed right now, honey."

Amelia wasn't amused by her mum's plan. She had been lazy and tired, complaining about being exhausted always.

"Five minutes mama, just five minutes please." Amelia ran away towards another performing puppeteer down the square.

"What the heck, AMELIA!" Rita shouted and dragged herself, chasing Amelia, swearing, murmuring when she saw a group of annoyed tourists flocked around some stupid tour guide with a mixed foreign accent comparing Jan Palach's self- immolation with the suffering of Afghanis and Iraqis in this festivity.

"Asshole!" she mumbled.

"Jan Palach," The tour guide raised his voice and turned towards the group where Rita was holding her gaze in distance.

"Meer..."

Rita's heart paused, her breathing stopped, as her eyes turned her into a silent picture of amazement when 'life' moved inside her, throbbing hearts...

If I would be a silent picture
Waiting for a moment
To breathe into life
And if I would have a choice
I will wait for you
Throughout this life
For your one gaze
For your one sight
A moment with you
In a lonely night
Kiss, under the moonlight

Christmas lights were brightening over the bored faces of tourists waiting for a break from Meer's history lesson. Yawning tired souls had had enough and Meer realised his foolishness as he ran his eyes over them.
"Beautiful ladies and handsome gents, please feel free to take some pictures and maybe some quick shopping from the Christmas market. The nearest toilets are located to your right and please take care of your belongings. We will be here for the next 20 minutes. If you have any questions, please feel free to ask. Thank you."
Meer took a deep breath as he turned back towards the national museum where Palach burned himself to death on the 16th of Jan 1969 as a political protest, against the invasion of Czechoslovakia.
"Jesus Christ, why am I so emotionally charged by Palach's story? I'm glad that I didn't start telling them about the execution of Jan Hus at the old town." He shook his head in disbelief.
Double standards of this world frustrated him. Different principles, a different yardstick for humanity and justice used by hypocrite liberals of the world inflamed him.
"Self-immolation doesn't help any poor motherfucker in third world corrupt nations," he thought "Nothing changes. No one takes any notice. Maximum some small headline hiding under giant Multinational Corporation's advertisement fills the extra space."

Poor, hungry, sick, homeless, who think about them in poor shameless so-called democracies? 'Go fuck yourself' is really a slogan of the elite class in shaming lands and if media gives the proper coverage, then probably the aim is to sell the thrills of weak majority to ignite rage in society and in return, the pressure group gets *what they wanted* as planned.

Who cares honestly about poor people of poverty-stricken countries? The first world throws the money towards the hungry politicians, pseudo-NGO's, ill-minded, manipulative and propaganda-based sellers of humanity, busy with a sole task of filling their black hole bank accounts draining into offshore properties and economies.

So, the money goes back where it comes from.

Charity begins at home, they say… sweet.

"Who cares, who cares?" was buzzing inside Meer's head when someone very tenderly touched his shoulder.

"You always wanted a daughter, didn't you?" Rita kept her palm still and whispered softly, as she wasn't talking to Meer but with her own self.

"This isn't possible Meer," he thought "This can't be true what you feel, this familiar sensation. Your mind's just playing to calm you down. Maybe an enquiring tourist wants my attention? But why is this palm waiting longer than usual?"

"Meer," Rita gently squeezed his shoulder.

Cold winds blew through Meer's hair, frozen tears on his cheeks slowly melted away by the warmth of Rita's hand. She moved her hands on his arms, clutching his shoulders, rubbing his back. Overwhelmed, Meer couldn't close his surprised eyes. He didn't believe on what was going on and tried to distance himself from the situation to analyse. Rita was all over her.

"Meer..." She pushed herself away, blushing as Rita noticed Amelia was staring at them, standing behind Meer with a surprised face.

She caught them red-handed.

"Honey, this is Meer." Rita tried to smile towards Amelia.

Meer turned to see the cutie with a ponytail, a little blonde with beautiful blue eyes where Meer could see reflections of Rita.

"How are you?" Meer shook her hand.

"I'm... fine?" Amelia looked at him.

"We went to see you at your flat." She felt a bit more confident now.

"And you know Mama is going to have Millie?" She quickly shouted with excitement.

"Millie... What's that?" He couldn't figure it out.

"Amelia, shut up." Rita snapped at her.

"My baby sister, my baby sister." She shouted.

Astonished, Meer looked at Rita, nodding her head as her tears broke. She ran towards Meer like a scared child seeking shelter. She had been everywhere, inside, outside but her comfort nested in his arms. And she was home now when Rita reached them, leaving Meer in a state of shock. Emotions overwhelmed and brain overloaded with fear, joy, excitement and surprise. His mind was swinging, spinning like a cricket ball. Everything happened so suddenly that he lost himself in translation and detached from his surroundings, forgetting where he was.

Rita was hugging him and shedding tears on his shoulder, Amelia cuddling her mother, and Meer supporting both of them, and all three were standing as a work of art observed by a bunch of tourists returning to continue their tour.

"Would you like to join the walking tour, Miss Newman?" Meer whispered quietly.

"I would love to honey, but I'm very tired and," Rita moved her hand over the belly "I am feeling very peckish."

"Listen, I'll give you keys. Go to the flat, make yourself comfortable; get something to eat and I will see you both later in the evening." He thought about his promise to Sahanara about reading her a bedtime story this very evening.

"I think I will go back to my hotel. I will see you around 8 PM at your flat, maybe we can go for dinner."

"Mmm... Yeah, yeah sure," Meer agreed a bit hesitantly, his brain was stuck at 'bed-time story'.

The tourists were getting a bit frustrated, and he could see the anguish on their faces, but he wasn't in the mood to run the tour anymore, wishing he could dump them in a local pub and fill them with beers, spirits, and cocktails so they wouldn't remember a thing next morning.
He really wanted to be with Rita now...
"Good people, my apologies for the 5-minute delay but I am glad to share this great news with all of you that I am going to be a father!" Meer spread his arms wide with an entertainer's smile, gathering the crowd for applause.
"Aww, congratulations, wow, *Wunderbar!*" were showered on them as Meer grabbed Rita, stood next to her carrying Amelia and making her feel jubilant as they receive an ovation. Clapping, best wishes, handshakes and some hugs rejoiced them. Love was over the moon, so was the dreaming hope to be in rapture forever. Arm in arm, kissing cheeks, the warmth of holding hands, steamy coffee and a kiss under the falling snow. They looked at each other, smiling eyes, understanding the stillness within the silent love, the magic of the unsaid words, unspoken love...The mystery of serenity holding riddle over centuries playing quietly between the two, sharing a known/unknown string, dancing at the same tune, falling on the same notes together but opposite as two shadows merge to cast a unique soul emerging under the burning stars.

The Pleasure of the Last Midnight on Another Day

Amelia was quietly snoring...
As they undressed each other in the dark corner...
Running hands over bodies, polishing the familiarity of past to ignite a spark, brushing off the rust, hesitance and reluctance in presence of a light sleeping child on the other side of the room.
Both acted like first-time lovers.
"Quietly," Rita whispered as she pushed Meer to recline, lowering, kissing his chest slowly, sliding her finger over a treasure trail promising to take the life out of him...
from where he sowed life inside her. Lips and tongue offering worship to tame a stray master whose mind was wandering away from the moment to the past pleasure of last midnight. He was gauging inside the body, analysing the scale of sexual gratification as any other man who's enough trained with abundant, frequent ploughing opportunities.
Meer was piling her hair into a loose bun as she pleased him.
"Is this a replay from last night, with a different woman?" He thought.

His mind was drifting, and he felt nothing much sexually. The excitement evaporated and he felt sorry for Rita, trying hard to stimulate him. He was kind of disoriented in presence of the child too, couldn't fake anything, wasn't allowed to moan or talk dirty.
"Let me lick you." Meer bit Rita's ear lobe and flipped her to return the favour, though unsurprisingly he wasn't starving tonight after the previous evening with Kumari but his 'work experience' was coming in handy at that moment. He was on it, but miles away from Rita, thinking about Kumari.
"Why was I thinking about Rita with Kumari and now the opposite?" He thought.
Meer was self-questioning his imbalanced emotional state and very hesitantly he asked himself.
"What about Kumari now?"
She broke into tears last night after reaching her well-earned orgasm.
"You shouldn't throw yourself at women for money. I am sure you know that you have me. We could get married." Kumari reluctantly said this morning, leaving Meer with some serious thoughts to re-evaluate his situation.
He was an illegal immigrant, waiting for an opportunity to change life but by choice too.
"I was never emotionally inclined towards Kumari, but after meeting Sahanara I felt different. I enjoy her presence. She changed me with her smiles."
Meer hadn't felt good in a long time. No wonder he went to see Sahanara today after his tour, though Rita was waiting desperately for him.
He was 15 minutes late when he reached his flat.

"Where's your mobile phone, Meer?" Rita was shivering with cold.
"I have been waiting here for the last half an hour." He could hear her complaining tone.
"I am so sorry for being late. I missed the tram and the next one took ten minutes to arrive. I am sooooooo sorry." He smiled like a kid.
"You could have called us. We are freezing here outside your door, wondering where you are, and I can see you are not excited by my arrival."
"I don't have a mobile phone anymore."
"Why not?" She protested.
"Long story. Let's go inside. I need to call a taxi. I booked a table for three in a Greek restaurant." Meer pushed open the door and looked at Amelia wearing a beautiful skirt.
"Beautiful dress! How are you?" He smiled gently, but she ignored him.
"Meer, are you happy that I'm here?" Rita looked in his eyes.
"I am super happy that you're back in my life and please don't be worried. Let me just get changed quickly and... here." Meer handed her a taxi card.
"Call them. Just say M wants a taxi. They know me. Listen, the phone is near the refrigerator." He shouted as he closed the bathroom door.
"M, wow...That sounds like a spy's name. You sure you are not doing something dodgy?" Meer heard a suspicion in her voice.

Panting as he locked the door, breathing hard... he still couldn't believe his luck that Rita was here. He never thought about this surprising twist. He massaged his tensed eyebrows.

"I should tell her the absolute truth about myself. But will she want the child of a gigolo? Maybe it's better I get rid of her and tie the knot with Kumari. She knows all about me, and Sahanara would be around me. I would have a job and regulated immigration status."

"What the fuck I am thinking?" Meer banged his head gently against the wall.

"She's pregnant with my child, she's pregnant with my child, she's pregnant with my child!" He repeated the sentence as a shaman in trance shaking his head, seeking the secret answer from the world of unknown.

"The taxi is outside M." Rita knocked on the door loudly.

"Coming."

"Cumming... I'm cumming Meer!" Rita shivered in rapture and pulled him back from his mind.

Wet... wet, soft spot of hidden known pleasures whitening the edges inside out with foamed bitterness... proud magic of his finger and tongue.

He smiled a lot over the dripping happiness of sheer feminine bliss.

Rita was laughing in rhapsody as she turned into a pleasing rainbow, coming over to colour me.

"I'm going to fuck you now Meer." She was drooling on his chest, laughing loudly.

"She's loose." Meer felt unimpressed as he reached inside.

"I will wrap your desires inside my body and will subtract you from reality; the way you left 'YOU' inside me. I will nullify you tonight from yourself; RITA will sweep all of Meer inside her. You wouldn't be left alone now, honey."

Meer wasn't sexually excited or amused by the 'extra passion session.'

"I just hope the girl will not wake up." He tried to look through darkness where Amelia was tossing and turning.

"Rita isn't going to leave me until I cum, FUCK!" Meer turned her like an expert wrestler into missionary position, forcing his hands over her wrists, wanting wildly to thrust his shaft, shake the bed madly as a violent earthquake, stroke hard to bring the genie out but he couldn't.

"God, she's pregnant and I need to melt my freaking-self inside her before I can go to sleep." Meer was all grumpy as he couldn't get his self to ejaculate. He kept missing the wave of pleasure that could lead to an orgasm.

"Aren't you excited honey?" Rita whispered as Meer stopped to catch his breath.

"I am just afraid; I don't want to embarrass us in front of Amelia," Meer said hesitantly.

"You've been masturbating a lot, bad boy." She giggled as Meer's exhausted tool slipped out of her.

"Did I have a choice?" Meer fell on his side and squeezed her softness as he shrugged in the dark.

"Are you sure? No hanky-panky?" Rita rubbed her nose sensually over his cheek.

What could Meer say? His nerves and body were worn out. He couldn't think of a thing that could comfort his feared thoughts of coming days. He was in a lose-lose situation, ending without the love and compassion of one, wrecking the life of someone again when life had brought deceitfully some happiness their way, to stab them in the middle of the road to dreamland.

"Oi, are you snoring already?"

Rita pinched him gently, but he kept his eyes closed. She snuggled against him, and Meer was covered in warmth of comfort and soothe of love, breathing deeply like a child. Rita moved her face to feel his breath; slowly she moved to hide her nose on his hairy chest to extract the fragrance that she wanted to wear for the rest of her life. Sleep was far from her...

Rita couldn't believe her luck that she's next to Meer as the baby inside holds to life. She was excited, happy and astonished at the same time. She moved closer to Meer to see if life inside her can recognize the origin. She held his unconscious hand and laid it on her belly.

Something swished very, very gently.

"Was that for real?" She smiled.

"Or maybe that was a just a shadow of imagination."

Rita slid her smooth fingers on Meer's dry cheek in hope of seeing his eyes again. She really wanted to talk to him, but he was deep asleep, snoring softly.

His presence next to her was turning her on sexually; she could feel that her body demanding more.

Rita very quietly moved her hand between Meer's legs, gently sliding her fingers on his crotch... sexually provoking him.

"What am I doing to this poor man? He must be tired, and I am being just a horny bitch." She tried to behave herself, but basic instincts couldn't be tamed by a good girl's empathy.
She was on it; her mind was on it. Physically, her hands were playing with him and her.
"I want to stop it... stop it... STOP IT..."
Meer's manhood was slowly empowering, shaping into lingam, getting ready to be pleased and pleasured with an arrangement of returning the favour, possibly?
A wet dream was slowly simmering into Meer's sleep... but he couldn't tell the following morning if that was a dream or reversed illusion of pleasure from half-awake last midnight.
This wasn't Rita; this was Kumari playing her Bengali magic in a dream where Meer was hanging upside down in the middle of darkness, spinning in a void, moving left to right, spinning blindly, calling... "Anybody, anybody?" Meer feebly mumbled.
He couldn't see a thing but can feel the presence of many in that room. They were coming one by one and sensually touching his ribs, belly and inner thighs. Once a tongue sexually soaked his smaller head...
"HEY!" Meer hardly shouted.
He tried to move his softly tied hands to catch the abuser, who was taking advantage of him, leaving him undone, in temptation... But who was there, in that cold darkness...?
His arms were struggling blindly in blankness, for freedom.

"Pull up; I should pull myself up." He thought when suddenly Kumari's laughter sprinkled on his nudity running a chilly sensation arousing goosebumps.

Meer felt that her laughs were echoing within the hall of mirrors where he was hanging in the centre of the pentagon. He pictured himself suspended five feet above the ground by a thinly visible thread.

"Kumari... Kumari..." Meer shouted her name as the pinch of sweet needles reverb in his body.

A sensation of pleasure ran into his bones as someone from the dark moved fingers above his prostate.

"That's your punishment for making too much noise. I'm here, and you can't see me honey." she giggled.

A lubricated finger left a rubbing sensation with menthol tickle on his sack followed by a steamy dip on his shaft. He felt fluids over his erection, dense and slow...

A moment of silence waited before a warm wave of tenderness soothed him and left Meer tempted to reach the climax... he was undone...

"Why can't I see you?" He heard his hesitant voice back.

"Does it matter?" Kumari sounded a bit distant.

"Is there something wrong?"

"Maybe you don't deserve me. Maybe you don't deserve anything." Kumari silenced his questions forever.

A sharp beam of white light shredded the mysterious darkness.

"Can we have sex?" Rita whispered, throwing her cell phone torch on him.

"Hon... Yeah, yeah... yeah." He was still hanging between the dream and reality. Drooling in a deep sleep, struggling to find where he was. Figuring it out. But Rita didn't miss a moment to lean on him quickly.

Kumari was in front of Meer, he could hear her, he could touch her, and he could tell with close eyes that the fragrance of sweat and the strong odour of her slipping wetness which he inhaled every time. He looked down to watch the action.
Rita's nowhere...
No one's anywhere....
Dreams and clouds were nimbuses, gathering outside the doors of the unknown as Meer was gasping next to Kumari when Rita reached her orgasm.
Lightning flashed behind the curtains before thunder roared to merge into ecstatic moaning and silenced all...
A silence that smoothly passages its way towards temporary disengagement from the world of matter and consciousness.
Raindrops were playing soulful rhythms on the windowpane. The deep night was slowly lifting its veil when Meer opened his eyes.
"It's dark and windy outside." He thought.
Lightning flashed the edges of the curtain and slipped into the corners of the room.
Meer saw wrinkles over slight puffiness under Rita's closed eyes.
"I should really go now before Amelia wakes up." He looked towards the other end of the room.
Meer felt tired and sleepy, but he promised Kumari to run the tour. He slowly moved out of the bed to find his pants somewhere on the carpet.
"You're leaving?" Meer felt her eyes on his back.
"Are you leaving Meer?"

Rita was blinking her blue sapphire eyes, turning bluer and the waters inside were two lakes of immortality where his eyes reached to find his own truth...
Emptiness.

She Is Mine

Steam's coming out from every pore, filling the dark shower room with layers of mist, waving in murk raising unclarity, ambiguity, like whirling smoke in a shrine of mystic, wanders you between worlds of practicality to spirituality, moving us away from the bonds of usual unreal, detaching us and revealing another truth between the journey of two halves of the world.
New endings, sudden endings, dramatic endings or new beginnings, a circle of life joins the dot from where it all started and from the same dot, time forms a new ripple in the ocean... ocean within, ocean above.
And I must die again, before the curtain raises for the final act.
God's entertainment business replays and shines brighter every day.
Entertainers. Aren't we all entertainers, entertaining one another with powerful performances, superb dialogues, thrilling climax? Romance, power, sex, games, lust, and thirst of life hangs our fiction of life in the air of reality and soon before we know it curtains fall, the show's over, lights are out... fiction is lost in thin air and reality prevails in the unknown truth. But in darkness, we stay, but we don't stay the same. Act two, you look at you, you ask yourself... who are you? Are you, or are you not?
I was not the same as I left Rita in tears and crossed the threshold of the hotel room.
She wanted me to stay, and I wanted it too... Did I want too?

I was rewinding recent memory as the hot shower tried to wash away the fatigue of last night and invigorate me before the start of a new day. Actually, there are no new day; all days are old in soul. Faces change but stories and hustles stay the same. Tiredness stays the same, laws of destiny, societal boundaries, economic disparity, good and evil, religious differences, shitty norms, all are constant.

Rita's pregnant and surely, she wanted me to be with her as much as possible, holding her hand, talking, making her laugh and getting her comfortable, confident for the biggest day of our life. I must make sure she feels safe and secure next to me. That wasn't possible till… I decided that I will not see Kumari again. She's kind and supportive, but I have more responsibility towards the woman who's carrying my child. I love Sahanara, but she can't take the place of my own blood. I mean, if I were the child's father, wouldn't Kumari have told me by now?

Don't take me wrong. I love Sahanara, but what can I do. "What can I do?"

This question haunted me throughout, all the way, every second I spent in Prague. Whatever I did, the thought of how to break free from this misery of decisions chased me. What's the next step, a right step towards a beneficial, healthy future? A future with uncompromised life filled with happiness and independence. But it seemed to me that a final sacrifice of my soul is unavoidable. I can't seem to dodge the emotional shock before I try to get back to normality.

I kept thinking about some tricks, a master plan of manipulation that liberates my trapped soul within the double triangle of Kumari/Sahanara, Rita/Millie and me. Feeling joyful and disgusted on the emotional roller coaster of Rita's arrival, I remembered my dad's response to his cousin when he complained a few months into his second marriage.
"Your ass will rip apart if you keep your feet in different boats."
Reflecting upon on my dad's opinion about polygamy, I stepped out of the shower, rubbing the towel gently against my body, juggling with my final decision to ditch Kumari and erase her once again from my life forever.
It was my last day as a tour guide, as Kumari returns from Karlovy Vary this evening. Christmas was around the corner and business was getting quieter as Prague filled with more locals and less international tourists.
I was heading to our office located in Staré Město, where I decided that I should meet Kumari for the last time and tell her about Rita's arrival. I had no other way out of the game. I had lied enough and played with her emotions long enough that now she deserved an honest goodbye. I didn't want her to hang on to the idea of our union.
I was chewing the story, the opening, the ending, constructing the dialogue in my head that how I am going to break Kumari's heart, softly of course, as possible when on the other end across the road I saw Dilafroz anxiously marching in front of the closed office wearing a long fur coat with Ushanka, breathing out the winter smoke, flatting the virgin snow under her shoes. I wasn't quite sure for a moment if that was her.

"Why isn't she with Sahanara? If she's here, then where's Sahanara? She would've called me if there's some urgency. Holy crap!" I was scared to find her like this. "Is that really her?" I walked quickly, smashing the muddy street snow under my boots, waving unenthusiastically through the fog to get her attention. I looked at my watch to confirm the time. It was five to eight...
"*Dobry den, všetko dobré Dilafroz*, all's good?"
"*Ano, Ano.*" She smiled and nodded her head in affirmation.
"Where's Sahanara?" I struggled to smile back at her.
"Kumari came back unexpectedly late last night, she's home and I'm here just to talk to you, can we sit down for a coffee, I bought some fresh *buchty* from a local bakery." She shook a brown paper bag of sugar buns with the grin of a happy child.
"Not again," I told to myself. "What sort of game is this... no, not again." I saw my huge sigh turning white in the air.
"You don't look very happy."
"I'm definitely surprised to see you this early morning, I can't deny that." I made sure to wear an annoying face.
"Can we talk quickly? I have things to do." She was all stern now.
"I'm listening Dilafroz."
"I thought... but anyway, that doesn't matter now." She chewed her lips and looked in my angry eyes with a hint of disapproval.

"I'm just here to tell you that Sahanara's your child. She's your daughter and Kumari didn't tell you about it for an obvious reason." She pointed her fingers towards me to brush me in shame. "She deserves better than you. Both Kumari and Sahanara, I don't know what you think of yourself." Her hatred pierced through me "Do you think you are royal?"

The frozen wind left me covered with white flakes as I laughed hysterically on the street... laughter turning into cries and cries into laughter insanely as Dilafroz left me humiliated in her silence. Numb, absolutely numb. I couldn't think what was happening inside as I laughed dementedly. The power to analyse and understand my conscious was snubbed instantaneously, paralysed in thought and action, powerless, utterly powerless.

I was blank in a spin. Spinning as I collided with a roller coaster. Shocked to know who I am, what I am, where I am. Silence rattled in my ears as self-disgust hit my gut. Filth ran through me as street noise poured life into my ears, slowly pulling me towards existence again when laughter burst out as Dilafroz was about to disappear from my sight. She must've heard me.

Frost was freezing my tears as the pain inside couldn't hold a tear more. Frozen wind crying in my ears, and I yelled harder and louder, mourning... mourning my own demise. I grieved the loss of my own existence. I lost me; I lost the final bit of my own self. Life ends here, life ends... nowhere. But here, now, when one couldn't give the love which seeps in the soul quietly for a revival of life after cold, dark and harsh days then... death is what awaits you.

Snow spots grow darker on the coat, seeping to my skin slowly. My nose drips as I sob with hiccups, suffering the pain of thoughts, sipping tightly gripped vodka in a corner of a long street, remembering everyone who took me close to their hearts and what I did to them in return. Mishki, Kumari, Norika, Babel, Ji-Su and now my own daughter... no one's spared, no one. I took a long burning sip to empty the bottle, slipped down against the wall, and fell on the snow with a wish not to wake up.

Silent Whispers of Ji-Su

The plane took off from the Lahore runway. Packed to capacity, a direct flight to London... carrying some snobbish dual nationality holders' busy discussing the imperfections of their motherlands. Frighten students with dreams of better lives. First-time flyers excited by the newness of the experience. Visitor visa holders, some with genuine plans and some clueless to where this leap in the dark will take them. A stroke of luck can change everything and anything. That chance, that probability of turning all into comfort and happiness by taking that one extra step drove every migrant of the history.
And history repeats itself.
"I'm not going to come to this hot as hell shit-hole ever again." I heard a teenager whispered to his older sister. Surely this British kid was falsely lured by Pakistani parents with tales of an exotic holiday.
"Absolute waste of my summer holidays." He continued.
"Why are you bothering me?"
"Bitch!" He silently whispered as he slipped his headphones back on.
The plane continued to ascend as the infant on my left decided to match his volume to the heights of the sky. The child was crying ferociously. Was it the noise of the airbus or the lowering air pressure, dirty nappy or hungry rumbling tummy? I couldn't say. But that poor mother, travelling alone with the child, very hesitantly asked me if I can carry her 6-month-old boy for a minute.

My Asian features were coming in handy.
"Sure, sure." I politely smiled with a gentle head nod and took the baby reluctantly in my arms.
I promise I have zero experience in taking care of kids. But when this little boy came to my lap, he magically stopped crying, started smiling when I looked in his eyes. A sudden peace entered me just like when I sat opposite Buddha in Haedong Yonggungsa Temple... silence soothed all around us.
"You must be very gifted with children, because this little man," she fondly looked at her son "is very hard to please." She looked at me with surprise as she mixed warm water with formula.
What could I say? I smiled and looked deep into the dark brown eyes of the baby, thinking Meer had similar eyes.
"Where are you from? Are you Chinese?" She asked innocently.
"I'm from the South-Korea." I smiled, as this question was asked nearly a thousand times in the last one week in the exact same pattern. I don't blame people, because I also belong to a very homogeneous, curious society.
 "Oh, you must be visiting Lahore. You know what we Lahories say about Lahore?"
"Tell me." I kept my eyes on the baby's smile, as I immersed within the flowing happiness after a long emotional journey to Pakistan.
 "We say, Lahore is Lahore and..." She paused for a moment to smile.
"If one hasn't seen Lahore, his birth journey hasn't been completed."

"So, my cycle's been concluded." Ji-Su was very amused by the saying. A big claim by a city covered with dust and dirt, pollution, moral corruption, piles of rubbish and illiteracy running naked in streets. Suddenly the sense of a nationalist pride evoked inside her.
"Lahore's Lahore." She thought about the slogan again as she looked momentarily on the young mother's face, returning the happy baby.
"Thank you." She gratefully smiled at her, adjusting the nipple of the bottle. She elevated her elbow to equalise the milk flow as the infant comfortably sucked the milk. She satisfactorily looked at the contented, sleepy face of the child with drowsy eyes slowly closing to open in the land of fairies.
"She looks as old as me, or maybe a bit younger." Ji-Su thought to herself as she gazed out from her window seat.
Clouds were lost floating dreams in the sky, waiting for the imagination of someone who see through them, could reveal them to the world.
We all wish to be found and find something, don't we? I wonder if that's something to do with our childhood. Hide and seek.
We all are looking and being sought by someone in the crazy-busy jungle of the world, every day we are losing and finding each other.
We want to be known and unknown at the same time.

The duality of human psychology leads them to a state of dissatisfaction. A need to be excited in finding treasures from the unknown paved the path of spirituality but the material world. Nine to five jobs, harsh living conditions, ever bigger cities with ever bigger challenges, the ruthless competition of power grab disillusioned most of us. We are still seeking what can't harmonise us with the spirit's goal... liberation.

All the rivers flow towards the same ocean. We don't realise that early enough, do we? Choosing sex, drugs, crime, cheating, manipulating or power-hunger to feed the need, to find the path, collectively harm us much longer as a society and as an individual before we set on the path of 'oneness'. The clock's ticking; the sand's slipping, slowly bringing the end of our time. Liberation?

I wonder how long the cycle of birth and rebirth can continue? A journey of sin can last? The succession of error can prolong? And how long Ji-Su can survive... on a lonely road? Finding Meer, turning every stone to find a clue, trying every contact in every city of every country where he could have been in the last three years, but...

I have this feeling now that he isn't in this world anymore. But my heart doesn't agree with my fears. So, I just can't stop my search until I get some news about him... dead or alive.

If he's no more, then I want to find his grave where I can sob for one last time. My eyes are dried and tired. I can't cry anymore. Trying to melt the sorrow that's choking every bit of life from me, frozen tears... refusing to share the fixed grief, to help me. Nobody can really help me, regardless of how many police stations, hospital telephone numbers I rang, people I asked, all efforts ended in smoke.

I landed in Pakistan. Bomb blasts, target killings, street crimes, murders, kidnappings. I heard and read about them all before I came to Pakistan, but nothing changed my mind.

Many years ago, I went to the Pakistani embassy with Meer in London to renew his passport. I wanted to take him to the South-Korean embassy and find out the requirements for a visitor's visa. He made a lot of photocopies of his new passport and national identification card to submit with his original. We had a file where he kept all of his documents, but one of bad copy ended up in the inner pocket of my old jacket. I'm sure he handed that to me so we can shred it safely. Last month when I was taking out some clothes for charity, I found that forgotten copy.

That was the sign.

Go to Pakistan.

Many thought it was a suicide attempt, an act of immaturity and childish obsession. My parents told me that I would be risking my life for an illusion. What could I tell them, that I see my life as an illusion without him? I knew the risk, but I didn't care. I wanted to find Meer. Probably I saw someone else inside him, someone greater than both of us... who could that be?

I set myself on the journey of madness to find his presence, his love, his care, his silence, his words, his passion, with a hidden wish to have him in my possession.
I left for Pakistan.
But that wasn't the beginning of my journey. Really, it wasn't the start of my investigation. Years ago, when I met him, intrigued by him, hating then falling for him, this all started by then. Later when I lost contact, I understood who Meer was, for me at least. He told me many things from his past but always hesitantly. He had an uneasy childhood. He said to me many times that his heart turned to stone. Life made him a violent man, a sad man, a very bad man. He avoided the details and silenced his words, but I saw the depression of a sensitive, sensible man escaping from a haunted past. I never entirely understood what he had done, why Meer couldn't come out of his misery. It was only now when I visited his village that I really came to know who he really was and what he was. So much has been revealed to me in the past week that I couldn't comprehend everything. I wrote all in my diary ... what my translator told me; now what I look at seems like a summary of an epic drama.
I'm sharing a few pages of my diary with you, for you to know what you don't know... though we never know enough.

12th July 2003/ Saturday

Yesterday on the staff notice board somebody pinned a pamphlet about charity collecting shoes and clothes. I'm planning to donate all my stuff before I leave Newcastle forever. I don't like my job. I can't stand the biting cold, and I can't live with this loneliness anymore. Meer isn't here; I have only his memories and for how long can I live with memories? I can't spend the rest of my days listening to songs that we enjoyed together or eating dinner alone at the same table where we used to spend evenings. Life wouldn't be the same after him. And probably everyone's right too. Now is the time for me to move on.

But the haunting question still stays the same; where is he? Why did he never come back to me? Why did he do this to me? Why did he never tell me that he sublet the property to illegal immigrants and using them to run a chicken shop for him? I thought he hated to abuse people. I thought he was different, and he was, but then? Why didn't he contact me? Could be that he's in an immigration detention centre and authorities aren't telling me? Did they deport him? Is he in Pakistan? Where is he? WHERE IS HE? No one knows anything. No wonder Meer kept people at a distance, never initiating a conversation, leaving an impression of superiority because he had secrets and life taught him how to carry secrets. Often wearing a blank face or a bothered expression sitting on his face to keep people at bay, he looked at others with a policeman's attitude... scrutinising, looking deep into them, very closely monitoring their body language, watching their actions, paying attention to the tone and the vocabulary they use. He wanted to be a step ahead of others, always.

I still ask myself why he chose me as his girlfriend. Did he really love me? Or did he love my silence, the way I gave him my attention without annoying him, the way I looked at him while I listened to him... we talked for hours while drinking sake. What did he like about me? He told me once that Arabs and Asian Muslim men prefer meat on the bone when it comes to food and women. That very night I taught him a lesson on what a woman with less meat can do to a man...
I miss you Meer...
I wish I never went back home without you or had just gone on the Euro trip with you. I wish I never had to plan to go earlier than you to South Korea, to discuss your presence, a foreigner boyfriend, whom I intend to marry. I never wanted to fight that battle in front of you. You never spoke to my parents, because they didn't know about you. And even if they did, they wouldn't like you. Without knowing you well they wouldn't approve you. The language barrier was another disadvantage. I'm not certain, but you got a bit worried every time you saw me shouting over the phone and I'm sure that was enough for you to understand how different my opinions were from my parents'. Otherwise, you wouldn't bring a glass of water for me every 15 minutes during my calls, making me smile.
Where are you now?
I couldn't sleep again last night.

This city is a sorrowing curse without you. I'm tired, I'm tired and I need your hugs, your arms around me, your breath whispering. Come back to me and lay by my side while I listen to your heartbeat and caress you, my fingers sliding on your chest, feeling the smooth skin hiding under the fragrant dark thick hair and when I breathe in, I infused myself with intoxication, spreading inside me as love pumps the madness, setting myself on fire, and in that scorch 'You' open new dimensions in me, unleashing my inner animal.
Come back honey, to attend my un-nurtured dreams. We will fall in the fantasy before night falls and will wake up under the warm sun. Breeze touching our skin and your flying hair, and I move my fingers through them, as we sail to a distant lonely island, come back... The night is deep again.

13th July 2003/ Sunday
I am sure finding his home address is an absolute sign that I should go and look for him in Pakistan. I'm sure he's there, where else he would go? Definitely a progressive politician now, striving for a change in society, working hard for the brighter future of the people, with big plans to alter the backward thinking, a hope in sight for the young people. A real man, empowering the women and vulnerable. That's what he talked about, helping the weakest of society to lay a strong foundation.
You had big dreams Meer, big dreams to pursue, dreams to realise us who we are, dreams to beautify the world and you let me borrow 'one dream' of yours too.

Do you still think of me? Maybe you think about the time we spent together, thinking about my shy kisses, my gentle touches. Maybe someone somewhere reminds you of me. Reasonless melancholy fills your heart and reasons the emptiness. Falling eve, the colour of the sky, a broken star, thoughts of autumn, a white breath of winter, a forgotten fragrance, an old book, a burning cup of black coffee... something that makes you think about me? When you see an emerald dress, a pearl necklace, a moonstone, French manicure... nothing reminds you of me?

Maybe you are already married.

A fear slithered like a snake inside my chest just now.

"That's why he didn't contact you." I heard the whisper of my inner Gollum.

"That's why he asked his wife to wear moonstone with French manicure; emerald dress suited her well with a polished pearl necklace and a thin gold wedding ring"

"No!" I shouted in my mind.

Did you ever think of contacting me, Meer? To apologise, to explain what happened? How did you manage to fall from the face of the earth? No telephone calls, no letters, no emails, nothing, just nothing. I heard nothing from you, you never came to Busan. But still, I went every day to the airport for two weeks, looking for you at arrivals, on every single flight which came from London, on crutches, in pain with a fresh bouquet in my hand... every time! And I never disrespected those flowers, which disappointed me just like you in the end. They accompanied me when I went for a conversation with the 'ONE' and floated them in the waves of East Sea, thinking helplessly, that these flowers would meet the waters of the river encircling your city. And one eve when you will walk by the river, all the flowers will gather in front of your eyes and in that second you will remember me, you will miss me, emptiness will capture your soul and you will remember that you withered me just as these flowers lost themselves what nurtured them. But all that was an illusion, fiction stirring in my head, possibly a result of bad lifestyle, lack of newness and excitement, pain and disappointment.
Flowers and hopes sunk long ago. Nothing reached you, not my prayers nor my sorrows. Days gone by and news of spring arrived froze in the winter of the time. You never unlatched the door of my room to walk-in and brought the fragmented memories. I waited and waited for so long that I can't remember where the past splits from the present and bloomed to the future. You are everywhere but not here...
So, Pakistan, here I come....

18th July 2003/ Friday
I'm in London. Took a sick day from work. I need a visa to visit Pakistan, so here I am, to submit my passport and application following a brief interview.
"Why would you like to visit Pakistan?" One embassy official asked me in the least friendly way possible.
"I want to visit Lahore." I smiled as I remembered what Meer told me about the city.
The history and the festivity of the old Lahore, colourful weddings and celebrations of the city, famous kite flying festival on the arrival of spring and warm-hearted friendly people knocking jokes to each other as they enjoy traditional sweets, sweeter than sugar and jaggery. Deep-fried, spicy crispy snacks rolled in Gram flour, seasoned with exotic spices. The breakfasts, the brunches, late lunches, midnight dinners... Meer told me all about his youthful adventures in Lahore. 'Food' is the magic word for the real Lahories, he said. Curry style foods immersed in strong aroma cooked with a generous portion of "ghee" enjoyed with thick naan bread and on special occasions this naan bread's dough is also layered with clarified butter and baked in the clay oven and brushed with 'ghee' again, once it's out of the oven.

"Wow!" That's all what I said nearly always when Meer told me excitedly about food recipes and blends of exotic spices, which would taste different in one food and completely different in other if used individually or when added in the different steps of the cooking. But maybe it wasn't about the cooking what excited me, but the way you orchestrated your stories Meer, the way you added flavours and colours to them, the way you spiced them, seasoned with laughs and jokes and fist-pumping excitement.

Undoubtedly you were a big foodie though, always looking for some particular taste and flavour, looking for new restaurants where you can go for contemporary Punjabi food. You always moaned about Indian restaurant food standards, almost every time when we went for a curry.

 "This is not right, that is not right, flavour isn't the same, the proportion of spices isn't balanced, and texture should be different."

"Oh Lord Buddha, what to say to this man?" I used to think when I saw you complaining.

I think about how love changes us, how we think, how we act, how we see our self. The way we adjust our goals, our life, our dreams, our passions...And how so many things give-up their meaning and value, often temporarily, but they do go in the background for a while.

Is it that human nature is seeking submission always, even in bedrooms? I heard very manly men; powerful men of society often get caught in submissive role plays? Meer, did you notice that I think like you now, thinking about sex like you used to do?

"Dirty hobby of yours" I used to call it and now I understand your thesis. The triangle between human behaviour, society and sex. I could see the bigger picture now probably because I'm starving for sex...? You left me undone.
I miss you. Do I have to say that again?
I wonder how many secrets are in my heart that you would die for, the thoughts you'd love to know. I remember you always complained about my 'quietness'. But tonight, I'm thinking how much I have to say to you? How long I can talk to you? And if I write my every single thought of this monologue, this night will be over and the night after that too. It's better that my breath would run out before the pages of my diary do.
I'm spending this eve in Hammersmith.
Yes! King Street, Hammersmith. The same hotel, where I stayed with you Meer when we visited the Pakistani Embassy. Earlier today when I was on the way to London, a million memories danced like Norwegian fairies around me. I went to drink a latte at that same coffee shop, sat at the same table thinking about you. Rewinding in my mind those few seconds when you turned with two massive white cups of coffee and looked around with a blank face for the table where I was sitting. I loved that confused expression on your face. I kept rewinding it and it always made me smile.
Tomorrow late afternoon I'll make my way back to Newcastle.
"And you will return with me too." I joked with you as we boarded years ago on the Piccadilly line.
"I will return to you, wherever you will be." You replied.
Meer, I'm right here, where you held my hand, but....

Next week, I will be returning to pick my passport and I will return to you on the next flight... Good night, it was a long day.

23 July 2003/ Wednesday
"So, do you know any Pakistanis?" He looked keenly at my face before handing my passport.
"In England, yes!" I smilingly said.
He seemed a bit disappointed with my answer.
 "I meant will someone accompany you during your visit?"
"No, I'm going alone and I'm sure I will be able to manage my trip perfectly."
He wasn't sure about something, and I could see that on his face.
"I understand that, but I would highly recommend a translator or a tour guide to accompany you. Please do contact your embassy in Islamabad on your arrival." This official was polite and clearly concerned about safety.
"Don't worry, I already contacted my embassy to arrange for a guide and they are waiting for my dates to be confirmed."
"Thank you." There was some relief on his face.
"I hope you enjoy your stay in Pakistan." Officer smiled with dry professional courtesy as he returned my passport.

Now I'm near Durham sitting in the coach to Newcastle with a hurting bum and hungry tummy, sleepy...
Honestly, I think I have no patience to travel on intercity buses anymore. This romance of travelling by road is getting old, like me, who's 26 but feels like a hundred and twenty-six. Too soon, I would say, but hey, age's just a number... funny to me to say that.
This morning I went to see my manager and reminded her of my annual leave.
I'm taking two weeks off. A week in Pakistan and another week for something, I don't know yet. So, tomorrow's my last day at work before I embark on my quest.
I got on a coach from John Dobson Street and made it just in time to Knightsbridge to pick up my passport and then back on the 18:30 coach from Victoria, nearly 15 hours on the road.
The idea behind doing these exhausting journeys was to connect somewhere... Somewhere by my intellectually created spiritual method which separates 'The self' from the thought, parts one from the vagueness of life, from ideas. Helps you in creating a distance between 'YOU' and the life which you pretend living. Entangled thoughts, psychological mess, unrealised tension and bothering 'cause' underneath the busy and occupied brain floats on the surface of the consciousness. You see the way through. A lonesome journey is a friend who talks with you, about you, inside you in isolation, which is a blessing. Seclusion is a way towards God...
Separation, detachment, all are the names of the same journey which return you to the ultimate source.

Today I was talking to my mom just as I was inside her womb again.
I didn't say a word, but all's understood and responded.
We were one.
As I'm 'One' with the Lord.
Here I remember what you told me Meer about the concept of "I'm the truth" by 9th-century mystic Mansur Al- Hallaj, which lead him to his execution.
Perfect annihilation.
The driver just announced that we are approaching Newcastle upon Tyne...
Good night.

25th July 2003 /Friday
"Good afternoon, ladies and gentlemen. This is your captain speaking. We are currently flying at an altitude at 33,000 feet at an airspeed of 400 miles per hour..."
The announcement continued as I took my diary out to scribble a few thoughts.
I was never passionate about keeping a diary, but I think writing helped me to ventilate my thoughts, the stress, pain... My psychology professor said in her very British accent "Writing stimulates ideas and put thoughts in an orderly fashion, Su."
So here am I trying to sort my life logically by visiting 'Pakistan', to find a known man at some unknown address in an unseen city with the help of a local guide? Surely my mother would be on her knees in front of the Lord for the next whole week.

Earlier this morning I flew from Leeds Airport.
Yesterday evening I was in Leeds city with my luggage for the first available flight I could book. I also booked a hotel in Lahore and later gave a call to the South-Korean embassy in Islamabad and updated them about my arrival. Afterwards I went to change some British pounds to Pakistani rupees. A few hours later I received a call from the tour guide, confirming he would be at the airport to receive me.
All was happening in a rush...
I was following my instincts and intuition to plan my mystified trip.
At first, all that I wanted was a taxi from Lahore airport, to go straight to Bahawalpur. I would never have found him in such a densely populated city without the address on his ID card. So, I assume it mustn't be a trouble to locate his whereabouts from the locals.
My expected arrival time at Lahore airport is 19:55, local time.
I'm excited and afraid. More afraid probably, but I don't want to think of my fears. I'm trying to focus...to triumph in the battle of the ill thoughts.
Yes, I'm fighting with myself... again and this makes me weak. I'm so tired of being me. I'm wishing to sleep but my mind is not at rest, nothing's at peace and the pace of my heart accelerates with every passing minute. I wish to order a glass of wine to ease the stress, I hope they offer some...A potion of my favourite dream...waking me to the life... drawing us together below the blue sky and above heaven, where life meets ecstasy and dreams turn to gold, tears are stars and stars are crystal and you wear them on me. I wear you on me...Forever...Forever...

27th July 2003/ Sunday
Is it...that every impossible dream stems from a self-lie? Crashing us right into our reality, the smoke of disappointment, delusion that shreds our hopes or... could it be that a thought opposes to the currents of practicality, defy the logic and convincingly succeed over the 'set pattern', makes us believe that 'truth' 'reality' can be reshaped by effort.
I guess I'm disappointed. I'm trying to get better, though this trip's been a let-down since arrival.
I felt here, somehow weird. The way people look at me is out of my understanding. Meer, you warned me years ago and advised to dress modest and I did... but still I feel like a 'thing' here. The gazes of the men pierce my clothes, and the heat of lust is on my skin. I could feel it. No wonder a burqa seems to be the right choice for living among animals.
Adeel, my tour guide, is a full-time student at a local university, completing a Master's in history program. He was my saviour at Lahore Airport where I was ambushed by taxi drivers, who fought over me. I was so consumed by the situation that I couldn't see that someone's holding out a paper with my name on it. He was looking at me and all the drama with a confused face. I waved at him to get his attention, and within 30 seconds I was out of that place. He grabbed my bags and rushed me out from the crowd by shouting something in Punjabi with a mixture of "OOY hello, hello... OOY!"
We were at the car park in the next five minutes and in ten, I heard probably half of his life's story.

What he does, what he doesn't, who he loves, what he likes, what are his plans for future, how much he feels blessed, how society let him down... religious views, political commentary and Lord he was loud... loud chatterbox. Then he started my interview. Why am I here? Do I have a boyfriend? What's my plan? And then without listening to my answer he told me what he thinks and what I should do during my visit. Oh Lord Buddha, I hated it, but I kept quiet and very patiently told him that I would like to visit Bahawalpur tomorrow.
"Bahawalpur?" He couldn't believe what I said.
"Yes, is something wrong?" I sounded stern.
"No, nothing's wrong but that's South of Punjab maybe a 7, 8-hour drive from here, maybe longer in this hellish weather."
"Yes, I know that. I'm here to meet a friend." I smiled.
"A... man?" He asked me hesitantly.
"How does that concern you?" I got annoyed but smiled immediately.
"Yes, a man."
There was a long silence suddenly in which he drove quietly.
"Boyfriend?" He couldn't hold his erupting curiosity anymore as we stopped on the red signal.
"We are nearly married." I sighed and surrendered to his question eventually. Luckily that was the last one for the day because we were already on the famous and historic Mall Road of the Lahore.
He was enthusiastically talking about the brief history of the city and the importance of the road and some details about the buildings on our left and right as the Toyota moved slowly in dense jammed traffic.

I was exhausted and drained. Fortunately, Adeel sensed my silence and silenced himself.

An easy check-in at a luxurious hotel and Adeel left me with a promise to come back at 10:00 in the morning, though he didn't show up till noon.

"I'm sorry, I'm sorry, I'm late... I'm late." He shouted as he saw me.

"Bad traffic, terrible, terrible but here..." He took out a mobile phone from his pocket. "My number's here, so you can contact me if you need anything. Let's go, let's go and let me show you a bit of Lahore and we can discuss your trip to Bahawalpur. We will go there tomorrow." He was constantly moving restlessly and talking loudly since he walked in the lounge.

"Did you visit any shops here? They are good... very good." He smiled foolishly towards the people and felt immediate disapproval of them.

"So, let's go, let's go... follow me, follow me." He disappeared as the madness appeared earlier. I'm sure we all felt like an audience of a bizarre theatre, who couldn't quite get what happened in the last act and just blankly looked at each other for a clue.

Life does the same.

A situation, a character, an irrational performance, but you still get lost in translation and shake your head in denial. Perception dodges you; logic defies.

"That couldn't be what it is, it must be something else." And within these thoughts, destiny defines us, the secret of the 'Unknown Hand' hands you the deeper truth. It's always a matter of split seconds. Decisions are decided somewhere much before the action-reaction cycle begins. Ripple turn into tides by that pebble fallen from the sky, sea monster evokes, lighting and the strong stormy winds changing one's passage...forever.

I've seen Lahore for three hours today...

Slow traffic, pollution, overpopulation, dust and curious gazes aside, the city does have a character. And what one could see without stepping out from their comfort zone, I had seen that.

We were just here on the Mall Road today...

Undoubtedly the road is the heartbeat of the city, but this heart's congested now. Jammed traffic, busy in the pleasure of horn honking, polluting the city with thick smoke and often loud music is left played from several cars to intensify the choke of the noise. Adeel was awfully loud too. That made me so miserable that regardless of my interest in the city I requested him to take me back to the hotel and liberate me to my sanity.

We agreed to meet at 5:00 am at the hotel's lobby tomorrow. From there, with a beating heart, I'd be on my way to Bahawalpur. My heart's racing as I'm writing these lines... deep breaths... deep... in and out...in and out, slowly. I'm calling Buddha, chanting his name inside loudly, remembering that all's been decided before. All...you, me, us, the universe. I'm trying to detach my pleasures, my hopes, my fears from myself. Happiness is a wave which reaches one's shore regardless, so is the sorrow. So, I go my way and you go yours, if Lord willing, we would find us, if not, don't despair, he's in you and I'm 'YOU', I reflect you in me. But you too... do you? Do you mirror the fire of my heart inside your quiver, as you think of a union? Does this move you when I look in my eyes here? And in the mirror 'You find you there', in the red drought cracks, salty waters of painful unknown distances, and I will drown in them tomorrow when you are there no more for me in hope to see me. Then I'm falling for the life of another world where you await me, waiting to see me and I know how it is, so I wouldn't let you burn in the fiery desert of loneliness under the blazing sun. Oasis... I await you, till you... DO.

28TH July 2003/ Tuesday
Wouldn't pick up a pen...wouldn't breathe, wouldn't see another dawn. Wouldn't live...

I thought of a black hole. You spin into it as death lures you innocently. Fear? I'm sure death isn't that terrifying, but the mystery of that transition made us all frighten. We don't want to die; we don't...who wants to die? But we die. We die every day; we die as we breathe, as you read... I'm thinking that fear of death is a fear of relocation, or of possession of this body? What is death? I asked again myself, and never felt so unafraid of it. I felt I'm ready to embrace it and free myself forever from the pain of this circus. Detach, as I thought of detaching myself from all... pain, pleasure, happiness, disappointment. Life's a gift, but what gift is it? People you love disappear, things you admire change, youth turns into nasty decay and colours fade from your eyes... is that the gift?

Meer isn't here...

I think, at the back of my mind I saw it coming all the way. My fear backed the bravery, and I landed in Pakistan for this...nothingness, emptiness.

I feel someone's taken my faith away from Buddha, I can't feel him around me, I can't see what I could before with his eyes.

He's testing me, testing again and again and again... Today I'm feeling I need to use my head and leave Buddha aside for a while, he's...

I need to take the matter in my hand and act more practically, more rationally with more logic but what difference that would make, anyway. I expect a miracle deep down, like any other dreamer, or should I say loser... who couldn't achieve anything and then God- A fiction, miracles- A super fiction and we are made believe. We are conditioned by religion, by media, by society, that good things happen to good people. Bullshit, absolute bullshit! Meer used to say that being nice and kind to the world, being humble and compassionate leads you nowhere but at the bottom of the society. This world is made by autocrats; God is an autocrat... if he's real.

What to write... I don't know what to express and how to explain all to myself that he's not here. Yes, he's not here and no one knows in this town where he is. His family... his dad was shot dead, and I was told that older brother of Meer was the killer, a drug addict, supported by political rivals, and later was abandoned and turned to the police by them. And with this classic move, they wiped-out Meer's family from politics.

Most of the people thought Meer was still in England, including his father's secretary who confirmed us that he spoke with him on the day his dad was shot.

"When was it?" I asked Adeel to confirm with him.

"30th June 2002."

That was the same day when the United Kingdom Border Agency raided his chicken shop and later his sublet flat, where illegal immigrants were staying. I thought.

I was rewinding the past once again...

On the 28th I lost my phone during hiking after another terrible argument with my parents about Meer's arrival. They plainly declined to host him and told me that a 'foreigner' wouldn't be welcomed in 'their' house. And when I reminded my father about his Japanese 'origins' on that day, my mom slapped me.
I left our holiday cottage...
The tension was on the rise, and I couldn't speak with Meer until after 24th when he was in Berlin. I didn't know what to tell him. He wrote to me on the 26th when he reached Prague, while I tried to think of a way to convince my parents. I just wanted them to meet him...but they kept ignoring me. They had other plans for my future. So, when Meer tried to ring me on the 27th I didn't pick up his call. I was afraid... I didn't want to disappoint him by telling him the truth, yes! The truth...that's what it only does, disappoint people. You were right Meer; it just frustrates people by exposing their flaws. And I didn't want to lose you... I didn't want to make you feel bad, feel sad...for me, for us, for our future.
I regret not answering your call... every day. I don't know what happened to you after 26th June. I couldn't contact you after getting back to Busan. And now I wonder what it would be if I knew on 24th June that it's the last time, I'm talking to you. When you were calling on 27th I would know that destiny is giving me a final chance to make a difference in our life. But who was stopping me from answering your call?
And as I'm bleeding my heart onto blank pages something started blinking inside.

Prague, I should go to Prague... I should go to Prague... I should go to Prague, started ringing in every corner of my head.

I was still in Bahawalpur when I first thought "Did I just solve a part of the puzzle?"

We were driving to a local guesthouse when Adeel very quietly said.

"Miss, I'm sorry, you couldn't find him." His voice was tuned into sympathetic notes.

"It's ok, thank you for bringing me here and helping me throughout."

He was muddling into deep thoughts.

"Miss, you remember when you told me that you want to go to Bahawalpur to see your friend; I knew it straight away that it's the matter of the heart."

I smiled as he looked in the rear-view.

"Miss, I understand this is your private matter and I'm just your tour guide, but I have one advice for you." He sounded someone else suddenly.

"Yes...And what's that?" I kept my eyes on the back mirror.

"You should pay a visit to the shrine of the patron saint of Lahore, Ali Hujveri, he would listen to your heart, and I would love to take you there if you allow me, Miss."

I kept looking at his shoulder in silence.

"Miss you can talk to me, you can tell me anything, I think that would make you feel a little better and if not then definitely our beef stew with a seasoning of clarified butter, some ginger and lemon juice would. I'd order dinner for you and our Asian tea would do the magic what Scotch whisky couldn't pull off." He tried to joke as he parked the car.

I looked around with an absent mind in the dark. I was somewhere else and didn't want to be disturbed. Quality Guesthouse... was modestly lit behind my back.
The receptionist very warmly and loudly welcomed both of us.
"Good evening *jee*! Welcome, welcome, most welcome to our 'Kawaalti guesthouse.'"
I looked into the eyes of a middle-aged man who was smiling with great joy behind the reception desk.
"Myself Akram Sheikh," he extended his chunky hand towards me, "I'm the owner of this guesthouse." Sheikh looked keenly towards Adeel as he shook his hand.
"I'm giving you the best, the best room of our beautiful, beautiful guesthouse, *jee*."
"Rooms you mean, I booked two single rooms for tonight." Adeel meaningfully corrected him with a clean threat in his voice.
"Yes please, same, same, I want to say sir *jee*." Sheikh moved his head like a robot and handed him a couple of room keys.
"Breakfast tomorrow between 8 to 10, Enjaay your stay *jee*." He was smiling tirelessly towards me.
Adeel stared at him before he turned towards me.
"So, I will see you back in half an hour at the reception?" Adeel tried to reconfirm his doubts, deep down he knew my answer.
"Ok." I noticed the porter, who was already waiting for me.
My brain's wavelength was in a different world as porter carried my luggage and I followed him in silence.

"Can you please tell my guide that I will see him in the morning now? I don't want to be disturbed at all by anyone and if you could get me some sandwich and some coffee, please, thank you." I dismissed him but he stood still, slightly confused.
"Do, you, have, room service... sir?" I ran my eyes over the room as I broke my sentence after every word for better comprehension.
"Yes, yes, very good food. Chicken *tikka, malai kofta*, roast chicken, very tasty, very tasty." He shook his head back and forth with a huge smile just like his boss.
"This please." He ran to grab the room service menu from the table.
"Thank you." I grabbed the menu from one hand and the door from the other to show him out. He didn't like it; I saw a surprised face.
Probably he expected a tip, but I was so cocooned in myself that I couldn't see outward. I was missing my parents. I thought of my father and my mother, their nonstop arguments, loud lovemaking and sudden indifference to each other for days but they never divorced, their marriage was a taboo...
A South Korean girl married to a descendant of Japanese imperialist in 1979.
Japanese thought of Koreans as inferior people, a dirty and lazy race. They took our land and our lives too when we protested. The same kind administered our innocence to the bottomless pit of brothels for their pleasures.
"Reward for today's brutality, a Korean beauty, a Filipino darling or a Chinese sweetheart. First come first served soldiers, first come first..."
My imagination was shouting at me.

"Oi, Korean dog of our king, come here for a bit of some Korean meat we brought you. Bastard was a right mess today with the gun. Come here cunt and have your sisters too."

I see a middle-aged soldier; hands drenched in blood with broken teeth stained by tobacco walk up with his tough back and muddy hair towards this 14-year-old as she stood still behind an armed Japanese man.

"Public toilets, these bitches are public toilets." Someone shouted before he slapped her.

"Use and abuse them, use and abuse, use and abuse, use, use, use..." I heard shouting as soldiers started raping the virginities and when they couldn't, how comfortably they shoot the comfort women.

And the unfortunate some, alive-dead, gave birth to kids of those soldiers. Who were they and the one who died in the womb of their mothers, who were they? Where were they? Who were they? How were they?

And as Meer use to say, one needs to dip the pen into his bloodstream in order to right the injustice and brutality done in the history of this world. Without sleepless nights and sanity, one can't do justice... and he just shouted in my head now. Give voice to injustice!! Give your voice to injustice!! It's a sin to be weak and poor, to be dependent on the power of the system which tilts the balance of the scale of justice as per wishes of the *rule makers* of society.

That's the only justice one gets... the injustice.

And I, got also that sort of same 'just' too. A hint of the imperialist was in me and the blood of a freedom fighter too. My maternal grandmother, who was born the same year Yu-Gwan Sun died in the prison of Japanese Korea at the age of 17.
She died because she didn't give up and neither the torture on her.
"Japan will Fall!"
She wrote from prison.
It was mid of Feb 1919 when Gwansun knocks the door of my grandmother's father's house.
"Please join our peaceful protest on 1st March for the Independence Movement, Korea is ours." She confidently looked at him.
"Aunae Marketplace at 9:00 am."
He hesitantly looked around in the street and without a word reluctantly shut the door.
"Long Live Korean Independence!" She said firmly and looked in his eyes when he was closing the door.
He never participated in the protest; he couldn't even think of leaving her young bride for a day alone, risking his life for a dream. A dream? He thought... Free Korea! Vicious Japanese, hunger of life, hunger of freedom. His thoughts contemplated throughout that night as he broke sweat between the legs of the young bride who felt the burden of his soul for the first time late at night.
But he hid behind his logic, practicality won over his wishes and next morning, he nearly forgot about yesterday as the pleasure of last night soothed every inch of his soul.
But all that was temporary...

"Nineteen unarmed people died in protest by the hands of Japanese Military Police." He overheard someone on his way home; his feet froze near that man.
"These bastards killed the parents of this 16-year-old kid, Gwansun. Someone was telling me she's the same child who was in our neighbourhood, knocking doors and she was taken into the prison."
Gwansun died on 28th Sep 1920.
And when my grandma opened her eyes on 27th Oct 1920, she was named after her by her father.
That was his only action against oppression. I always think what else one could do when life's so hard that a tear is even afraid to shed?
A tear is a sign of revolt!
A tear is a mark that times are changing, and a tear can make *them* scared, as now they know that it's 'No More' to what it used to be. So, if they suppress you, that is the golden moment, marking of the new beginnings...
"Japan will Fall!"
Gwansun wrote from the prison.
And it did in 1945... The year my grandmother got married.
She was an ordinary girl, wasn't that brave as her father wished her to be. Carrying unmet dreams of her *appa*, a lot of expectations and hopes, his regrets and wishes were the constituents of her soul, but like her father, she wasn't capable of achieving the best of the life.
But a window of hope opened when she met in 1941 my grandfather, Dae-Jung, a member of the Korean Liberation Army, who fell in love with her. He was an idealist, revolutionary of his own kind, but it didn't take him long to fall for her.

I think a man's always looking for a woman who opens the door to his dreams. He wants recognition, the throne, the acknowledgement. And a woman, she looks for a window manifesting the colourful rainbows over the sky. In the pursuit of this happiness, often women are the ones jumping out of the window too.
My mother was their third daughter who was born in 1962 and this story that I told you is passed over the decades and reached to me finally by my mother when I was in Busan last time when I told her about Meer...
"This isn't possible girl; this will never happen." There was a firm finality in her voice.
"But why?" I shouted.
"You know why, Ji-Su." She tried to calm her voice as she felt the astonishing resemblance of her current self with her deceased mother.
"Because he's not a Korean!" My eyes sparked with rage as I confirmed to rewind the past.
"I'm not saying that you are saying that Ji-Su." My mother struggled to keep her calm posture.
"Dad's not Korean!" I mumbled.
"Shut up! I said shut up!" She was trembling.
"This is how we raised you? Disrespectful and ill mouthed?" What went wrong with you? You think you are old enough to be rude to your parents? Let me remind you, your father was born here, he's Korean, it's not his fault that he was born in the house of those bastards, and he knew what we stand in South Korea for, he's one of us. Him or me, we don't need your approval for life! We had fought our battle with society, and we can again if you desire for one!" Her eyes were blazing like a tigress.

"But look at yourself, who are you? You are half of him, aren't you? For you we changed the city, so you don't get bullied at school, we gave you a Korean name, we protected you throughout and for what? For what Ji-Su, for this day?" She was yelling on the top of her lungs and tears were running like a stream through her eyes.
"I'm glad your father's not here to see all this, I understand that love is blind, I know what it means, and I know what price one must pay sometimes - just to be what one wants to be! And how and where!" She wiped her tears with the back of her hands.
"I love him! And I want you and dad to meet him. I can't think of a life without Meer, he will come for a week, and we will fly back together." I said plainly and stubbornly to my mother.
"What's so special about him, why not someone from here?" She sounded exhausted in her voice.
"Who's here? Perverts fixing hidden cams in female public toilets, ungrateful and underestimating men, who think they are Gods because of a few inches of extra meat between their legs, busy gamers, pornography addicts, alcoholics, gamblers, spoiled sons of extra caring mothers who would go on their knees once and I would end up on my knees for the rest of my life pleasing and pleasuring them."

"It's my luck or karma that I never met anyone 'normal' and I'm sure some men would be very different from my perception, but I never attracted them, nor they did, so..."
I saw a shadow of grief on my mother's face, as something broke and scattered to the corners of her soul. She never thought that words and situations can pass through generations. The trials and tests of the learning being, the unsolved matters, teachings and struggle to understand can run to last in generations, till we liberate. On that eve my mother spoke tirelessly till late. She told me in detail about her struggle with marriage and breaking away from society after marrying my father. She was content though, but her grief of not bearing any more kids after me consumed her emotionally. Her trouble in conceiving for the first 6 years of marriage, miscarriages and depression and how badly she coped with life with and without anti-depressants, my childhood memories, the struggle of my father and his nasty habits which made her jump out of the 'lasting forever love'.

She made me promise not to tell or discuss anything with my father until we come back from our holiday. And on holiday, I couldn't keep my mouth shut and ended up having another argument with both of them and the climax of the holiday broke with my broken ankle.

And today I'm sitting with a broken heart in Pakistan, in South of Punjab where once Meer used to live, his hometown, his birthplace, thinking of my parents, thinking about him.

My next stop would be Newcastle or Prague?

But I'm back in Lahore tomorrow and possibly if I can, I would love to fly back...

This trip seems to be just another link, another clue, another step in the quest of finding Meer.
Good-night or good morning, I should say... It's 3 am.

30th July 2003/ Thursday
I checked in earlier...
Tonight, I'm flying to London. Sitting at Lahore's departure lounge waiting for my flight, still in a sort of trance, as I was at the shrine of Lahore's Patron Saint, Ali Hujwiri, locally known as "Generous Lord" or "Benevolent Lord".
"Benevolent Lord's Town is another calling name of the city between locals," Adeel told me when we came back to Lahore yesterday evening. He was insistent about taking me to the shrine of Mystic Master and paying regards to the sanctified man. He told me, "Life could be changed by one gaze of 'The Mentor', so please let me take you."
I wouldn't say that I entirely understood the spiritual context of what he was saying, but I was trying to learn the logic behind his words and concrete confidence. His take on the entire thing was culturally, socially and spiritually very intriguing to me.
"Thousands of people doing charity or taking part in some form of charitable work in a day, offering food, sweets and snacks, doing volunteer work of different sorts to be the part of Saint's benevolence, but at the same time you would find pickpockets, con men, drug addicts, pimps, criminals..."
"But why they are allowed there?" I asked him.

"Saints of any religion would share one common goal... the welfare of the society. Their spiritual path leads them towards God and then God reflects himself through them as he reflects through all of us. But I think the passion of a saint to be in "oneness" with God isn't an ordinary one. I think in shrines and in all other sanctified, and holy spaces, godly manner is presented. Look at this world... rapist, child molesters, murderers, terrorists, they all live between us. God keeps them alive, feeds them too though he knows their intentions and actions. But just as a mother who never loses hope over her failed child, I guess God thinks the same about his creation. Nature is hopeful for tomorrow. So, we are and so are the saints, otherwise, this world is a doomed and damned place since at least for the last 500 years, but still, life is on." He smiled and sounded very different to me.
"I'm taking you for a unique cultural experience. I'm not sure you would ever see that many people engaged in various activities. Just one hour at the shrine and then we can do a short trip to the old city if traffic and time allow."
While driving, he told me something very mystical.
"It's quite possible you are going through this alchemy to turn you to something else." He breathed deeply and exhaled slowly as if he was contemplating a thought. 'The mentor' removes the veil from one's eyes and then you can see through all. I think you don't understand this, but you will one day, currently, you see someone behind this veil for example 'MEER' but when this veil is unveiled you might find something else. He was trying to select his words carefully.

"Are you trying to say that you can't step into the same river twice?"

"In a way, I can elaborate what I'm saying by telling you the story of Farid-ud- Din Attar's 'Conference of the Birds' but I will say that the Final Truth is yourself." Adeel kept his eyes fixed on the road as he confused me with his very philosophical talk.

"Ji-Su, life is easy if you perceive it simply; leave the complicated matters in the hands of the unknown when unknown fears haunt you. We can run to chase the prize, but we can't always be the winner. Neither we are running alone in race, nor do we know the meaning of victory and the cost of it." Adeel spoke as he was in trance.

"What's yours will get to you." He grew silent and Lahore's traffic filtered through the silence.

"But there's no harm in trying to win," I spoke my mind reluctantly.

"But no one wins when they are hurting themselves in any race and can you say that you've been not trying enough? Or exhausted enough?"

I nearly had tears in my eyes.

We were walking through a crowded passage that leads to the main entrance of the Shrine. Both sides of the narrow street were full of stalls, traditional sweet and savoury snacks, petals, flower assortments, kiosks where you can purchase pre-cooked food for charity, religious and devotional music sellers with unleashed speakers, men dancing on a wild rhythm of *Dhol*. The beat came into my feet and moved inside me like a swirling tornado reaching to the higher ends of my soul and swinging me into a different world, in a Darwish trance. I was tapping my foot as my conscience danced with the men who were performing a sort of shamanic dance in front of shining fabric embroidered with Arabic scripture. People were putting money in the centre of it, and many came to kiss and touch the cloth with their eyes.

"They are taking this for the Master's Shrine," Adeel whispered in my ear.

We stood aside to pass the proceeding and followed them into the main building where the white marble floor was packed to capacity. Women, men, kids, elderly, young, infants, everybody seeking the blessings of the benevolent saint.

"I'm going to hold your hand now, so you won't get lost. We will be going towards the shrine. One side is specified for women, but we can just stay in distance, and you can pay your regards to the Lord and ask for a blessing. "Adeel was almost yelling as he navigated us in the rush. The poor man got badly pushed around as he tried to guard me.

"Can we sit down somewhere?" I asked him hesitantly as I looked around after getting a bump at my back from the crowd.

"Let's see, come with me." Adeel pulled my sleeve and rushed further like a warrior into the floating crowd. I didn't know where I was, going through the rush, surrounded by the shoulders and sweating odours when I looked up to breathe some fresh air when I saw some Arabic calligraphic scripture on the face of the sanctum. "Treasure benefactor from whom the world benefits, revelating God's light. A perfect mentor of imperfect ones, so the mentor of perfect ones."
"Let's sit here." I heard Adeel's struggling voice when suddenly everything just went into slow motion. Silence moved between the spaces as the noise lost its pitch. We crossed the columns of the shrine. A strange familiarity stroked me. Something was reminding that I'm aware of this. Buddha surrounded me and covered my wounds in comfort. I was in his care and my heart floated towards Mother Mary attending the little Jesus. She bowed and caressed his forehead. I didn't look up, but a soothing and reassuring contact submerged peace inside me, and I physically felt my body's weightless, and I rose, just as someone floats in the air and waves of moonshine passes through. I could see I was growing and transforming into what I was when I was a part of heaven.
"All's one and one's all." My pumping heart told me.
"Who's one and all?" I span within as a galaxy.
"You." Someone spoke.
"Me?" Moving towards the source of immense light in a tunnel reaching infinity at the speed of light, I repeated myself.
"The one who knows one's self is the one."
"But I don't know anything." A pain moved towards my temples from eyes, freezing the nerve.

"If you know that you don't know, then you know that you will! Because the negation of 'I' is the path of 'one' and that's what you are looking for inside yourself, outside, in Meer, in this journey, in your every breath, in and out, around and opposite to Buddha."
"So not knowing is the 'Knowing' all..." I confirmed.
"With correct direction, yes,"
"Where's Meer?"
"You carry him around. You should know where he is."
A massive jerk brought an end to the roller coaster of unbearable light. A universe collapsed and recreated; source shrinks to a dot disappearing within the darkness between eyes as I despaired myself.
"Don't be sad, you want to be with him, you will be with him and that will be just you around him, but not the way you thought it. You can't play someone else's role in life Ji-Su; destiny isn't stopped by death either. Embrace what you have and strive for what you want, but don't lose your mind and life over it, though that's destiny too."
And I saw Meer emerging from the darkness of my eyes. A dark curtain revealed him with a sarcastic grin and hate in his eyes, wide-open arms on the charismatic stage proclaiming some kingdom with a hint of the disapproval of his sheep audience.
"We are entertainers bound by our destinies, no freewill darlings, no freewill tonight I'm sorry. We are living by the night, living by the show and we shall role-play freewill but pardon me. Apologies, apologies, just amusing us and them... Entertainers. Entertainers only, sires."

"Are you ok?" I heard the Adeel's voice as I found myself sitting on the white marble floor with a garland around my neck. He was tapping my very shoulder gently as he was hesitant to intervene.

"I am." I looked around myself as I woke up from a deep, refreshing sleep as a new-born trying to observe its surroundings quickly but calmly.

"Sure? You look very surprised honestly." Adeel looked with a concerned face.

"I'm ok, what's happening?"

"Nothing. I didn't want to disturb you in your meditation, so I waited for a while. I think it's time we should head to the airport now. Are you hungry?" As he completed his sentence a middle-aged mother with an infant accompanied by an old man came around and gave us two naan breads with thick split lentil curry in middle, wrapped tightly in a small plastic bag. She looked at me and showed me the little baby boy with excitement and said something in Punjabi to me. Adeel jumped quickly to translate.

"She is saying she had the child after 15 years of marriage and she's here to thank the benevolent saint. She's here offering food to people daily for one month and she's requesting if you can bless her son."

I didn't know what to say, but I opened my arms to take the child and give him a warm cuddle and a little kiss over his forehead. He smiled and a nurturing love secretly infused deep in our hearts.

"Stay always blessed and married, would wash the faces of seven sons, heat wave wouldn't touch you ever." The mother blessed me as I returned her child.

"Did she really say that?" I asked Adeel as I was sure he was joking when he interpreted it to me.
"She's a villager. That's a traditional blessing. Just smile." And I did with a bow and the old man touched my head like the Pope.
I felt light as a feather on my way to the airport thinking about that child and the mother, about my mother, about my strange experience at the shrine and the message I had. That similar feeling of being at my temple, thoughts about Mother Mary and Jesus at the shrine of a Muslim Saint...
"All's one, one's all."
Does that mean me, and my reflection are one? And what's between is 'I' too?
My mother, father and me are one, my future kids, their father and I too, their father's parents and so on. The reflections of our parents in us and of our ancestors in them and when we reach the source, all is one and in that one is all! Though all are different and other, one doesn't match the other and what matches isn't the same.
 As a child, I was told that I looked like my mother and later the features of my father were prominent in my personality and now going through the old albums I can see my mother's jawline and father's nose in little Ji-Su. Some mornings when I look at a mirror, I find *Umma* staring at me and on other days my *Appa* would peek through my eyes. This repeats daily. I note the way I move my head, the way I look around haphazardly, the way I move my toes, everything I do has impressions of them. I miss them regardless even life isn't always easy around them. Criticism, cynical jokes, comparisons and so many 'DONT'S' because I'm a girl.

The boarding call is just announced as I quietly reflect on my day, on my silent stories of unsaid wishes, prayers and efforts to silence an alive illusion that whispered magic in my ears. But tonight's fading moon wouldn't fall to rise a new sun. Not-yet, just not-yet, till it's all over in this moon fall.

Beginning of the Happy Ending

What would you do if you couldn't stand to look at yourself in the mirror?
When filth runs in your blood and only you know what a miserable, cheap bastard, nasty cunt you are but you can't change yourself. Neither do you have the balls to end your life. You seek a bit of a fresh air to support your hateful self, to drag the baggage of life till the point of no return.
What would you do?
Alcohol, drugs, party hard, fuck? Fuck, fuck, fuck, fuck? Or you seek forgiveness for your sins? Try to avoid all the self-harming nasty habits, start doing charity, participate in fund-raising events, become a volunteer in a local hospital? Or are you like me, unaware how to relax, always ending up doing the wrong thing because we were not taught as growing adults how to calm from within? We were always given an external stimulus to force the change inside though the method should be more holistic, but who the fuck knows what that shit means, right? When parents have bills to pay and food to provide, luxuries to pursue, or sexy dreams to fulfil because that's all what they were taught and learned to preach, but then what choice do parents left with when it comes to mentoring kids? Tough competition, rising poverty, lesser jobs, increasing interest rates, devaluation of the money, housing crisis, food shortages... No parent wants to see their child suffering or struggling, caught up with criminalised thoughts. So, what does that tell you?

"The fucking system is broken." I'm not saying that but my kingmaker, politician father did when I spoke with him for the last time.

"Meer, we rule and decide for the sheep. How difficult is it directing the stupid, ignorant, illiterate innocent herd? Don't be afraid of power and politics." I heard a husk in his voice "Do you really want to work in some cubicle from nine to five or want to be a businessman? Who must lick the balls of the customers, shareholders, employees? And God knows how many times you need to bend over and split your cheeks for different governmental departments and others who use you as someone on the other end of glory hole. Fuck it, who needs that kind of bullshit!"

I was shocked. My dad knew about glory hole... fuck! That's learned on his secret trips to Europe and America. Well, who am I to judge? I'm no different and the same genetics corrupt me when my brain shuts down. Thoughts blind as bats throwing themselves effortlessly into a black hole of sinking conscious and drowning without leaving a sign. I had no clue how I ended up at Pushpa's flat on that evening after passing out on a snowy street earlier that day.

P for Pushpa, P for prostitute.

Have you ever heard of a gigolo using the services of a *Prostitutka*?

I know this sounds odd but come on, we are normal people involved in the pleasure business who want some fun too. We need support when depressed. We need love and care just like you, just like others who hate us. I'm still looking for ones who love us, not just accept our presence in society because we pay taxes, but truly appreciate what we do.

Do you know any?

We are entertainers performing in the darkest streets of the city under the brightest lights with the least respect. Forget admiration… the clapping we are used to isn't the one you heard. But you did hear our kind 'nicknames', society use them every day to show their sheer gratefulness towards us.

Whore, slut, pimp and other unimaginable disrespecting words in all languages of the world, paying tribute to the world's oldest profession of absorbing and accommodating the filth of society to keep the purity of the hypocritical cultures. Throughout centuries double standards prevailed because of prostitution. It's the blood of the scum of the earth, which drew a line between wrong and right. But who was drawing that line?

Pushpa and I are acquaintances, not friends. But she seemed bizarrely familiar to me. I must accept that fact reluctantly. In the real world we know each other for the obvious reasons. We did a customer together once, one obsessed with tan skin and Indian culture, history and spiced food. We were kind of experiment for her that involved some tantric practices of which I had no clue but my colour tone, creamy Kama sutra and Pushpa's well-practiced 'yoni' massage and tantric techniques did the job. As a professional, I've great respect for her work. The way she comforts her clients like a 'geisha' and the way she acts and carries herself. I'm truly a fan of her style, impressed since the beginning but as always, class comes with a price. She's on the higher end of the market with a registered therapy business under her belt.

"Oh, don't tell me, I came here... Shit!" I saw Pushpa sipping red wine, peacefully resting her feet in a cosy blanket on a gigantic comfortable sofa while reading some thriller.

"I won't tell you." She answered without disturbing her concentration.

"Oh *Panchod*, I fucked up." I knocked my forehead against the pillow. "Please tell me please, what did I do?" I felt worse from the guilt building inside.

"You puked Meer, that's all. No harm done and please... no foul language in my flat." She didn't bother to look at me again.

"I'm sorry, but I vomited? How did I get here? Did I go to your workplace?" I was annoyed that Pushpa wasn't paying any attention to me.

"No, you didn't. How can a drunk man walk 3 miles?" She turned to look at me for the first time. "I was driving this morning to work when I found you on the street, drunk, lying in the pavement, covered in snow. So, I picked you and brought you back to my flat."
"So, I was sick in the car?" I looked at her hazel eyes over the slightly darker olive tan.
"No, just on me, when I tried to get you up." She smiled.
"Holy shhh... I'm sorry, I am extremely sorry Pushpa." shaking head in regret, my eyes wandered on Pushpa's body, her long neck slipping into a low-cut, sleeveless vest. I felt my fingers running over her smooth arms, reaching her shoulders grabbing and bending them to lean, pulling her hair...
My lust was stroking deep in her waters.
"You messed your cloths when you threw up, so I took your clothes off. By the way, why don't you wear any boxers?" Her gaze returned to the thriller with a meaningful, mischievous smile.
"Yeah, just trying to be professional." I laughed as I jumped out of the bed hesitantly but shamelessly... to piss, to ease the hard-on, instigated by sensual goddess sitting across. Shaking her anklet carelessly in black underwear, vibrating sensuality, visually shagging me in cold, dead, dark corners of myself where I lost ignition long ago.

I realised older you are, more pervert you get, harder to excite. No wonder adult toys industry, pornography and all the other businesses and services of prohibited pleasures flourished leap and bounds by the help of narrow boundary conservative cultures, so does the outrageously open, free, easy access sex societies had done their damage in decreasing regularity level of 'Normal Sex'. But again, what the fuck is normal? Is monogamy normal? Doesn't it bore anyone to death after few years? Polygamy fucks you up in the ass, obviously, for several different reasons. Free sex and casual nudity undoubtedly decrease the thrill and charm of nakedness, what's hidden is exciting and enticing.
Didn't you hear of blindfolding and role-play... acting to be someone else, isn't pretending is an invisible blindfold on both parties?
And doesn't that make the idea of *burqa* sexy?
From what I heard modern wealthy Arab women wear nothing underneath *burqa*, only posh lingerie... what a tease, jeez! So new Arabs are not only just rich but dirty too! And from what I recall, the 'indecent darlings' of red-light district Lahore used to wear '*NIQĀB*' when leaving the old town to mingle with the regular crazy society or going out for the 'on call' jobs. And not just them, but also the city girls with conservative background too, when embarking on an illicit and illegitimate date always used *hijab* for safety, after bunking the college for secret naughty spotty date behind the doors of underground hotels and cafes.
Head scarves are famous to hide messy, un-shampooed hair or grey hair with full makeup. Just check with girls for more alternative benefits.

So, *burqa* is oppressive? Think again!

And again, I looked at Pushpa's beautiful, slim tan legs shaking her gold anklet vibrating to stir sexuality in my ill intensions. Little pink bow below her navel on a nearly see through underwear and Pushpa's sexy legs drawing from them. Her anklet resting on one knee playing an unknown rhythm. Something moved within, moistened below the bow...

"I'm hungry." I smiled with a meaningful gaze at her lips.

"Biryani's coming."

"I guess... we can manage 'something' before Biryani?" I winked at her and swiftly stepped closer, moving my fingers sensually over her silently exciting nipple under her vest. I was perfectly provoking the stormy pleasures inside the dark berries when she said breathlessly.

"When was the last time that you were in bed with someone, someone whom you're in love, with someone who's attached to you, with someone who loves you for what you are and not for the heavenly orgasm you give?" Startled... Rita flashed in my eyes as I grabbed her firm boobs.

"Do you know I'm married?" Pushpa mumbled.

"Meer, do you remember when was the last time? That the person whom you love isn't in the same room where you're naked with someone else, shuffling intimacy to forget your insignificant half?" Pushpa pulled my hair to unhook me from her.

"Answer me, when was the last time?" I saw an evocative threat raised in her voice reaching her red eyes.

"Last night."

"That's good, good..." She rubbed her nose against mine and said, "I will make you pay before you leave." And pushed my face where salt was slightly stronger than my taste.

"Can you lick me stronger?" Pushpa's sweet but blunt voice crossed inside me as I wrestled feebly against Rita. It was a darling's request, initially.

I stroked my tongue disobediently as Rita's face haunted me. Her nipples were aroused under the bra. Goosebumps on her arms, waiting anxiously as her heart pumped passionately. Rita secretly moved her fingers to reach where unknown thrills flooded her. She was waiting for me, as I dreamt of her again in the bed of a different woman, mumbling in a familiar language reminding me of Mishki for a second and her orphan kids. Where were they now?

Pushpa garbled in Punjabi.

"*Amritsar, Amritsar...*" She had her forefinger rubbing her forehead in a pleasing trance, where a healed wound left a horrible mark, turning blood red. I was bothered, shivered by the scare to fall through the fading crack and soak into blood. I wanted to stop her, interrupt her during the unfaithful ritual, I wanted to talk...

So does Rita, waiting for me with my child inside her.

"I must return." A gut feeling shook me.

"Go to her and hold her in your arms. Tell her how much you missed her, how much you're in love that not another thought shared your mind, just her... all around, wishing she would be all day with you, walking by Vltava, holding hands..."

"For fuck's sake can you please lick me stronger?" Pushpa's annoyed, shrill voice reached me.

"Lick my clit like a Punjabi man down on his favourite meal using his fingers and tongue passionately. Don't be a shit. You owe me this and 8,000 Koruna for what you are doing my Paki honey."

A wave of volcano raised, erupted and melted to run and burn all inside me.

In that second my arm moved quicker than angry thoughts like a python, choking, sinking Pushpa's life, drying final breaths as I wanted to slap this bitch trying to degrade me for her gratification, seeking compensation for my sin. I pushed her face into the wall with the other arm, ignoring her weak punches, losing the fight for her life. She was nearly blue when I eased my grip, and a stream of blood ran down her nostrils. Hate and fear returned my unforgotten past as I pulled her hair and slammed her against the bed frame again and again ruthlessly. I tugged at her half dead face and shouted...

"Bitch I am not yours! I am not your slave, I'm Meer... Meer!!" And threw her face into the wall.

Lava was running in her veins when Rita smiled, waiting for me with a soul inside her. "Come home now, come home." She whispered, and I didn't take another second to decide what to do. I looked around for clothes and didn't spare a gaze for Pushpa.

"Push PA, living by your name, yeah? Push of English and Pa (enter) of Punjabi!" I mocked her as I slipped on my pants quickly and looked around for my T-shirt when I suddenly fell powerless. A sharp pain in my ribs and spine handicapped me, landing me flat on the face. Pushpa was roaring, standing above my head with an iron lamp that she thundered again on my collar bone, nearly missing the face as I turned to see her.
"I will kill you bastard. You're a snake who bites the feeding hands." She aimed at my head again when I kicked her stomach and ran breathlessly towards the door. Pushpa targeted the lamp on my spine. I fell on my face as she ran towards me and threw herself on my back, leaving me numb. Pushpa pulled my hair and chewed her sharp teeth on my earlobe before she smacked punches on my neck. I tried in vain to move away from her brutal hammering, but my body couldn't move, and I laid as a dead punch bag on the floor when my fingers touched a piece of glass, already covered in someone's blood.
"Fuck you Meer! Fuck you! Fuck you! Fuck you!!!" Pushpa was punching and cursing me as she was on revenge from a past life and now, she caught me for her vengeance. She was nailing elbow blows on my spine, drilling them hard in joints as I yelled in pain.

"I have hated your face since I met you. I knew today's my day when I saw you on the street, drunk as fuck! My husband is on his way, and we will cut your cock and cook it for you, before I shave your broken legs and my husband shaves doner meat from them. Imagine the pleasure, imagine the pleasure!" She madly clapped her hands from excitement and bowed to whisper, "cannibalism"

"What?" I fastened my grip on the glass as I shivered within, seconds before I thrashed the sharpness powerfully with a reverse fist and filled the crack with blood. I stabbed the glass where the fading mark was bleeding from her fresh wound, blinding her right eye. Pushpa's screech pierced the walls and fountain of blood sprinkled and streamed everywhere as I threw her on the floor and smacked a powerful punch to shut her up.

"This is it, this... is... it!" I pressed my left hand on her face as I started choking her with the right. A vision... blurred to clear suddenly, caged for decades, freed to reveal itself as I took her life slowly, her heart pumped faster to beg for life, fading the existing reality into an old one.

I'm staring at Pushpa's corpse, just as I stood on her old body, thinking... this is the beginning of the happy ending. Happy! Ending! What could be a happy ending? A Bollywood finish, an end with happy tears, balloons and love. Where all goes well by defying logic. The "lived happily after' notion is bought by us all. The pasture is greener on the other side and in chasing dreams, hope and satisfaction life becomes a circus of choices. Entertainers like somersaults...High to higher to highest.

And I just hit my highest as I plunged Pushpa to the darkness of annihilation. I laughed at her mortifying screams reaching me from hell, wishing me to burn eternally. Laughing at her helplessness, I poured a large peg of whisky with a hand dripping with her blood to treat my internal and external wounds. I rested my feet on Pushpa's face as I tasted my drink and looked at her boobs, a bulging urge to fondle those tits rose within. I wanted to learn the difference between breathing boobs, pumping a full of life heartbeat behind them and the cold dead breasts. "Are they still suck-able?" I thought, when something scolded me for my temptation.
"What the fuck are you doing?"
"What the fuck, what the fuck, what the fuck!" Echoed inside my head.
I shamefully moved my feet and wandered off with my wounds and whisky. I wasn't rushed, instead calm and relax. Comfortable, in fact, with my animalistic instincts taking control of me. I felt like a wild, powerful beast that isn't afraid to kill another if he must. Basic survival instinct turned me into a vicious, cunning monster looking around for prey. I wasn't afraid of Pushpa's husband, who would be coming in any minute, or the police called by a suspicious neighbour. I was ready to shed blood for a safe escape. But how I could do that cleanly? Sharp pains in my body, a severe headache, probably a broken rib or two, signs of nosebleed with a swollen face and blood stains everywhere.

"Is there any other option, a safer option?" I asked myself, knowing that the police would enter this property soon to investigate this murder and my fingerprints, blood, hair, could lead their forensic team to me... if I didn't take care of this mess.

"My exit must be clean, without a mark of me left." I told myself, limping around the two-bed property for few minutes before reaching to a decision.

I locked the flat and hopped into the shower for a quick wash to clean myself and sponge down blood from my body. I used a fresh towel on my painful body before I walked into Pushpa's wardrobe. My eyes were looking for a long skirt and some thick black tights that could fit me. I selected a deep blue dress, a grey trench coat and a black scarf with navy blue woollen tights. I ran back to the bathroom to shave.

Next step, make up.

To date, like any other masculine straight man, I knew nothing about applying makeup.

Men have seen women taking off their makeup, applying makeup remover on a cotton pad and rubbing it against their skin, washing their faces before they slip into bed. But who saw them applying makeup? Painting a mask to beautify themselves, enhancing their features or hiding the flaws. I had some good luck to witness a few ladies doing their makeup on the tube in London, turning ordinary faces to deceiving beauty pageant contestants within minutes on a crowded train.

I know there is some base they apply on the skin, before stroking blush-on over their cheekbones.

"Is this foundation?" I looked nervously to a bottle and squeezed some liquid out and rubbed it on my face.

"It's not a good idea, not good." I looked at myself in the mirror, reflecting a perfect idiot with shit-coloured liquid on my face. My hands grabbed some cotton pads to even the foundation. I looked odd because the foundation didn't match my colour tone, but I keep rubbing the cotton pad to smooth the layer. I pulled the leggings on and slipped into the dress, put the trench coat on, adjusted scarf and used a black wig I found on the side of the dressing table. I jumped into my shoes and looked at myself in the mirror... a sexually confused depressed man, who desperately wanted to run away from his identity looked back.

"Fuck my life!" I shied away from my own reflection and went out of Pushpa's bedroom with a bottle of nail polish remover to find something flammable. I wanted to destroy all the evidence. I ignited one magazine and threw it on the bed to burn and turn my sins into ashes. Fire was moving quickly when I limped out of the flat. Luckily, I didn't come across anyone in the corridor. I limped across the alley, struggling to move quickly away from the building...hoping to find a taxi or a bus stop. Streetlights are few and cars are fewer. Snowflakes are on my face washing off my ugly makeup. I come to a main road to bus stop. But I'm not feeling confident enough to face people with my current getup of an undone drag queen.

Luckily a taxi pulled over and without wasting a second, I sat inside the taxi and without looking at driver I said "*Hlavní nádraží*, central station." He was staring at me. I could see he wanted to say something, but he returned his gaze back to the front as he started the engine. He was driving but his curious eyes stayed closely on me through the rear-view mirror. 536 Koruna. I counted the fare.

I thought again to ask him to take me directly to the flat but didn't want to risk showing him my address. I stuck with central station, the meeting point of the good, bad and ugly of the society.

I left the taxi and flowed into the crowd, seeping into the central station. No one bothered to waste their time on me, and the ones who did on the escalator I passed quickly, making my way to the metro.

I was in a rush to be at the flat, change and meet Rita. I was already late, but I couldn't dare let her see me dressed this way. I start to feel sick in the carriage but held my breath to stop the nausea. People were moving away from me. Undoubtedly, I looked bad and smelled worse, a weird foreigner. How hideous this would get if I puke? I thought.

Spinning head, red eyes, snow fall...Don't remember how I made it to my street.

"21:14" I looked at my watch.

"I'm late! I'm late!" Shaking head denial, I ran towards the flat to save a last chance to be with Rita. I didn't think about anything else but to go and meet Rita and then ask her to take me to a private hospital. The broken rib was killing me; I felt some bleeding wound at my back, and a jagged pain in left thigh. I felt worse as I neared the door. Earlier I took two painkillers with last sips of whisky from hipflask, but as I enter the flat, I fell on my bed unable to move, cold and pain sawing inside my rib cage. I dragged myself to the kitchen for a glass of water and some alcohol to drink and to disinfect my wound when I heard a knock at my door.
"Oh, for fuck's sake!" I shouted with frustration as the doorbell followed the knock.
I was still in a long skirt, leggings, makeup on the face, only the trench coat and scarf were on the sofa. I was annoyed as hell, when buzzer rang again and I smashed the glass against the wall and pulled the leggings down and swiftly freed myself from skirt as I cracked my bones in the effort and splashed water quickly on my face to get rid of the makeup, I threw the wig in the bin when I stepped on the glass shard.
"Fucking hell!" I yelled in pain.
I stared at the mirror, a puffy face, red nose, burning body, bleeding wound... I was in perfect condition to visit the A&E, when I opened the door. Kumari was freezing in the snow, fuming, and her expression melted as snowflakes disappearing on her coat.

"What happened Meer?" She worriedly stepped forward to enter when gravity pulled away my balance as frosty wind cut through the bare body, sawing flesh and bones, lashing unbridled pain to my heart as million needles pricked it at once. I fell on my weight, powerless... like bones melted to dilute by a poisonous alchemy of blood in a reversal of life. Kumari rushed to hold my helpless existence before I crash to shatter in an unknown on the floor. But...

This is a beginning of a happy ending?

Back to Origin

All's dark and I don't remember a thing. The last memory is the worrying face of Kumari and her shout... losing voice in the depth of my mind to raise and emboss an impression on my memory but all's just vague in deep darkness. Kumari's cold fingers on my face, bow... to put her lips on mine, the comfort of warmly soft lips sponged the last memory and then it's all dark. Some voices left shadows behind, whispers around me, just as dew drops fall silently in desert, no impact... silence pertains, pattern follows...

Life brought me back to the origin of my existence. I'm awake but I'm not. I swim inside myself as I look outside to understand the life around me. I see colours, I see patterns, I hear voices, I understand, yet I don't comprehend. The communication isn't embedded in the existence and one day I opened my eyes to reach where I was, yet. I wasn't decided on subsistence.

"Meer, are you ok?" A kind voice rose in the darkness, whispered in my ears before I heard an ocean, waves surrounding me but a deep silence behind currents held a holy secret within. Disciplined quietness, a sacred spot where stillness is law. I submerged by mighty authority and again I heard an uncommon voice coming through, passing my partial blindness.

"Are you awake?" I thought I heard myself... a feminine voice.

"Kumari?" I moved towards the whisper.

"She's at her flat."

"Rita? I don't... Who are you, where am I?" I moved my weightless head towards the sound.

"Rita's doing a pregnancy scan now." She silenced my conscious. I saw Rita's lubricated belly being scanned by a sonographer and Kumari in a kitchen, while Amelia played with Shahanara. I was inside the living room, also next to Rita looking at the screen.

"What's that?" I asked.

"That's all of us."

"All of us? I'm sorry, who are you?" I felt within unrecognizable warmth of being as I glowed like a firefly for an instant.

"I'm you; you can call me Meera." She smiled within my blankness. "When you were decided to be a man as our mom conceived, I was there too. You were born and I took the birth too. It's just not me but 'you' are in hundreds, and we are alive together with you but now as you are clinically dead, you can hear us, feel us, talk back to us."

"I'm dead?" I moved restlessly.

"Clinically, yes. We brought you here and now we are waiting."

"Waiting?" I felt a cold breeze.

"So, you can be through this transition."

"I'm not ready to die." A deep sadness widened inside me.

"Who is ever ready to die?" Meera was amused by my answer. "We just die. That's why we are created, to experience and then fade. Everyone dies. But don't worry, I might get a body next time and you would be my alive invisible counterpart, or we both could be invisible unknowns in another dimension."

Silence muted all as something melted within. I passed to an open sky where a wish of being alive swam swiftly again inside, cold wind blew over and I froze on a point between will and action, conscious and unconscious. Colours, waves, marks, stars and sounds around the unseen breaths went into a dark tunnel and I saw my mother smiling opposite me. I recognized at her not from the memory but from the love blossomed in heart infinite ages ago and bloomed. My dad was behind her, a pale face and my brother?

"They are here to welcome you." Meera said softly, whispering.

"And there's no turning away?" I confirmed as I seek the other end of the ocean where world would be moving in an old pattern without me... carefree.

"Yes, not from across there, once you move to the world of conceded souls, but..."

"But?"

"Life isn't what you left. Life is what is left after you. A wish to be alive and be in love, wish to nurture one's offspring and give another opportunity to self, to complete and satisfy the immortal urge of completion is an obsession of mortal psychology, evolution means that you reborn with your child. So, it's not you but the calling of your unsatisfied life Meer, forcing you to go back. You are not dead. You are held between life and death but your stubbornness clinging to life will not change the past. You can go back and wake up at the hospital where you are in a coma. Between this, Kumari and Rita came across each other and Amelia and Sahanara played together. Babel's planning to visit your flat because you left her hanging way long to dry and..."

"And?" I added.

"And the police are reviewing the building's CCTV recordings from the night you tried to burn Pushpa's flat."

"Ji-Su will visit Prague soon; she's constantly looking for you."

"I expected that." A grief of losing precious pearl of life was spreading within.

"The world isn't an attractive place anymore. It is all downhill and you will go down very soon as you get back." A sensation to silence or differ aroused sturdily. "And I know you will ask why but you have all the answers too. Decisions are decided in the moment when conscious is creating unconscious. Reactions and results are merely mirroring us, reflecting our destiny. Choices are limited and fixed, here and there too." A polite pause pushed me powerfully towards my mother as she blurred with all in deep darkness spin, an unknown pain spiralled me down to an unending tunnel opening in a circle where a flood of transparent entities fired like bullets towards my vacuumed free-fall. Dropping in nothingness of future I expected zilch but a joint to my previous life as I invisibly raced towards a suicide in nature's den... darker, vaguer, quieter. I lost sense slowly as I was forced to rest in an uncomforting spell releasing to reality from unknown. Light of life changed to unseen colours within cataracts when I heard strange voices as I floated in a bubble of surrounded darkness. Waves, rhythmic waves playing the song of the lost river, dried to desert as distant shores wrapped in dense darkness dawned to life drifting towards an open-end question.

"I was there... but I... wasn't ...wasn't where I..." Whirling as a burning moth in midnight darkness, hammering madness against circled cage to escape from the reflections enclosed in the mirror of the future.
"I was there... but..."
Days passed when I was crashing like a wing-clipped bird slicing blankness of a different divine space in lust of life but didn't wake up from my permanently brief death on the blue planet but behind the end of a long, odd, dimly breathing tunnel, opening to unknown. A mysterious awe enticed me to set foot on a passage full of small, faintly sparkling pebbles, sharp as broken glass pinching themselves painfully in my essence, seeking attention, to reveal something, to warn... "Don't, don't." whispered by the air holding her breath silently as I curiously glided with an evaporating body towards the dead silence and smoke with a wall dragging itself behind me, filling the only escape, pushing me out to face the destiny at destination. I'm lighter and lighter... bleaker... when an unbearable pain burned my feet, resisting to move like an animal who know it's being lured towards its death, a gunshot, a sharp dagger to slit the throat and pump all the breaths of life out with blood... I know something is coming.

Probabilities

"Blair vows Britain will not be intimidated as more than 40 killed and hundreds left injured this morning as terrorist attack the capital."
A dark room is splashing in glaring colours coming out of a muted television. Walls, windows, tightly covering curtains all painted by the gleaming light, shadow and dark rainbow of television covered the hue of this miserably stinking room I entered.
"Four terror bombs blast commuters in London this morning killing over 40 people and left hundreds of Londoners injured as Al-Qaeda cell claims responsibility."
Stunned & bewildered by the horrible footage of severely injured, harshly wounded people, pictures of the blasted bus and trains running on telly, I was witnessing the catastrophe of 7/7 bombings as audio descriptions blinked chaotically on the television screen. I noticed there was someone else in the room, someone waiting for my attention. In the room's corner, standing quietly. A hue moved forward from invisibility to the light of recognition, when familiarity sparked my eyes with astonishment.
That's me! Meer.

My astral body looking plainly towards me, detachedly indifferent, rather bothered by my presence as he isn't willing to be there, looking at me hypnotically in a paused deep silence before he pointed his finger towards the door on my left, facing a long rectangular mirror against the exit. My eyes followed as the finger moved in linear motion from the other end, turning my head remotely to witness the tragedy.
I was murdered.
My corpse was lying in a frozen pool of blood clutching a grand kitchen knife stiffed below the heart.
"Is this really me?" I looked in denial at the corpse.
"Really, this is me...dead? Murdered but not brutally slaughtered in an unknown flat rotting in my own flesh."
I looked at my astral body quietly fading out in thin air, leaving dissatisfaction behind, when I modestly requested a few moments of presence and focus.
"No!" A large vibration strummed inside me to quiver my essence.
"No?" I humbly repeated the answer opposite to the rebellious prisoner shouting with his questions inside the cage of my erratic conscious.
"Who am I, where am I? What's all this circus of death, life and life beyond the death... soul, spirit, astral bodies, angles, protectors. Who are you? WHO ARE YOU?" He shouted, madly, angry vibrations strummed as I looked back at my corpse and returned the gaze to the Master Astral body.

"You would know all in right time. I'm not here to unveil 'The Unknown' which's beyond the boundaries of our understanding. But an answer to your stubbornness is this, that all's recorded, it's the matter of dimension you travel in or could exist in. Life and death are hidden in several layers, each completing a 360° cycle before returning back to the point where all started and that dot matches another vertically increasing or decreasing stage, rooted to other parallel universes in a sequence to infinity. No one ever knows all and 'All' will never know *'One'* if one isn't aligned in any pattern with a specific element of existence. You survived surprisingly and more astonishingly here in the world of the final mirror but who brought you here?
"I." he said.
A bubble boiled in the pool of blood as I turned towards the corpse and popped with its only breath. But before I understood he was gone and so does the host seeking annihilation rather liberation from the tiresome journey of individual existence leading to nowhere unguided. Quitting isn't an option.
And what options did I have?
Me, my dead body and disturbed darkness exasperated by lunatic television, spelling addictive blood pressure shooting vibes, poisoning the space within the space when furious machine strangely started blinking to corrupt and died abruptly with its last flash.

Darkness howled from the gut of silence as noir splashed to the corners, blinding the seeping blankness as feathers of mysterious shadows wrapped all to breathe the stillness... incantating murky illusions to haunt the gloom as captured silence whispered to the ears of my shadowy loneliness.
"Am I alone?" I thought.
"You are not." A deep voice dawned from the depth of emptiness.
"It doesn't matter who you are or where you are, I invited you to see for yourself and decide. What matters is how you reached your end. Destination matters!"
"Destination matters..." I mumbled.
"And what about the journey? Hey, who are you... hello... hello?" I heard an echo back as I spoke in a deep cave of blackness where darkness was darker than the sleep of the dead... Sleep of the dead? How did I know that? Did I depart?
Could be... could be that I'm already consumed by death, or I tasted the death and my claustrophile soul is having nightmares in the final resting, there's no home to go to. Universe is my oyster but reluctant to accept that unexpected liberty raised mystified sensations of fear and unsurety, spitting poison of horrifically ugly questions to utter loneliness.
"Where to now and for what, to whom? Did I survive a prison for another prison?"

I thought the initiation of death rolled the same question I faced after every emotional trial of life! Or is it a joke? Just as life fools us throughout. What is life? What could be the answer to this simple question rooted deep in complexities of the spectrum of existence spread across the universe and beyond the wild imagination of an intelligent conscious constantly going through identity crisis. "Who am I?"
What could be a perfect response of this? As I coexist simultaneously in parallel universes, unknowingly correlating to my counterparts and their Karmas then who am I? Am I the one living with my active conscious or am I the result of over 90 percent of brain activity that goes beyond the conscious awareness? Could that be that same 95 percent is acting as a central controlling hub for the rest of 'Terminals' working 'Differently' in different spaces then no wonder that my 'conscious daily routine' goes through several minute, unusual responses during the day in result of the 'Same brain' work process, juggling trillions of activities in each fraction of a second, energizing life through at least ten parallel universes each containing a form and a physical brain.
The question stands the same, "Who am I?" Making me wander in unknown territories to wonder about 'Life' swinging me from a point to another, extreme opposite and back... back towards where I started. Am I suffering from action paralysis in the afterlife too?

Suddenly the room trembled as I was lifted in the air and spun without gravity in whizzer of darkness to the point where blankness turns into a bright star, far in a galaxy on clear dark night as you twirl in tornado. Shooting, rocketing towards that source of energy with the speed of light and with every instance the majestic gets greater, grander and intense in its power and attraction that one realises it's not the speed but the magnetise of the reflection of 'The essence' of the essence which sparked once on the mount of Sinai. I was mesmerized by the purity of that brightness which unveiled till I was blinded of the sight, where all revealed to my conscious as I was asleep and now, I woke with an understanding of the secrets behind what the natures conceal and behind that logic connecting to unknown yet known facts. I looked at planets; I looked at numbers; I looked at karmas; I looked at eras; I looked at challenges and passions; I looked at revenges and punishment... I understood. I learnt... I understood me and I understood her... I understood death!

1 / ∞

Scene opens as I arrived to a quiet corner of a German bordered Czech village in outskirts of Liberec, silent as an alchemist, watching the last moments of his dream turning to 'Perfection' when birds with golden wings flapped across the skies as sun melted behind the trees, floating gold in lake waters reflecting to blind the birds, flying to the unknown skies to seek the truth of the world... were they Farid-ud- Din Attar's? Searching for the truth? I looked at them and followed to find "where's my life at?" But as they crossed the deserted main square of the village they disappeared, as God hides in his silence after a glimpse.
A gentle summer afternoon is caressing my essence, blossoming a field of sunflowers under the warmth of bright sun sparkling me as a golden star twinkling on a dark clear night. I'm glittering with yellow sapphires within, soothing me in this strangely quiet village. I strolled down the street by the church looking at the unfamiliar faces for a clue. No one approached, no one spoke, and no one even looked at me. Teenagers, elderly silently walk in streets wearing the same expression on their faces, saddened on arrival of the unwelcomed. I looked on their long faces closely, but I couldn't tell where they held the pain in their heart holding away from stony eyes, but they were perfect in their sorrow.

I ignored their hypnotic presence around me and looked at the gentleman's club, waiting for animals to be unleashed in the rich corner of this village. It's still early for 17:00 till late night business to be ready, after the yesterday's hard work of the 'Gentlemen'.

I peeped inside to see the long brushes and wet mops in an effort of sparking the stage floor, where beauties spin in their high porn star heels complimenting their long legs, strong grip and powerful gaze cutting through the faces of audience as they swing craftily around the pole, judging who's the one with uncontrollable lust in their eyes for her body, seeker of her private dance... is he alone or with his mates? Are they a couple? Could be a woman burning in a desire to melt near her, dying to sniff the musk hailing under her armpits and yearn to dig her nose where 'The Lips' splits. Or could it be that middle-aged woman taken her older and now incapable husband for this erotic night-out to stir excitement to produce a *hot* and full of *fun* night, out of him? Is it possible that the man smiling handsomely in that corner with his new girlfriend known in club to be trained bastard in getting the 'Bi' side out of young girls, will he buy a private dance for her?

Lost in the thoughts of the entertainer, I looked inside the old-fashioned strip club to find the broken hopes of past dreamers, now haunting inside the barren emptiness of the building.

I moved away...

A narrow passage leading to a wide street was carpeted with the sunlight. A blank canvas brushed by the rays, raised a dot in the distance turning red as I moved left. A pregnant woman blond slightly curled hair was on the road, panting, covered in blood.

"Rita!" I shouted in an instance as I raced towards her.

"HEY, WHAT HAPPENED?" I yelled as if I could shout through the past to the future.

"Rita!" I ran my shadowy hands on the blood-stained clothes as she continued to bleed between her legs. Her pale face was drenched with fear, tears running down as she suffered the delivery pain. The horror of death was visible on her face; blood dripped from her vagina as cramps and contractions shot arrows of pain inside her, signalling to be ready.

"Hey, keep your eyes open." I saw her eyes rolling as I helplessly looked around feeling the throbbing worthlessness, beating the guilt and shame inside me.

The sound of a roaring Jeep approached, nearer and nearer, slowing and stopping at a safe distance from Rita. I saw a German couple in their 30s running towards her. Within seconds their youthful, sparkling with happiness, smiling faces turned to gravely concern. And without wasting a moment, the guy carried unconscious Rita in his arms while his girlfriend pulled the Jeep next to them and rushed like a wild horse towards nearest hospital as Rita continued to bleed on their back seat.
I rushed with them but as I followed the speeding Jeep my movement halted. I was static.
"You reached the end of your leash." Someone whispered within.
"This is where you stop, move away." An unknown voiced as I exhausted my essence from unrestrained worthless failing efforts, trying tirelessly to follow Rita till the car disappeared in the bright invisibility of melted sun at the end of the road crossing the Deutschland borders.
I turned around hopelessly, dejected in the sorrow of losing her again, just as before and after. Frustratingly confused, questioning, I followed the blood marks, trailing her breaths, following fragrance of her scent perfuming the air calmly and stirring quietly the nostalgia of our surreal past into my existence. I looked at the blood spots marking the road and noticed a nearby farmhouse.
I floated seamlessly towards it, when my gaze wandered to find Jan lying in puddle of blood, dead, stabbed on the side of the building.

"What happened here?" I moved closer when something pushed me away.
"Go to the door!"
"No one's inside." I learned immediately as I saw the facade. Blood stains splashed across the firmly locked door, drawing tear lines of pain towards the frozen cascade of gore carpeted beneath the door gap, peeping through the invisible dark alarming me of the horror quietly breathing behind.
I was prepared...
Dead already, what else could I lose? A spot in Eden after inflicting hell over the people, leashing out pain over innocent hearts? I knew like all of us - where I'm heading after life, in life.
So, when I entered to the other realm of gloom, I was painfully fearless and sad when lightning thundered to shock me to witness the repeated tragedy of my death, stabbed, murdered, stiff, holding a huge knife in abdomen.
"Who brought you here?" Someone asked with authority.
"I?" I heavily replied sorrowfully.
A bubble boiled in the pool of blood and popped as I stepped away from the corpse. But before I understand and grieved my betrayed death, I saw myself opposite shaking in fear looking at some fading entity as he returned his gaze from me.
I knew where I was...

My corpse was celebrating its death by the hands of the passionate beloved who coloured her love and hate with a splatter of crimson... dark, stark, fervour turn to deep ruby blood. I stared in shock at the large kitchen knife firmly resting in belly, slicing the pancreas, lancing stomach and sharpening its blade in my spleen.
"So, it was Jan? And who killed him?" I shook my head sadly in negation as the dead television resumed with a blink, splashing the sparking glare on a confused expression, standing across from me stressing in blindness of finding reason of presence when I noticed familiar faces moving on the screen. "That's me and..." I shouted to myself as Rita appeared on the screen boarding on a coach with me...

Illusion within the Final Dream

Meer and Rita were at the Prague coach station heading towards the terminal, boarding with the Prague- Liberec route passengers.

Rita looked weak and stressed out, bothered by his presence walking beside her in his stylish round glasses with a neat beard, sparkling ear studs, holding a blind cane, rolling the white ball slowly at the end of the stick perfectly to find a passage at *Černý Most* bus station behind his purposely closed eyes and Rita... pulling away with resentment in the shared frame with him, carrying her big belly as she dragged a small luggage, forcing a failing smile to lift her spirits as she showed tickets to the driver with a tired face.

They were miles apart yet trapped within unhappiness of each other's disappointments. One could tell that life ran over them. Reality happened in the background of stern expressions boiling over their unfriendly faces.

"What am I doing, lending a hand to a criminal, assisting a murderer to escape, who happens to be the father of my child." Rita anxiously looked around as the child kicked sharply to distract her worried mother.

"I know, you can feel my distress darling, I know." Rita moved her hands gently over her belly to comfort the restlessness inside as seclusion entered the moment to withdraw her into the serenity of motherhood... absolute bliss.

"Are you ok?" Meer whispered.

"Please, don't talk to me." Rita quickly leaned over to pull the curtain to avoid the sun and the two police officers on patrol.

"What happened?"

"Nothing! I never thought you are this person, Meer." Distressed Rita exhaled, biting her lips as she swallowed her saliva to smooth her drying throat.

"Please, drink some water, please." Meer politely offered a smile as cold air gusted over her sweaty face. The bus finally decided to move.

"And I'm sorry... we can talk later."

"Surely, we will talk more! Once we are there!" Rita replied sarcastically, looking at his silly smile directed in air. Sulking on his flawless acting, thinking 'How perfectly he controlled his expressions as a trained entertainer since they left the house this morning.'

"Do you realize, I'm carrying your child?" She paused to stop her aggressive attack halfway when Meer slapped his thigh in despair.

"I know what you want to say honey but not now, please!" His voice trembled in a struggle to manage the situation.

"Fuck you! You can't control me or drag me into your shit. I can't stand lying, LIAR!" Rita nearly shouted as Meer turned his face knowing the shit storm heading his way.
"If I weren't carrying our child, I would never be here with you Meer." Rita locked her hands together in fear of losing her temper.
"Thank you for being with me." Meer mumbled and tilted his head against the head support.
"Don't bullshit me; don't even try. How can a man can abandon his daughter? What precedent you are leaving there Meer?" Rita was fuming.
"I'm sorry."
"Don't be, because I'm sorry to myself and to our child and to Amelia who's waiting for her baby sister at Kumari's place while I'm..."
"Stop it, PLEASE!" Meer raised his voice.
"Don't you dare to stop me mister!" Absolute anger flashed in Rita's eyes.
"I did not know Shahanara is my daughter! Kumari never told me, and this was all before I met you." Meer clenched his fist.
"Yeah, and before her, there was a South Korean girl; do you have a child with her also?" Rita hatefully looked at him.
"For fuck's sake, what's wrong with you? I was in university back in Newcastle when Ji-Su was my girlfriend."
"Ji-Su, Ji-Su..." Rita repeated her name like she was memorizing a *kototama*.

"So, this Ji-Su and you lived together? Where does she live now? Are you still in touch with her?" Rita raised her right eyebrow as blue eyes turned bluer with fury.

"How do I know where she lives now? And yes, we lived together, but she stayed in her dorm too!" Meer struggled to stay compose, withholding from grinding his anger into words, he was avoiding any more agitation to exaggerate the already exploded situation.

"Just tell her full name, so I can find her and tell her what a selfish, sick bastard you are!" Rita tried to look into eyes that were avoiding her eye contact. Meer was about to ask why she's so hostile today, but he stopped himself from asking the stupid question. He knew what her answer would be... a blunt answer.

"You know Meer, I believe nothing you tell me. I don't believe a thing about your past. I still feel there's something fishy about you. You are hiding something, just as you are hiding now from the police."

"Now you have crossed the limit!" He whispered as he clutched her hand.

The bus was speeding on the motorway while Rita fell emotionally and psychologically apart from Meer. She was massaging her hand with the other and regretting another mistake of believing another wrong man and letting him into her heart. A murderer, an illegal immigrant, a terrible father and possibly a womanizer who lies tirelessly about himself with everyone around him.
"What's there to admire about Meer?" She thought. "A bad choice, no, a worst choice!" Rita boiled her blood more as she feared the nightmares, he could trap her in, as Meer already dragged her in this *bordel* by seeking her help to escape the local police. "What the fuck am I doing?" Rita repeatedly asked herself. "I don't need another headache in life and certainly I can manage this child on my own. This baby is a blessing from God."
"Blessing of God, blessing of God, this baby is a blessing of God." Rita enchanted her affirmation immediately to overcome her fear, to brave her shaking faith. All the Catholic teachings, which she was taught to believe were losing grounds.

"Why did I book the holiday cottage, so he can cross the border and seek an asylum in Germany? What proof does he have that his life is in danger if he went back to Pakistan? And why he came up with this idea *only* when I told him that I don't want to marry him anymore? Why doesn't he seek asylum in the Czech Republic? I'm sure he wanted to marry me to just get residence. Love, child, his emotions all's just bullshit, a big bull shit. He's a good actor, an excellent liar. He would be an amazing entertainer if on stage." Rita hatefully stared at Meer as he stood outside the bus, waiting, while she queued to collect luggage from the driver before they took a taxi to Hrádek nad Nisou, a small village next to Germany.

Rita thought she knew what Meer was planning but he quietly, unsurely kept thinking about the choice of the village. He wasn't definite. A constant blank havoc plagued his thoughts every time he spread the maps of the uncertain future. He had no clue what to do or say since Kumari told him about Prague police raiding his flat. He never said a word to anyone. He wanted to leave Prague soon as possible and staying near the border was an intuitive decision. Meer was utterly quiet as Rita and Kumari were in awkward silence. In the background were noises of Amelia and Sahanara playing together.

No one knew what to do.

Meer was recovering. Rita was pregnant. And Kumari was suffering an emotional shock. They all lived in Pandora's Box. Silence of misery, past mistakes and psychological manipulation wrapped in insomnia, and decency of diplomacy burdened all when Meer decided on his departure. He wanted no more troubles for Kumari because of him, suffering from depression and dejection, Kumari avoided any conversation with him since Rita was there and her pregnancy came as a life shaking shock to her. She wasn't sure what to do, anxiety ate her soul, yet distressed Kumari supported everyone around her. She was happy to see Amelia and Sahanara playing together, and their joy kept them all together.

The day Meer was discharged after a week in the hospital, Kumari brought him to her apartment against his insistence on going to his flat. She knew already the reason for his resistance.

Money.

Meer mentioned the hidden cash to Kumari as they arrived home and within a few minutes, she brought out two massive black bin bags and left Meer alone with them. Piles of currency, personal rubbish, condoms, sex toys, porn, pills. She had been already to his place 'tidying' the mess and money while he was in a coma and very smartly, she used the cash from the hidden stash for funding the hospital admission and other expenses without using any real names or addresses in a private hospital.

Meer was thinking of her since this morning after he left Prague with Rita.

"Did I make a mistake to choose Rita over Kumari?" His thoughts were running in a loop, judging merits and demerits of his decision. Clearly, he regretted abandoning Kumari.

"How I never understood her love, never regarded her as my saviour? She was there every time when I needed her the most and God, I have a child with her, Sahanara my daughter... Sahanara, my lovely daughter." He was in absolute meltdown every time he thought about Sahanara or the unborn child during last few days.

"I'm imprisoned within emotions, logic, needs and dreams... bounded within a triangle." Meer sighed.

"Did I need Kumari? She could have brought so much ease, money and freedom to life." Meer thought and felt disgusted instantly by his own selfishness.

"I can't truly love anyone, can I?" He frustratedly boiled within "I'm incapable of giving love; I see my ease only.... emotional ease, psychological ease, financial ease. I look for my comfort and nothing else. This is the problem, I'm the problem, the true culprit, no wonder nothing goes smooth, and this beginning doesn't seem to resonate with our romantic past. Or maybe it's just the destiny of love, happiness and excitement to meet disappointment, depression and regret, polar opposite of dreamy expectations of youthful love." Another deep sigh came out of Meer as he scratched his head in frustration.

"I bet he's regretting to have me in his life. Typical man, can't take stress and surely not from a woman." Rita shook her head sadly over the shattered dreams. She was hurt, deeply upset with him or with life...disappointed on her for making mistake after mistake, and not learning from the past.

"Don't believe in men. They're vultures, pathetic, hopeless creatures and God, why on earth we show our kids fairy tales. Handsome, perfect prince, saviour of the poor troubled girl, my foot! Women don't need men; men need women! Women don't! And we can do everything, I can do everything, girls can do everything!" Rita repeated her second affirmation when the taxi pulled outside the modestly stylish self-catering cottages for urbanites seeking rural breaks in a quiet village with decent pubs and few restaurants.

Mysterious birds crossed the clear skies slicing the tranquillity of final days of last parallel dimension with their golden wings swishing towards the end of time as Meer unfolded his white cane and quietly waited for Rita. Meer patiently stood aside till the driver reversed and drove away from the cottages. Rita was fuming in silence, breaths away from bursting and tearing Meer apart, but he smartly carried the luggage and gracefully walked ahead of Rita towards the door. He knew another rough conversation is the last thing he wanted today. "She's pregnant, behave! Behave!" Meer reminded himself when Rita quickly crossed him to enter the code on a digital lock. She looked unwell, stressed and angry. Lack of sleep, pregnancy, an uncomfortable journey full of fear with a wanted criminal completely drained her. She was a mess, and all she wished for was a pillow and comforter's cuddle on a decent bed, an uninterrupted sound sleep.

They picked up lunch on the way and the fragrance of freshly roasted chicken and thick cut American style chips was voiding their argument temporarily.

Meer went to the kitchen and added food to the plates, served it nicely and called Rita, busy in getting rid of the tight bra squashing her sweaty breasts. She undressed herself to underwear and walked towards the kitchen with nearly eight months belly and enormous breasts swinging happily on the rhythm of her feet, swollen nipples, raised Montgomery glands on wide areola and fuller thighs. Meer looked hypnotically at her rounded belly and breasts nearing the table. Saliva flowed and collected under his tongue from the juices squeezing from pleasurable thoughts, stroking within sticky waters of lustful intimacy.
"She's beautiful, isn't she?"
"What's so amusing mister that you left your hot food on the cold plate?" She taunted.
"Oi, what you are on about? I know about this smile of yours." Shrill tone of Rita forced Meer to ground.
"If you think you will melt my heart with your stupid smile then you are mistaken." Rita mockingly laughed.
"I'm part of your soul already, I'm breathing inside you with every single heartbeat Rita, I admire you and I find you sexy, my sexy!" He smiled. "You are angry, I'm annoyed but that solves nothing, you want to have a go at me say it all, I won't stop you or taunt you." Meer breathed slowly.
"I love you, regardless of my flaws, sins and inner clash. I love the way you are, and I thank you for being in my life. Thank you for..."

And before Meer finished his sentence, Rita rushed towards him and thawed in his arms. She was someone else when she breathed on his skin.
Moving hands on Meer, she whispered breathlessly "Don't leave me" as their souls swim together in essence of an unparalleled love, reaching infinity. Meer sliding his burning hand over Rita's cheek, slipping fingers over her ear, crossing her temple, grabbing and locking her head gently into an intense kiss, lips inseparable by sweet juices, bodies unanimous by flowing energies fused between them.
Meer raised her heavy thigh gently to seat her on a sturdy oak wood table, laying her over the tabletop, tucking heals on edges, her toes rested in air when Meer kissed them and moved his tongue, sucking passionately as warmth of his palms melt her calf and thighs.
Meer looked at Rita... closed eyes, exhaling heavily, biting lower lip in pleasure as Meer spread the shy thighs away to gaze at his delicious food, just before he scratched the folded knees erotically, sliding down the nails, scratching to mark the dry skin, nearer and nearer to the triangle splashing in waters of anticipated gratification.
Meer was on it, satisfying the lust of his thirst, quenching the deepest desire of Rita to be at peace in love. Meer was finding his way to the lost, hidden door to her soul, and every kiss was taking him nearer to the climax of his destination.

"Sex and orgasms aren't the end but the beginning of a smoother road to a strong relationship." He thought as he gently moved hand over her baby bump, kissing the dew drops over rose petals when Rita got up and pushed him away. Her toes were on his chest when she winked and ran towards their room.
She wanted to be chased... And Meer was chasing the dreams...
Lying beside each other, exhausted, breathing heavily to settle through the happiness rushing in their blood, Meer was revolving restlessly around the kisses and lips of the old Rita. He was thinking what has changed over the period... feelings, the passion, excitement of intimacy and the irresistible wait of when he calms again his body and frees the caged soul into stormy waters of pleasure.
Rita was floating on the waves of emotions, spreading and retreating on shores of love. Her mind was wavering between sure and unsure. What she wanted against what she felt and what's happening inside her was at war. Pleasure was still pulsing within her as she juggled her options of accepting him as an untrustworthy, deceitful criminal, a liar man or to take the loving, warm and very caring side of him...A person whose troublesome life led him to awkward, unusual and strange difficulties to survive.

"What's wrong in seeking the help from someone whom you love?" She thought. "What's wrong in finding a safe passage to a normal life? What would I do if I end up on a street due to unforeseen circumstances?" Rita kept thinking for and against Meer until he broke the silence.
How's your mom? How's Tim?"
Silence faded heavily into an uncomfortable quietness.
Rita inhaled a long deep breath and held it deep to control the floating tears in her eyes, raising to the edges as pain sharply grow deeper and dropped as she exhaled, a tear fell out from the blue lake.
"What happened, what's the matter?" A tear turning into a salty waterfall alarmed Meer. Rita was sobbing. And Meer felt that something is leading to a wrong way.
"They are no more Meer! They are no more!" Rita hysterically shouted in tears as Meer quickly moved to comfort her. She was yelling in grief in the arms of Meer, stroking and petting her back, caressing to sooth Rita into silence but she pushed herself away aggressively and looked with madly boiling eyes towards him.
"He died because of you! Your hate killed him! Your religion killed him! Your people killed him!" Rita Shouted violently.
"What nonsense are you talking? I didn't even know till now, what happened?" Meer raised his tone.

"What happened? What happened? I'll tell you what happened! Just as you killed that poor woman in her house in the name of self-defence, one of your Muslim brothers killed my brother for the same reason, jihad against intruders!"

"What the fuck are you saying Rita, are you out of your mind?"

"Are all of you the same Meer? Killers, murderers, terrorists... I wonder if I can leave my child alone with you Meer!"

"What's wrong with you? Wait, let me understand, Tim's martyred in Afghanistan?" Meer asked reluctantly.

"YES! Where else your Muslim brothers are Jihaading? To bleed our proud and brave lads! Why you idiots don't understand that soldiers are there to protect and save the poor, hungry and vulnerable Afghans and fight right wing Islamist terrorism!" Rita was yelling on the top of her voice.

"They killed my mum too! She couldn't bear the pain of her only son's death, what do you know about relationships, anyway? You are cold, stone hearted bastard who don't give a shit about family, kids or emotions!" Rita hatefully looked at Meer.

"What the fu..." Meer shouted halfway.

"What..." He lost words between empathy and lava boiling inside him. He dropped his voice and went through a silent trance for apathy with closed eyes, deep breaths, massaging his thumb and middle finger over the well-formed eyebrows, looking deep in his head, focusing, calculating the situation.

Meer calmly broke the stillness and raised the tone of his voice softly with all the love he could gather in the moment.

"Is something wrong, Rita? You don't have to do this to breakup with me, I understand I have flaws, I made grave mistakes. I killed someone in self-defence and tried to burn their body and flat to get rid of evidence because I knew no one would believe me. Who will listen to me if I get caught? You think I'm a bad and irresponsible father, I swear on my life that I didn't know that before I met you, I was clueless about my fatherhood." Meer breathe awkwardly with pauses.

"And I... love you so much that I was afraid to lose you. I stayed silent, couldn't tell you the truth about myself and I still couldn't draw enough courage to tell you what I have been through." Meer looked deep in the eyes of Rita, hypnotically losing senses into the depth of deep Blue Ocean, constricting and breathing, dilating his world spreading to the skies, falling, swathing in mist with musk hinting the passage through the jungle whispering out of time. Heartbroken, miserable, misunderstood and troubled Meer was unable to melt Rita.

That evening, he went out and chased an escape within empties. Downing alcohol, sipping beer between vodka shots he phased sadness to depression, freeing him to an uncomfortable ease in head, swinging between a Delphic state and reality.

"Fuck it!" He mumbled.

"Fucking do this, do that... For what? For what, tell me?" Meer laughed.
"No use of struggling for a woman, not worth it! No, no, no... Not worth it my friend, not worth it!" He looked at the man next to him.
"Child is important; children are... they are gold, Zlatá... Zlatá, můj přítel." Meer nearly fell from the chair when vodka influx churned with beer resulted in a hiccup. Something was coming out. Meer held his breath to calm the reflux but the next second he was rushing, knocking chairs, running blindly in street maze, finding his way, sick, throwing up on the corner of a cobbled street, breathless. Meer vomited all the way with an empty rumbling stomach and spinning head till he arrived late at night and slept like a dead horse on the sofa.
Rita was waiting for Meer, expecting his early arrival to apologize for throwing a tantrum but anticipation turned into frustration when she gave up irately on her last hope.
"He's hopeless; our relationship is in the gutter for him already. Why he isn't here, he knows I'm pregnant with his child and regardless of anything he should protect me, care for me." Rita pulled the comforter to her face promising herself to go back to Prague tomorrow and back to England day after, for good.
"End of the story, and I will make sure I won't see his shit face again." Rita grumped and closed her eyes.

The night quietly passed, dipped in darkness and calm. World quietly swung on axis, spinning out of shadows of night, welcoming light. Sun rays passed through the clouds, moving through the trees, penetrating, shining on the leaves, brightening the spaces between, striking through the windowpane, brightening Meer's soothing sleep. Faded dark turned into deep reddish orange when he heard the shower.

"Rita's up." Thought of her alerted to raise him completely. "Surprise her, make a cheese omelette." His brain received signals from the unknown. "A yummy breakfast would cheer her up." Meer excitedly rubbed his hands and ran towards the door to get some groceries.

Cool summer breeze was blowing the trees, comforting warmth of sunrays was blissful, fresh air breathing the fragrance of freshly cut grass wrapped in hint of lilies refreshed him and a strong sneeze opened his eyes.

"Achoo!" Meer pierced the peaceful silence as a bird flapped its wings for an unknown destination.

"We all are the same." Meer thought.

"Terrified from the fear of unknown, afraid from the unseen hand of time, from the tides of life tossing us in air of unsurety to test the balance of entertainer, silently hidden inside, waiting for the change?" Introspecting psychology Meer reached the local convenience store.

"Six eggs, Gouda, croissants, butter, milk..." He was at the cashier's till when he noticed the stare of the shopkeeper as he stationed the radio to a British Network.

"London underground had been hit with multiple bombs attacks this morning, right now we have caller on the line, ringing us from Liverpool station area. Let's talk to him..."

"What! What did I just hear?" Meer struggled. Avoiding any eye contact, he rushed outside without taking his change or receipt. He was running as he was caught stripped naked in the city centre. Weak in knees by an unknown guilt, Meer was scared, his gut feeling was informing him that right-wing Muslim's are involved in it.

"Now all of us will be blamed for this incident, I hope this is not true, not true! This is just my fear, only fear, nothing else." Meer was brisk walking hoping that his doubts will turn false as day goes by and more clarity over the incident comes under the light.

"Why am I overreacting, I'm not in London! Why am I so stressed? I shouldn't be so much worried." Meer wiped sweat from his face as he confusingly navigated his emotional direction.

"Something's very wrong with me, I should be with Rita! She would be waiting for me." He hasted as clouds covered the sky and greyed the landscape.

"Hopefully, I wouldn't catch the rain." Meer turned left and looked towards the gloomy clouds gathering from North above him. He hurried to reach the alleyway when he noticed the opened door.

"Rita, door's open." He shouted as he locked the door behind him.

"Rita! Hello... Hello!" Meer followed the loud television on the left, broadcasting the most important news of the year, opening a new chapter of the history, written again with blood and tears of the innocent.

"An official unnamed source confirmed London's under attack by an Islamic terrorist organization." The news was flashing across the screen as Meer looked at the TV, stunned and heartbroken to see the city where he spent some wonderful days of his life, mesmerized by the cultural and ethnic diversity of London, now in tears cursing the 'enemy within'. He knew a new wave of Islamophobia is coming.

"Islam is a plague taking over the Europe. Stop immigration. Send them back. No more Muslims." Hateful slogans will become popular and accepted by the masses.

Meer was in shock of denial, imagining what's next for him. What should he do? An unknown fear crippled his thoughts just as hundreds of thousands of Muslims and culturally-Muslims felt in Europe, America and Australia after knowing about the names, faces and religious identities of 7/7 culprits. His mind was wandering between 9/11 and America's war on terrorism in Afghanistan and Iraq. He questioned himself where he stands in equation when he will be painted as 'danger to society' because of his looks, colour, name and religion... which he barley followed. 'Was falling in love and having a child with Rita and plans of marrying Ji-Su were a cover up apology to his self? Did he feel sorry for who he is? Having a child with different, socially and politically superior race was the card he played unconsciously to secure the place of his 'genes' in the new world where being Muslim is a curse and practicing Islam would be an 'easy label' to be called fundamentalist, possibly Jihadi, enemy within and threat to common culture. He thought for a minute that if he really wants to name the new-born with a Middle Eastern styled Islamic name, if he wants to share his surname with his child or ever wanted to visit a mosque with that baby, even raising a child on an Islamic faith seemed like a very bad idea. He kept thinking how he would raise and highlight the softer impression of Islam to the 'New Adam' under nerve wrecking societal and predominantly biased media's pressure. I don't want my child to be born with a

'natural inferiority complex' fighting and cursing themselves throughout their life for taking birth in the wrong household as they battle against world for their rights and personal space.
Does the child have to be a Muslim if he or she is born to a Muslim parent? How he will convince the child that Islam doesn't teach violence but tolerance, and would respond to the criticism on nearly obsolete and old cultural values of the past merged in local practices of Islamic faith and over centuries rolled and replaced true Islamic values? Meer thought of 'Rumi' and about the repressed, undervalued and generally unrepresented spiritual dimension of Islam in West.
Meer was busy with internal juggle while he waited for Rita, who had disappeared from the cottage.
"I just hope she is still here." Anxious, he got up and looked at the television, punched the power button to shut up the devil and went to their bedroom.
Rita's bag was still there, her maxi on bed, slippers on the floor. Meer took a deep sigh of relief as he laid down with her night-dress on his face. He missed her badly as tears fell from his eyes.
"I love you so much and I don't know why." He said and closed his eyes.
"Ding!" Doorbell rattled Meer, resting deeply in comfort of Rita's perfume.
"What time is it?" He looked at the clock.
"Ding!"

"Rita!" Meer smiled and briskly walked towards the door with excitement to welcome her.
"Just act normal... normal." Meer told to himself, brushing hair, he opened the door with a huge smile.
"Rita! Jan?" His eyes brighten with familiarity as a quick sharp pain pierced him above the left rib cage. Rita fell over Meer as Jan pushed her with jagged knife, lancing him through the stomach.
"Rita..." He grumbled as he grabbed to balance her, pushing the stab deeper, knifing intestine, rupturing the spleen as blood bubbled to drip from the corner of his lips.
"Aaaaaaaahhh..." Meer shouted in pain as wounded Jan limped outside.
"Meer!" Rita screamed, smashing into him. She turned to chase Jan, when Meer pulled her forearm.
"Stay!" He said breathlessly.
Meer's fist was holding Rita's palm fixed on knife, when an unexpected tug from Meer imbalanced her.
"This is the beginning of our happy ending." He murmured.

Pain pulled the arrows of sorrow and grief inside him, luring sad life towards death when a final smile played on his lips as he looked deep, in deep ends of her eyes, shocked, scared from unknown known, shivering in pain as the child moved restlessly inside her. Meer lifted his iron filled fingers to release her arm carefully, liberating her in finality. He looked at Rita's belly, the child was tearing her abdomen apart before Meer closed his eyes and fell into the black hole of immortal annihilation.

"Meer!!" Rita yelled.

Silent darkness filled the space, exhaling stillness of painfully quiet death as shadow moved inwards with the shutting door blocking the rays of light over the lifeless body, clockwise casing the dead, lying in a pool of blood, stiff. Then slowly a ray of sun sneaked through the door gap turning the blood into ruby red, stopping right above the base of eyebrows where his third eye was opened, observing Rita's blank face as the white door shut on her face, separating them forever in two worlds.

"What I had done, what... what I was thinking, what had I done?" Rita looked to her clothes bathed in Meer's and Jan's blood, shivering in cold sweats, trembling since Meer clutched her arm making the child move inside her, manically shifting, increasing pressure on pelvis, cramps crushed her abdomen with pain and panic when Meer eased his grip... her waters broke as Rita sobbed in tears of fear and guilt.

"What have I done?"
She cried in pain as she moved away from the cottage to seek medical attention, struggling to keep her balance as she walked, holding walls, polls, dustbins. Rita was dragging herself for a haven.
"I should die too, I should... what's the point anyway and... what would I answer when this angel would ask me about the father, what would I say? Who's he? Where's he? Who killed him? This pain is a sign that this is my end too but what about Amelia, what's her fault, why would I want to make her life more miserable? My lovely daughter, unaware of paternal love, who will take care of her? I can't be that selfish. Yes! I'm murderer but I can't run away from my responsibilities. Yes, that's right! I also have a duty to bring this soul on earth, I'm chosen, I must do that, I must! This child must experience this beautiful world turned ugly by humans, maybe this baby would do wonders if opportunity given. This world needs Messiah, we all need is Messiah, don't we? But can I live with a lie? That could last for a lifetime? A lie to live for the rest of my time, for a smooth life of my angels? I can do that, I can... Yes, I can do that for my children!"
Rita was dragging her clueless self, struggling to walk as pain raised and falls inside her...
contractions. The child was moving relentlessly as she heavily breathed to contain herself. Her focus was to calm herself. She wasn't due till next month but...

"Is this the will of God?" She thought vaguely as she looked around. She completely lost her sense of direction as fear of life, death and new life captured her.

"Where am I?" She found herself on a quiet road, not anywhere near the village centre. Crying with pain, shouting as the child started to push out, Rita nearly fainted as blood splashed between her legs.

"Oh God... Oh God!" Rita sat slowly, holding her belly and yelling in pain, lamenting, cursing. She cried for Jesus to bless her as she closed her eyes and prepared for her last breaths.

Amelia's face, Meer's smile, her mother's voice all drowned in her conscious.

"I'm hallucinating, this can't be real, my brain is distracting me... Am I dead?"

Rita hoped for life as she looked at the clouds focusing her breath and tilted towards the side finding comfort in the cool breeze blowing on her face, relaxing her pain as blood discharged on her thighs turning the pink linen pyjama red when pain suddenly soothed within darkness behind her closed eyes into insensate.

"This could be the beginning of my happy ending."

A final thought recorded before she unconsciously drowned holding the last string of life into an unknown world.

Far in distance speeding tyres were rushing towards her...

Eternity

Ji-Su heard another airplane taking off from Prague Ruzyně Airport in the departure lounge.
"So, this is it." She closed her eyes and rested her head at the back of the seat.
"Really, this is it... the end." Ji-Su was holding her tears, ready to depart when another plane headed in the sky leaving her obnoxiously restless.
Ji-Su was waiting to board on her last-minute booked flight out of Czech Republic in miserable depression. She had enough in the last few days going back and forth to the police station, hospitals, hotels, train stations of the city. She hired an English-speaking Czech lawyer, spent a fortune on him to bring him to a police station and filed a report of a missing person about four years ago in Prague, but nothing happened just as the inspector frankly told to the lawyer...
"Within days... in case like this - nothing would happen, no definite clue, just a name, passport number, an old and out of service international phone number, few pictures. I understand this seem like a matter of heart but..." He paused to stop himself from saying something harsh as he looked at innocently confused and concerned face of Ji-Su.

"Please leave her contact details and your contact details *pány*, we will contact if we get some information worth to share, *Děkuji*, thank you." Next day she was there again and again on the following day, sitting silently, waiting for some miracle to transpire while she quietly conversed with Lord Buddha, but nothing happened until she was politely asked to remove herself from the police station. She went to Pakistani Embassy too, a bizarre conversation full of personal questions lead to a situation where she was insisted to explain their love story to them. Ji-Su even went to the local mosque as her best bet, with a great hope that someone might know him there.
"Maybe Lord had turned his heart towards Him, and he started remembering the God." She hopefully thought on the stairs of the mosque.
"God is misunderstood by everyone." She recalled Meer's verdict.
"People who ignore themselves at any conscious stage of life by blindly following the worldly pleasure are dumb, just as the ones following the religion soullessly without understanding the essence of religion. I'm proud of not following the religion completely rather than half-heartedly."
And half-heartedly Ji-Su decided to spend the rest of the day in sightseeing to refresh her low morale, to rejuvenate the energy level and think of something new to locate him. She felt she's at the end of the rope after meeting the disappointment at the Mosque.

On her return Ji-Su bought a walking tour. Following instructions of the guide, looking around, watching crowds of the people, Ji-Su felt suddenly Meer around her. She could feel his presence as they crossed the Powder Tower, entering the old town. When Meer slowly left his body in the parallel world near Hrádek, spreading into the energy fused within 'ether' and for a few moments he was everywhere before his conscious faded into dark and brighten again in the world of visual sounds. He was breathed by Rita, yelling in pain at a hospital delivery suit, by Shahanara and Amelia busy in playing with Dilafroz and by Ji-Su walking in Prague city centre behind a group of tourists with sad eyes, while Kumari carried a purple umbrella and chattered cheerfully about the facts of the famous astronomical clock when she caught her eyes.
Ji-Su was completely out of touch, busy within, though her quiet eyes searched something around her, sparking with intelligence on her pale complexion, with a gaze pausing on every face around her.
"Hello! Seems like you are looking for something, aren't you?" Kumari smiled as she walked up to her, leaving the rest of the tour with their Old-Town photo stop.
"I thought I might be a bit of help." Kumari looked at Ji-Su' wide jaw line.

"Yes! Yes... I'm actually looking for someone." Ji-Su hesitantly looked at Kumari. She didn't expect that the tour guide was noticing her so closely.
"I'm looking for my boyfriend." She confusedly said.
"Is he on the tour with us?" Kumari looked in direction of Ji-Su's eyes, wandering still at every face.
"No, no... I think he's in this city but I'm not sure." Ji-Su spoke gently as she's in a dream.
"I'm sure he's very handsome and precious that someone gorgeous like you, my friend is looking for him." Kumari softly nodded as she understood her pain and devotion.
"Four years, about four years I'm looking for him. Even went to Pakistan too, to his hometown to find him."
"Pakistan?" Kumari went out of breath.
"What's his name?" She asked quickly as a thought flashed in her mind.
"What are the odds she's the same Korean girl Meer told me about?"

"Meer Choudhury, do you know anyone with this name? Asian, Pakistani, tall guy with dark hair and brown eyes... wait I have a picture." Ji-Su didn't notice the change of the colour on her face when she looked haphazardly inside the bag to pull the photocopy of Meer's identity document and some printed pictures. Kumari quietly sipped the water to calm the shock she was in. She didn't know what to say when Ji-Su flashed old photos of Meer under her nose.

"Have you seen him, ever?" Ji-Su hopelessly asked while Kumari held her breath flipping the pictures. "Do you have a child with him?" Kumari managed to hide the tremble shivering in her voice.

"No, we are engaged to each other but no, no kids. Have you seen him ever?" Ji-Su looked innocently on Kumari's fading face.

"No, unfortunately I haven't. No, I'm sorry." Kumari abruptly replied and left awkwardly quick, leaving Ji-Su even more confused than before.

"What's wrong with her?" She thought. Ji-Su couldn't comprehend what bothered the tour guide. She wasn't even looking at her as they went on to proceed with their tour.

"Am I upset? No, I'm not. Definitely not!" Kumari told to herself as she wished to run away from the constant pain and hurt.

"The moment she said Pakistan, I knew this is coming, didn't I? I'm not hurt, I'm fine! I'm perfect... I'm great." Kumari reminded herself as a strange pain in stomach made her sick.

She wasn't feeling well for months now and every time she taught herself to settle and accept life, something happened to shatter her confidence and psychological health. Rita, Amelia and now... She didn't know what to say to this much younger and beautiful Korean girl who was desperately and hopelessly in love with Meer too. She wished to break her heart by lying to her that he's dead, he's the father of her daughter and he died last year in a car accident, but she couldn't agree with her evil thoughts. She felt unwell by withholding her anger, turning into depression and emotional meltdown when Ji-Su approached her hesitantly.
"Are you ok? Are you feeling alright?" She was anxiously careful as they stood next to Jan Hus memorial.
"Yes, what happened?" Kumari smiled frankly over Ji-Su's concern.
"I thought... I upset you."
"No, you didn't. I just had a similar experience like yours in the past and..." Kumari struggled to hide the truth.
"I'm sorry; I made you feel bad, but here..." She extended a post-it note towards her.
"My number and my email address, if you ever come to Newcastle or go to Busan, please...be my guest." Ji-Su smiled and left without saying another word to her.
That evening Ji-Su booked her ticket back to Newcastle.

"I'm done with all this, with Meer and especially with my unconditional love. I guess my tour guide in Pakistan was right, sometimes we don't have to run behind our dream but to wait and let our wish swish towards us. I think now's the time I should withdraw the forceful stubbornness and let the life flow and take its course of choice. What's mine would be always mine and will reach me regardless and what isn't will never be golden caged and would disappear on one fine, bright, beautiful morning, like an illusion. Just as mortals vanishing in front of us from this beautiful world, nothing keeps them occupied and dear departs. Where do they all go? Where does everything go? A thought, a dream, our hopes, wishes?"

Ji-Su quietly went back to Newcastle and finally handed her resignation. And on the same day a meeting between her and the GM was arranged in which she was offered her managers role with an attractive salary and benefits, who resigned with immediate effect during Ji-Su's absence.

Ji-Su very reluctantly accepted the manager's role for six months on insistence of his colleagues. All she could think of was going back to Busan, stay near the parents and probably date someone of her mother's choice to keep her blood pressure normal. She felt guilty to put her parents through stress and now she wanted to restore their peace of mind. And she did... by letting her mom know that she's ready to meet someone once she's back.

Ji-Su was focused, positive, emotionally in the right direction to recover from self-inflicted depression till a telephone call from Prague turned the peaceful numbness to a chaotic storm of thoughts.

"Hello, my name is Martin Novák, I'm calling from Czech Republic Police, Nové Město Police Station in Prague regarding Mr Meer Choudhury. Am I speaking to Miss Ji-Su Lee?"

Ji-Su thought her heartbeat stopped with her breath and in an instant loud drum throbbed in her chest when she stuttered.

"Yes, I...m Ji-Su...H...H... How can I help?"

"We have some information about Mr Choudhury, and we are assuming he's the same gentleman you were looking for. Is it possible we can email you some photos urgently to identify him?" A dry and professional voice echoed within her.

"Identify him?" Ji-Su asked reluctantly.

"Yes, can I confirm with you Miss Lee that you are the fiancé of Mr. Choudhury, and you were not aware of his whereabouts for last 4 years, is this correct?" Policeman was unsure about the truthfulness of Ji-Su's confirmation.

"Yes, that's right, but what's the matter is he ok?" Ji-Su's heart was pounding louder in fear with every passing second.

"We can discuss the details, once you can confirm the identity of the gentleman, Can I please have your email address, thank you."

Ji-Su confirmed her work email address and waited anxiously for the email of Martin Novák. He promised her a call back after 15 minutes while Ji-Su sweated with nervousness. She was shivering in unknown fear when a different Czech number blinked on her mobile screen. She refreshed her inbox quickly before answering the call. Nothing arrived when Ji-Su confusedly answers the call as she slipped saliva to her dry throat.
"Hello?"
"Hello, Ji-Su?" A frank, sweet, feminine voice soothed her ears.
"Yes, sorry... whom am I speaking with?" She was nearly sure about identity of the caller, but she confirmed again.
"My name is Kumari B, I was your tour guide in Prague, you remember?" There was an awkward silence between them for a moment.
"Yes, yes, I remember you, how are you?" Ji-Su replied slightly distantly.
"I'm ok. Listen, are you still searching for your boyfriend?" She asked enthusiastically.
"Yes, kind of.... this matter is in the court of Lord now." Ji-Su breathed deeply and clicked to refresh the inbox again.
"Someone told me they know a person with the name of Meer and is also from Pakistan, working as a porter in the kitchen of an Indian restaurant." Kumari paused for a moment to judge Ji-Su's silence before she continued.

"My sister's going to Korea for two weeks from Italy and I bought a small present for you from my trip to Barbados." Kumari kept her cheerfulness as Ji-Su clicked, closed, reopened and refreshed restlessly her inbox.
"Thank you, I appreciate your effort. If you don't mind, can I call you back in a few hours, I'm at work now and I will text you, my details." Ji-Su disconnected the call desperately as the new email landed in her inbox.
"These few seconds can determine the course of my life?" Ji-Su hastily thought clicking on the email. She clicked and double clicked on the attachments as she dropped the call without saying bye to Kumari. She shuffled her thoughts within moments, her intellect and sixth sense went silent, and wavelength reached blank dead. She wasn't sure what to expect from life. Kumari was presented with a different information opposite of her fears, which she didn't want to sink inside her to avoid any more disappointments. And Czech police used vague words to confuse her to the next level of frustration.
A full body shot was on the screen. A middle-aged man lying dead on floor of an unidentified origin, with bullet wounds in his chest, curly hair, big ears, thick nose and pale skin, about 172 cm tall in a flashy red T-shirt.
Phone rang and Ji-Su answered immediately. Martin was on the line.

"Yeah, Martin sorry to disappoint you but that's not Meer. He wasn't any gangster or drug lord." She responded confidently as something was off from her chest.

"I did think that." Martin sighed, he didn't try to hide the unhappiness when he said, "one second please," And placed me on hold for about a minute before he came back on the line.

"I have one murder case here of an unidentified man of South-Asian origin, who was stabbed at a holiday apartment about 6 months ago at Hrádek nad Nisou." Ji-Su could feel him scratching beard, going through notes as he forced the receiver to stay between his ear and shoulder.

"We were notified by the owners of that holiday apartment who contacted us about 5 days after the double murder. Miss Lee, I just received this case earlier today, and I just started looking into the case. Do you know that Mr Choudhury was a friend with someone with the name of...Rita Newman or Jan Bartos?" Martin Novák stressed the question as he interrogates the matter with a deceitful witness.

"Mr Novák, I guess we are done here." Ji-Su blew off with rage.

"I'm not sure if I can co-operate with you anymore and to answer your question, Meer didn't have many friends and definitely not with the names you mentioned, thank you for your call."

Ji-Su nearly slammed the phone on her desk after she drooped the call. She was flushed with anger, boiling blood like lava steaming out from a volcano's mouth. She didn't know till later why she was mad at that detective who was merely doing his job. She learnt she couldn't bear the idea of Meer being with someone else. She didn't want to accept that he's dead, killed by someone and with his last breath, her fading hope would disappear in darkness of Meer's death. She felt sorry for both Martin and Kumari for disconnecting their calls rudely. Ji-Su texted a long apology for her grumpiness with her address, thanking in advance for Kumari's gift and gladly agreeing to speak with her sister about the South Korean trip. She requested Kumari to speak on her behalf with the man who might know Meer. She offered to email her some pictures of him over, in case Kumari goes personally to see this man working in the restaurant.

A week passed but Ji-Su didn't receive any response from Kumari. She tried to contact her over the phone but always reached useless busy tone leading to a call drop. She couldn't leave any voice mail and text messages were undelivered after her first SMS. Ji-Su wondered that what went so wrong that she blocked her entirely but soon she ignored the bother and life went back to the old routine. Waking up at 7 Am, leaving for work at half 7, playing classics while driving for 25 minutes and trying to avoid morning rush hour, reaching to office at 7:55 and straight into the office kitchen at 8. A large cup of coffee with a homemade sandwich from the previous night on her desk and sharp at quarter past eight begins the working day. She spent most of the evenings in bed watching some stupidly emotional film or Korean dramas filled with tears to unwind her lonely self before she meditates for half an hour and jump in bed at 10:30 pm. On Saturdays she drove to outskirts of Newcastle, often she spent a few hours on Whitley Bay walking by the coast or sitting on the beach on a rare warm day. Wind blows her away and her mind fly towards the distant past while she takes sips of the chamomile or mint tea poured out of her flask. Her batch mates and nearly all friends left the cold North-East for madly busy and super cosmopolitan London or slightly busier Midlands for better jobs and opportunities, but she couldn't think of living in a bigger city with a fear that one day Meer would be searching for her in Newcastle and... She would be sleepless, turning sides uncomfortably in her bed somewhere in the big city, fearing that tonight Meer could be in Newcastle and regardless of relatively an underpaid job, unsuited weather and foreigner incomprehensible Geordie accent, the city didn't lose its charm for Ji-Su. For her, Newcastle held the breaths of her beloved in its air. His memories turned alive with every rising sun... his words, his voice; his thoughts wandered under the moon light of this city. She felt Meer's emptiness in her soul every midnight within the darkness of her silent bedroom after a deep wet dream where she breathed passionately towards the heaven, turning the dimness of dark, evaporating into white cloud filled with radiance within closed eyes holding sight of bodies sweating in love, melting the wilderness of vacant selves to a hefty union pouring reflection on a shining lake.

Ji-Su was sure deep down that he will come back, and they will be together, holding hands, eyes locked in the gaze of the other, rubbing noses. Spend the rest of the days just like that, going for lunches and late-night dinners, watching movies, reading while she keeps her feet in Meer's warm lap sitting opposite to her, discussing life, cultures, languages, food, society, people, influences, heritage and history of religions and regions of the world. Together they never had enough time to talk about all those thoughts and ideas when they were blessed with each other's company. Sex was a part which flowed as unbound waters floating between them encircling their bodies and they dipped into one and other on waves of love and compassion. But Ji-Su knew that's not the end of it. This path leads elsewhere. A fire can only breathe till oxygen runs out and sex can only comfort till the fresh air turns into unbreathable. A moment, a noise, a child, a fear, a doubt, a miscarriage, an argument, a third person, anything could kill the passionate sex between them, and then he disappeared... leaving the space for 'Him', the 'one' who brought him in her life from across the oceans, like a spiritual mentor who moves away and let the 'reality' reflect over you. God immerse inside you, or you submerge inside God, but Ji-Su consciously tried to hide herself behind the goodness as she was afraid more and more with every passing day from the evil, turning the uncomforting motions and emotions inside her. Alcohol intake increased and her mind often slipped towards getting laid by multiple men simultaneously, shouting, spitting and abusing her. She started watching hard-core pornography and put herself on a dating site over one weekend and within an hour, messages with sexual motives were overflowing with nudes. Next working day was the payday on which she charity about 35 percent of her net salary for the cancer patients in Pakistan. Imran Khan Cancer Appeal collected charity for Shaukat Khanam Memorial Cancer Hospital and Research Centre.

"Who else deserves her help in this bad, rotten world more than a child suffering from cancer, born in a family earning less than her monthly morning coffee bill and, in that month, how many unpaid luxuries she enjoyed? How many sins she committed? Does a thought of a sin count as a sin too?" Ji-Su asked herself.

"My outrageous plans to get in bed with different men asking them to tie me, humiliate me, use me, turn me red for their pleasure or unleash my extremely wild 'dominance' to turn their faces and asses blue pleasingly hurting them, throwing alcohol on their bodies and making them piss themselves as I shove a 'Long John' inside their butts, pushing them to down several beers and urinate as I smack their cheeks.' She thought.

"What had gone wrong, what happened to me?" Ji-Su questioned herself.

"So much anger, hate and fury clogged within, but against whom? Why am I so unhappy, dissatisfied from life, what's wrong? Am I angry with myself, with people, with Lord? How much I remembered God since I came back from Pakistan, did I remember him at all? How much I missed Meer and how much I thought about the Lord? Is there a comparison between love and duty, passion and responsibility? Don't recalling Meer count as sin too? Maybe I'm so sinful because Lord wants me to sin, remorse and pay for my mistakes in form of the charity? Maybe my ill thoughts and wicked deeds actually don't matter to God, what matters to Him are the good deeds and actions, helping the humanity. People matter to God, His creation and their hearts, their emotions."
Ji-Su was manipulating the relationship between sins, benevolence and the God. Tired, exhausted by the Lord's silence, taking her faith away from the 'Godly wisdom' of the superior.
"There's nothing for me in His plans." She sighed hopelessly in despair as she moved her grounds. Time, situational reality and the western living changed Ji-Su. Spirituality which needs a length of time, confidence and blind faith seemed like a laborious and fruitless path and without a mentor to stay on an unknown journey which is just a journey, looked like a fool's idea in a materialistic world.
Path to oneness was losing its sanctity and meaning in her eyes.

"How could I ever know that I was on the right track? How could anyone find the correctness of their direction?" Ji-Su thought.
"And why the people on the right path always end up facing so many hardships? Why is patience tested till the last thread? God, time, destiny... what are they trying to teach the immortals on the path of oneness?"
Ji-Su kept thinking on these lines. More she questioned the 'unanswerable' more she fell apart from herself and the God. Her frustration took over her mind and plunged into a steep depression. She was angry, hooked on her remorse when a window to adrenaline opened for her attention. Her phone was beeping with a text from a handsome stranger whom she exchanged numbers on the dating website. Sexually enticing messages rolled in excitement and the thrill of a new charmer swayed her erotically. She was moved instantly from pain and sadness wondering during 'indulgence' that's why good actions are so dull and sins are so full of passion and tastefully breath-taking.

"This could be..." Ji-Su pauses the thought for a moment "Am I starving for sex?" She checked her psychological pulse to confirm the direction. "Am I desperate for a man to be inside me, over me, on me melting his self over my petite and unattractive body? Small breasts, thin legs, small ass, flat feet. Yes! That's not the standard of beauty or sexiness. Meer loved my eyes, my jawline, my laughter and the smile which played on my lips. We made love like there's no tomorrow, I felt his soul, heart and love when he..."

"STOP THINKING ABOUT HIM!" something shouted in Ji-Su's head.

"Concentrate on what you are doing, pull the fucking pleasure out of the moment and forget all. Get yourself hooked with that hunk and spread your legs for that hungry puss eater, bitch." Ji-Su scolded herself.

"7 pm, this Saturday, meet me at the coffeehouse near the Millennium Bridge, Quayside. We'll take it from there." She texted back confidently but shook her internal peace and replaced it with confusion, excitement and fear that forces bland women to run away from the unknown excitement luring towards fascination, but a wave of apprehension repels them towards the old safe harbour. They retract back to cosy cocoon not by choice but by the unknown's fright.

Next couple of days passed in swinging between deciding and deceiving the unrest conscious, throwing tantrums to back off.

"What is it that holds me back, what is it?" She annoyingly questioned her puzzled self.
"What stops me from leaping into the newness, risking a chance into the dark? Is this simply my hesitance and reluctance to try new things, immature shyness, or does this has something to do with my upbringing? Could it be childhood's lack of confidence? My stubbornness or too much faith in right and wrong against 'experimentation'? Or simply a psychological resistance to accept that I'm not what I thought to be...I'm someone else, who I looked down upon and detested, so I'm disappointed and ashamed opposite to myself? Or... or it's the silent Lord instilled himself so deeply within me that I can't change."
Ji-Su felt deeply upset and angry, frustrated wanted to break free from her old, tamed, obedient self. She struggled to distract her mind from the rage rotting within her when she texted the 'hot' date vulgarly provoking him as she switched on porn, sipping whisky after a large portion of Pho spread warm contentment of broth inside her. Headphones, playing female fantasy moans faded in clapping cheeks as her fingers slipped in sticky juices, softening hidden lips when the bad boy promised to sweep them with his tongue, digging his nose deeper inhaling the heat of her passion as he shadows over her diamond, sparking it, igniting her waters with soothing satisfaction of lust spreading across her soul.
"My taste buds are eager to know you." He wrote.

"Tomorrow!" Ji-Su replied.
The next morning was Saturday. A long bath with extended half an hour for shaving thick pubes and spending the whole afternoon in highlighting her beauty, trying dresses and matching footwear, Ji-Su played inaudible erotica on TV, provoking to incite her exhausting thoughts turning her powerless. She wanted to lay without delay with a temptation of redemption from self- inflicted misery of stupid love which fooled her golden years of life.
"Let's meet at 5 pm, if it's not too early for you." Ji-Su dropped a subtle clue for the player when the doorbell rang in the silence of the flat.
"Who this could be?" Ji-Su quietly tiptoed up to the door and peeped through the viewer. An unknown blond with slightly curly hair, blue eyes, overweight in fitted jeans was looking away. She looked a bit startled but harmless from her features.
Ji-Su heard a crying baby behind the partly open door. The unknown woman was pointing towards something... a child tucked in a car seat with a note on its handle 'Flat 1. Ji-Su'
"I was crossing your flat when I saw this child crying, and the baby bag. Are you Ji-Su living in Flat 1?" Ji-Su could see tears floating in her tired blue eyes. She couldn't understand what's happening there.
"Someone left a child on your doorsteps in this freezing weather!" She hesitantly looked at the astonished face of Ji-Su.

"I just wanted to let you know. Sorry for intruding. This is none of my business. Wasn't sure if I should call the police or talk to you first, sorry... sorry again!" And before Ji-Su replied, she disappeared, leaving Ji-Su unable to understand what to do or think. She was in shock, utterly terrified by the thought of someone leaving their child deliberately at her door. Perplexedly with shivering hands she carried the car seat with a crying angel tucked in a beige baby blanket. She walked back to the living room, quickly putting down the car seat and rushed back to close the door, welcoming winter chills into the cosiness of the flat. She picked up the baby bag and quickly ran to attend the crying tot.
"Child must be hungry or cold." Ji-Su's maternal instinct kicked in, but she wasn't sure where to begin. Her train of thought was running in all directions. Should she call police, emergency services, child protection agencies, the local council...
"Hold the infant and put her against yourself, hug the baby to calm the fright." Something instructed her.

Ji-Su hesitantly sat on her knees and slowly placed her arm behind the baby's back, sliding the other between the legs. With a fast-beating heart, she slipped the baby in her arms. Ji-Su was holding the baby boy in the blue jumpsuit closely against herself, returning him back to comfort as she covered him in a blanket. Sitting cross-legged on the carpet, she looked closely at his face. Sleepy dark brown eyes, natural blondish brown hair, light eyebrows, olive skin over big cheeks. He yawned cutely with his small round mouth, melting her heart when he started crying again.

"This could be because of a rumbling tummy or a full nappy." Ji-Su stood up and carried him to her messy bedroom. She smiled at the baby as she laid him in the middle of her bed, thinking about calling the police again. She didn't want to be in any trouble and for her safety and in the best interest of the child, Ji-Su decided to contact the police and report the incident after the child's feed.

Ji-Su ran to get the baby bag and some nappies. "Ooowaa, Oowaaa..." He clearly wasn't impressed by the efficient Ji-Su, protesting against having been laid without his consent and leaving him entirely on his own without a prior permission was a big no!

"Calm down, calm down... I'm here, here... I'm, I'm... I'm here, sorry, sorry I went to the other room. Look, I have your bag, see. I will make you a bottle of milk, just give me a minute. Don't cry please, don't cry." Ji-Su carried him quickly in her arms, started dancing gently on tip toes, swinging slowly as she sang a Korean lullaby.
My baby, darling mine... sleep now
Till morning, dream sweet... calm now
Stars, moon, fairies flying... peace now
He was calm, suddenly, all peaceful as he understood the warmth and wisdom of this lullaby playing from a forgotten past.
Her voice soothed his discomfort and the baby forgot about the hunger until Ji-Su took liberty to sit on the bed with him.
"Oh, you are a spoiled baby boy. Tell me, what is the matter, what is the matter honey, tell me." Ji-Su struggled just as a new mother in desperation of understanding the child, together untangling her own self. A mixture of happiness, frustration and incomprehensible rush of feelings, untouched emotions swished inside her.
"He's hungry and I need to boil some water for his milk." She learnt quickly.
"I will carry you but first I need to make your bottle. You are hungry that's why. So don't cry. Just give me two minutes." Ji-Su looked in his eyes firmly and disappeared to the kitchen with the milk bottle.

He was in her lap, sucking the milk contently and slowly closing his eyes in the comfort of his filling belly. The warmth of unconditional love was lazily rolling his eyes under the blanket of long lashes, reconnecting him to the world where he was conscious, lively and more alive than the rest of the humanity. Awake in true silence, unknowingly knowing the ultimate truths of life, breathing them from essence where 'one' doesn't reveal 'The Self' but sits opposite within colours of an ordinary butterfly. Unknown world entertained him when Ji-Su patted his back, deepening the widened circle of sleep as she curiously opened the letter she found inside of the bag while unpacking it for the milk powder earlier.

Dear Ji-Su,

Meet Meer's son. And mine.

And who am I? I don't know, even after so many years I cannot say who I am really. But this isn't important at all, because his actual parents are no more from this point on. I left him on your doorstep and now the decision to raise him or not, rests with you. He's 5 months old and his name now should be decided by you. Meer always wanted a girl. He never expected a son.

Love him the way you loved his father. I'm returning Meer to you.

Printed in Great Britain
by Amazon